Citizen and Traveler

Kétévi Adiklè Assamagan

Publisher: African Travelers Press—Wading River, NY
ISBN: 978-0-692-97479-7
Library of Congress Control Number: 2017959833
Citizen and Traveler/ Kétévi Adiklè Assamagan
Digital distribution I African Travelers Press 2017
Paperback I African Travelers Press, 2017

E-mail: keteviassamagan@gmail.com

Dedication

In memory of my parents, Marie-Jeanne Afiwa Nouho and Alphonse Koumou Lanta Assamagan.

Prolog

The story of Kovi is a semi-fictional memoir with a biographical bent. In many chapters, some anecdotes contain fictional elements to illustrate Kovi's personal views or aspirations.

The narrative has three sections. The first part, chapters one to ten, starts with Kovi's arrival in America for graduate studies. It follows Kovi until graduation, naturalization and life as a family man. Also, it describes the visits of Kovi's parents to America. The second part of Kovi's story, chapters eleven through fifteen, describes his return to Togo for his father's funeral. The third section, from chapter sixteen, follows Kovi's professional travels.

The reader will notice shifts of time prompted by comparisons of current situations with Kovi's experiences or recollections of previous events. In the linear narrative of Kovi's journey, he goes places, meets people or experiences interactions that trigger flashbacks. At that point, the story shifts to the past. In other cases, the account changes to the future to complete the description of an event. In either case, the narrative resumes afterward in a linear flow of time.

Chapter One
Arrival

Many years ago, Kovi left Africa for the first time. It was an Air Afrique flight from Dakar. The jumbo jet was full. It taxied for a long time on the runway before it reached takeoff speed. As the airplane gained altitude, Kovi watched, from his window seat, Africa receded farther into the distance, until he could only see the vast body of water—the Atlantic Ocean. He was taking a small step into America. He was young and alone and in the pursuit of happiness.

The day before he departed, Kovi consulted an old guru who performed rituals to contain evil spirits for a safe journey.

Kovi and his father, Kodjo, said goodbye in a few words. Before Kovi got into the car, he turned around. Many people had gathered—family and friends. Some were crying, for they were not sure when they would see their beloved Kovi again. Kodjo was a Christian who attended an evangelical church and members of the congregation—including the pastor—were among the people and they were praying.

Kovi noticed that Kodjo was no longer in the crowd. He had retired to his room. Kovi hugged everyone tightly, especially his mother, Afi, who, in tears, reminded him of the pitfalls to watch out for on his journey and to be alert to the angels in his path. To Kovi's embarrassment, Afi was wailing at the thought of letting her son go on a journey into the unknown.

Kovi traveled by car to Lomé, where he boarded a flight to Abidjan. After a four-hour layover there, Kovi changed to another Air Afrique flight with a stop in Dakar, before a seven-hour crossing of the Atlantic Ocean to New York City.

Kovi arrived at JFK Airport on a Saturday and immediately noticed that he could not understand Americans, despite being able to read and write English well. They did not understand him either; Kovi had a heavy accent. At the hotel, he switched on the television, hoping if he could just listen enough, he would understand little by little. It was not long before he switched off the television out of frustration and despair and sat quietly on the bed. He thought that the English conversation lessons back home were of little use and wondered how was he going to study and learn enough to graduate.

He regretted coming to America, and wished he had gone to France instead. French is the language of education and business in his country—Togo. From grade school to university, education is carried out in French. With a wealth of materials in French literature, Francophone African literature, and the contacts between the two countries, students from Togo get to be proficient in French and go to France to pursue higher education. Many of Kovi's friends and colleagues were making the journey to France. Why had he gone to America instead?

Before his departure, going to America generated a lot of excitement and envy. How on Earth was he able to get a university scholarship in the United States of America? The ultimate first-world country, the land of opportunity, the land of the brave! For many of his generation, going to America was the far better option, better than any other alternatives. Yet, there he was, alone and unable to understand anyone—not even enough to navigate the Big Apple through that first weekend.

Kovi had a handful of dollars for the entire weekend—the few dollars they gave him when he exchanged West African francs before he departed. "The currency exchange rate was unfair," he thought. But surely what he had must be enough to get him through the weekend until Monday morning, when he would report to the African American Institute (AAI)—the agency that managed his scholarship program.

His first purchase in the USA was a hotdog at the street corner. He converted what he paid into the currency that he knew well and the cost horrified him.

He had to make his few remaining dollars last until Monday. Worry set in as Kovi tried many times to ask for the price before he bought anything. Often people could not understand his heavy accent, and when they did, he could not comprehend their responses. Kovi had a cousin in New York City but he did not see her. On Monday morning, the AAI gave him a lot of dollars and an airplane ticket to his final destination in the Midwest.

Kovi boarded a flight to Saint Louis and sat beside a beautiful young lady who looked just about his own age. She was of slender build, had a pointy nose, thin shiny lips, and an auburn-colored long hair that often covered her blue radiant eyes. She was a friendly lady who attempted repeatedly to talk to Kovi. Unable to understand the woman and self-conscious about his heavy accent, Kovi shied away from saying anything. The lady might have thought he was deaf, mute, or both. She took it in stride and remained friendly to Kovi, who reduced his interactions to grins and smiles.

At Saint Louis, she helped Kovi find his connecting gate. Kovi took a few seconds to read the posting at the gate, and when he turned back, the young lady had disappeared. He looked around and could not find her. He could only observe the sea of heads—with different hair colors and styles—that were drifting toward the baggage claim area. Then he realized she must have been an angel sent by the Almighty specifically to help him in that leg of his journey. He recalled what Afi had said before his departure, that he must pay attention and give praise to God, for there were angels disguised in the flesh and sent to help. He was not aware that he was traveling with an angel. "Good Lord!" Kovi said to himself.

An agent of the AAI met Kovi at the airport in Carbondale Illinois. Afterward, he spent several days at the apartment of another student from Togo. They made this arrangement before his arrival, to give him enough time to find his own place with the help of the students who were well-established there.

Carbondale is a small town with a state university that attracts many international students. Some of them are there for further English lessons before they start their academic programs, which might be in an entirely different university, elsewhere in the country.

Kovi was one of those students, sent there as a precursor to his graduate studies.

Chapter Two
English Lessons

Soon after his arrival, Kovi wrote a letter to his family about his journey, specifically to assure them that he had arrived safely. He could not call them because his family did not have a telephone. He could have called them at the house of a family friend who had a telephone, but he did not arrange this before his departure.

When he finished his meticulously written letter, Kovi found out how much it cost to mail it overseas from the USA; the postage stamp had forty-four written on it. He became stressed and worried that it cost forty-four dollars to mail a simple envelope and so he held on to it for several weeks. He waited to better understand the costs of daily expenses and to develop a correct estimate of an appropriate budget. When he was confident that he could pay forty-four dollars to post the letter without running into financial difficulties at the end of the month, he went to the nearest post office.

They did not know about Togo. To Kovi's astonishment, a serious discussion went on for a while to figure out where the envelope was going, to calculate the correct postage. There were many wild guesses about locations in South America, Africa, and Asia. Kovi explained to the post office agents that Togo was in West Africa. They advised him to add that location to the destination address to ensure the mail did not end up elsewhere.

As for the cost of the postage, he was again told it was forty-four. Kovi took out forty-four dollars to pay. The agent appeared confused for a moment, then started laughing and explained to Kovi that he meant forty-four cents, not dollars. Kovi sighed in relief to learn that mailing a letter to West Africa did not cost as much as he feared, so he could mail as many as necessary to keep his folks back home abreast of his activities and progress.

When Kovi was leaving the post office, a man in the line behind him stepped aside and introduced himself as Josh. He was a big fellow, perhaps in his fifties, with a huge beer belly that hung over his waistline and partly covered his belt. He was wearing a T-shirt and jeans that were smeared with different colors of paints. He arranged his golden hair in a ponytail that hung down his back all the way to his waist and wore a baseball cap with a symbol Kovi did not understand. His fingers had a few small open cuts and his fingernails were dark blue. "This man must be a handyman or an auto mechanic. Papa Kodjo used to appear like that at the end of a long workday," Kovi thought to himself.

Josh had witnessed Kovi's interactions with the post office agents and curious, wanted to talk to him. Josh asked him about how he got to the USA all the way from West Africa, and Kovi said he flew over. Then Josh continued.

"I want to go there someday."

"That would be great. You would love it," replied Kovi.

"To see the animals."

"The animals?"

"You know, I want to see the lions, the leopards, the cheetahs, the elephants, and the savannas, and do the game drives."

"Okay, I understand. But there is more than just seeing the animals."

"I am sorry. I mean no offense. I know what you mean. There is a lot more we can learn, appreciate, and enjoy. Not just the animals!" said Josh. Then he added, "You know, I am involved in a charity organization at church and we collect donations for a school project in Africa. You should come to my church sometime; the folks there would love to meet you."

"Okay, thank you. I will think about it."

***

Kovi visited the church and to his astonishment they received him as a major celebrity. The church folks met someone from Africa in the flesh, someone from the place they were helping through their charity, though not exactly Kovi's village or country. It was Africa, and that was good enough. There was a sense of satisfaction as the unexpected presence of Kovi at the church came to symbolize the fruit of their charitable missions and provided encouragement to sustain their efforts. Kovi impressed some that saw him as a highly educated young man from Africa, a man who came from afar to further his education in their country. His courage in journeying so far from his home to a country where he spoke the language with a heavy accent was an inspiration.

Kovi made many friends at the church and returned as often as he could on Sundays, although the church service underwhelmed him. The first time Kovi went to church in America he thought the church service was flat and uninspiring. Back where he came from, the preacher displayed many qualities to drive the congregation into a frenzy of praise and celebration. At home, the preacher did not deliver the important message of God as someone who is giving a speech at a scientific conference, but more like a passionate politician with a determination to convince his audience while singing and dancing at the same time. As the sermon carried on, the preacher became the leader of the choir and the rest of the congregation, while the entire ensemble followed along in perfect unison. The decibel level increased as the preacher's voice became more authoritative with the support of the refrains from the crowd and the long interludes when the sermon turned into a celebration. It was not clear if anyone learned anything from the sermon, but the uplifting service made most people so happy that they escaped the struggles of life for which they came to church to pray. In comparison, Kovi left his first church service in America in the same somber mood he was in when he arrived, although the friendliness of the people and their interest in his exoticness gave him a few smiles.

In time, Kovi attended many American church services and noted that there were different types. Some, in their ambiance or cheerful spirit of praising the Lord, were like or even surpassed what he experienced in West Africa.

After a few weeks, with the help of church folks and local African students, Kovi found a room in an apartment complex within walking distance of campus. Every morning, when Kovi walked to class, he saw large crowds of people walking in many directions, like a colony of ants in a search of food. The number of people increased at particular times that coincided with the end of lectures, and the transfers of people to other buildings for the next classes.

One sunny autumn day, Kovi came out of his apartment complex and walked toward the university, but after a few hundred meters he turned back. The sunny day fooled him, and he had worn short-sleeve clothes, thinking it was one of those hot, tropical African days. He could not sustain the walk in the chilly wind, and turned back to his apartment at a rapid pace, almost shivering, to get a heavy jacket that he'd purchased several weeks earlier for the impending colder weather. Meanwhile, he noticed that the American students, perhaps some foreigners, too, dressed lightly. Some even wore T-shirts and shorts, and they walked comfortably in the fine autumn weather that was already giving Kovi a runny nose.

Kovi could not comprehend why the people appeared so resistant to the cold to the point of taking some pleasure in a weather that he felt was freezing. Back in his home country, people complained that it was cold and got into their heavy sweaters when there was wind in the evening or a cool breeze before the rain. There in America, on that day, it seemed much colder to Kovi than anything he had ever experienced in West Africa yet people carried on in their summer attire, insensitive to the cold.

Kovi came back out in winter clothes that comprised a heavy jacket complemented with a warm hat and gloves. He was warm and confident as he hurried to his lecture hall. Along the way, Kovi became self-conscious when he noticed that he was the only one dressed for the cold. Some people looked surprised at him for a moment and went about their business, while others found the scene amusing. Two gentlemen approached Kovi.

"Hi. I am Jesse. This is my friend John."

"Hello. I am Kovi."

"Hum… Kovi. That's a nice name. Where are you from?"

"West Africa. Togo."

"Hey! Kovi, did you check the weather today? A cold front in the forecast? Snow perhaps?"

"Check the weather? How? Where?"

"You know? On television?"

"No. I am sorry, I do not have a television."

"John. You hear that? The brother from Africa ain't got no TV. Why are you dressed like this?"

"It is cold today. I am feeling cold."

"John, you hear that? The brother from Africa is cold. He got his ass already frozen in September. Man! What is he going to do come December?"

"Jesse, let the dude be, man! The brother is cold. That's all. If we get you over there in Africa, your ass will be so hot that you will think you are sitting on a stove. Isn't that so, Kovi?"

"Well, I do not know. I do not want to know anything about his ass in Africa." They started laughing. Then Jesse continued.

"Hey Kovi, listen. We've got to take you shopping for cool clothes for the season. You got to look cool, you know? I mean do you see anybody dressed like you around? Wearing that heavy stuff now means that by December you will need to wear three of them to stay warm. You got to be acclimated to the cold, man!"

Jesse was tall and slender, with a dark brown skin. He was bald and his scalp was shiny. John too was tall with curly dark hair, and skinnier than Jesse. Both were in sports jerseys and looked like accomplished athletes.

After that, Jesse and John were at the street corner every morning to wait for Kovi so they could walk to the campus together. Kovi's new friends were members of a nondenominational church group made of students of different races and colors, committed to spreading the teachings of the Lord and helping members of the group. Some gathered at the student center to discuss and do homework. When they finished with homework, there followed moments of jokes and teasing before everyone dispersed.

One day, they asked Kovi which word in English sounded the funniest to him. They instructed him to not rush to the answer but to sit, relax, and think about it first. Kovi did just that, and when he was ready, they said, "Which English word sounds the funniest to you? Please tell us."

"Wow."

"Wow?"

"Yes, wow. The first time I heard 'wow,' I did not know what it meant, and I thought what a funny sound to make! You know what my response was then? 'Wow!' Naturally, like I just knew when to make the 'wow' sound."

Most of them had not reflected on the "wow" sound before and found Kovi's revelation amusing. When everyone went his or her separate way, Kovi thought about the equivalent of "wow" in his native language, and that sounded funny to him. So then, he wondered how people say "wow" in their languages, if they sounded funny, and, if so, would that teach us anything about the commonality of human reactions to situations and events that compel people to exclaim it. T

he next day during his English class, which was full of foreign students, Kovi asked everyone how they say "wow" in their native languages. It was a group of about twenty students and each one was from a different country in Asia, Europe, Africa, and South America. They became friends, bound by their heavy foreign accents, and diligently studied English to become ready for their academic programs. One by one, each student said, "wow" in his language, and after he heard twenty different "wows," Kovi stared at his colleagues for a while and said only one word in English, "Wow."

"Wow, what?" asked one of them.

"Just wow," responded Kovi.

"Is that all you have to say? You started the exercise and we want to know what you think after you heard everyone."

"Sometimes 'wow' is the last word. It says it all and there is nothing else to say after wow."

"But Kovi, we have not heard you. Tell us how you say 'wow' in your language," asked another student. And after they heard Kovi say "wow" in his language, their responses were "wow."

A few did not see the point to the exercise and walked away unimpressed. Others turned it into a game and asked each other repeat the "wow" word in their languages, and they learned how to say it in fifteen different languages, and each morning before class, they carried out an exercise to see who could remember the most versions.

Although he was there to learn English, Kovi developed a few insights about other languages, too. Sometimes, they reviewed each other's essays and the consistently different grammatical structures in the formation of sentences surprised Kovi. It then dawned on him that one of his colleagues had written a beautiful essay in his own language, but used English words.

Different idiomatic expressions, unknown to native English speakers, came up and became standard among the foreign students. For example, in an English conversation class, an African student stressed her point by concluding with the phrase, "Not everyone has the same head!" Their English instructor, a lady from Canada with the beautiful elocution that only a native speaker can aspire to, was bewildered. "Yes, we do not all have the same head. We know that much, but what is the point?"

Some students offered their viewpoints and explanations of the statement that then became the subject of debate. The instructor listened for a while and interjected, "Oh! You mean to say that we do not all have the same skills, potentials, desires, aspirations, et cetera." Then, there was the "wow" moment as she continued, "Wow! Is that how you say it in your language?" For the rest of the semester, the expression became popular among the students who resorted to it to tease each other and justify any differences in their grades and performance, to the chagrin of their instructors, who could not get them to use proper English formulations. Often the students said to each other, "Hey, don't worry about it, man. It's okay. And remember, not everyone has the same head."

***

As Thanksgiving approached, Kovi and the other foreign students heard a lot in class and from American students about this important holiday. Most people left to celebrate the holiday with family and friends, and the bustling university town became a ghost town. It was an unpleasant experience that many foreign students went through, when they were stranded at the university alone during Thanksgiving.

In class, the instructors asked Kovi and the other foreign students about their plans for Thanksgiving. Some students who had been in the country for a while and appreciated the scale and the importance of this holiday, or who had family in the country, made plans like the American students did. Some foreign students had already tasted the deep feeling of loneliness and isolation during the Thanksgiving holiday season and did not want not to let it happen again.

Some locals organized themselves into an association of "host families" to assist foreign students. During the holiday seasons, these host families invited foreign students and other stranded-ones to celebrate with them.

A few students seemed not to care and appeared content to stick around and study. Fortunately for Kovi, Jesse and John approached him and asked if he'd made any plans for the holiday.

"My brother from Africa, you should not be alone on Thanksgiving Day, man. You got to be with family or friends."

"I have a cousin in New York City, but I have not yet contacted her and it is now too late to just show up for Thanksgiving."

"Okay. Come with John and me. You will celebrate Thanksgiving with my folks in Gary and after that, you will join John and his family in Chicago."

"I cannot stay for too long. I have English classes next week."

"What's wrong with you? You can miss classes for a week. You will learn English more by immersion. Immersion, man!"

"Immersion?"

"Yes. By conversing with the native speakers. You talking every time with them foreign students will just make you learn a different English."

Kovi thought about the suggestion for a while and visited Jesse and John's families in Gary and Chicago. The three men journeyed together to Gary first, where Jesse and Kovi stayed for Thanksgiving, while John continued to Chicago. Jesse's extended family had gathered at Jesse's parents' house by the time Jesse and his friends arrived. It was late in the afternoon. Everyone was excited to meet the "brother from Africa" and to be the first family to offer him the uniquely American experience of the Thanksgiving dinner. Jess's Uncle, Jamal, took care of the turkey. He cooked with a special recipe that he did not want to share with anyone for fear of competition or to lose the special privilege of being the "turkey-man."

Jamal was a short man with a dark complexion. He appeared to be his sixties. He had a nicely trimmed dark gray beard, large sideburns, and a mustache that meshed into one smooth set of hair around his face and contrasted with his shaved head. Jamal had been in charge of making the turkey for thirty-some years, and everyone looked forward to this delicacy on Thanksgiving Day. They cooked the bird to a shiny golden brown. When they took it out of the oven, one dared not destroy the scene by cutting it. The spiced meat was radiating an appetizing smell that made Kovi's mouth water. After a moment, probably meant to showcase his turkey-cooking skills, Jamal was sure that everyone knew of his achievement, and he carved the turkey with an elegance and precision worthy of a surgeon.

They served dinner in a buffet style, and when Kovi approached the table, the quantity of food astonished him. They had turkey, ham, chitterlings, and an array of vegetables, including corn, collard greens, stuffing, and mashed potatoes. Some family members brought dishes with them, including an impressive array of dessert items. Kovi thought to himself, "This is too much food for so few people." He saw a drumstick laid on the side and told Jamal that was the piece of meat he wanted. When Kovi finished his plate, Jamal yelled to him across the room.

"Hey, bro! How was that drumstick?"

"It was good. Thanks, Jamal."

"Anytime, anytime man. It's my job to see people eat well and be satisfied."

Jesse's father, Steve, joined the conversation. Steve too was short and of a dark complexion, like his brother Jamal. Kovi paid careful attention to his appearance. He maintained thick black hair that he elegantly combed. Unlike Jamal, Steve must have shaved his beard, but he had a mustache trimmed low and his sideburns extended from his hair and descended from the side of his ears to just about halfway down his jaw.

"Hum, I don't know. The meat is not as succulent and juicy as it was last year. Don't you think, Aunt Jean?" said Steve.

"Hum… Yes, now that you mentioned it. There is something missing this time, but I can't put my finger on it," responded Jean.

Jean wore beautiful earrings and bracelets, and a hat full of various ornaments. She had radiant brown skin that appeared to glow and illuminated the entire room. She sat dignified and her presence commanded respect, but Jamal did not consider her and Steve's comments as the definitive assessment of his cooking skills and he asked the opinions of others.

"My brother from Africa, what do you think?" asked Jamal.

"Well, I was not here last year, so I cannot compare. But, this was a great meal. Thanks for having me," responded Kovi.

"Man! The dude is diplomatic. Well put, man. Well put. But we were here last year, and this isn't the same. Something is missing. Aunt Jean agrees," said Steve.

"What do the rest of ya'll think?" asked Jamal. Everyone kept quiet, except Jean and Steve who kept insisting that this year's turkey was good, but not as good as it was last year. Exasperated, Jamal climbed the stairs and yelled that he would never make the family turkey again.

When Jamal left the living room, Jesse and the other folks started laughing uncontrollably, and Kovi did not understand what was so funny. When Jesse finally got a hold of himself, he told Kovi that he had a lot of nerve to have taken Jamal's drumstick. For over thirty years, he had been sharing the two drumsticks, the best and tastiest part of the turkey, with his brother Steve. Then Kovi, fresh from Africa at his first Thanksgiving dinner, dared to claim the precious drumstick reserved for the head of household.

"My father and mother tease Jamal each year over the turkey and it was only this time that he got angry because he did not have his drumstick," explained Jesse.

When he heard that, Kovi became concerned that he may have missed an important cultural clue and offended Jamal, who had put such effort into cooking the turkey.

"Don't worry, son. I am glad that you enjoyed it. Jamal is fine. His heart is in the right place," said Jean.

"His heart is in the right place? I would hope so. He was not born with some abnormality, was he, Jesse?" responded Kovi.

"Don't get scientific on me, son. Jamal is a good man. His heart is always in the right place," Jean insisted.

"Hey, listen Kovi. It means that he meant well. His intentions are good," interjected Jesse.

"Oh, okay. Thanks," said Kovi.

"Except that time at the store when he yelled at a store agent to get his way," said Steve.

From upstairs, they could hear Jamal complaining about the fact that Steve brought up that story again. Jamal thought the story was unnecessary for the occasion, especially in the presence of a visitor from Africa. But Steve was unmoved and continued to narrate the story with a great deal of excitement, to tease his brother even further.

Jamal became a fireman after he served in the Vietnam War. He retired from the military with many honors for his years of service to his country. He was a respectable and trustworthy man.

One day, he went to a store to buy a new television. While in the store, he insisted that they checked and tested the device before he took it home. He did not want the unpleasant surprise of buying a defective television.

When he got home, as he was getting the box from the trunk of the car, it slipped out of his hand and hit the ground hard. Inside the house, he hooked up the new television, and despite his best efforts, the set did not work as it did in the store. So, Jamal carefully repacked it and took it back to the store. When he got there, the person who had assisted him before was no longer around. He explained to the new agent that they sold him a defective device and caused him the inconvenience of having to make a second trip to the store for a replacement.

The agent checked and verified that they had tested the device sold to Jamal and it was in perfectly good condition. Hence, any subsequent issues might have resulted from inappropriate use or operation not covered under the warranty. So, Jamal was not entitled to a replacement. Jamal got loud and visibly angry, and when he did so, he attracted the attention of the store manager.

The unfolding scene surprised and frightened customers, and they started to leave the store. To avoid any further embarrassment and keep customers shopping, the manager pleaded for Jamal to lower his voice and agreed to replace the device. Jamal got the new television, but he did not hear the end of the story that his brother and his wife told repeatedly, and each time with embellishment in the loving and good-natured game of tease among family and friends.

Just as Steve finished telling the story, a boy of about eleven years old was having dessert and belched loudly. "Excuse the pig, the hog is already out," responded Jean.

Kovi looked at Jesse with a face that asked for a translation of what Jean just said. Jean looked at Kovi, surprised and wondering about the English he was being taught at the university. She suggested that Kovi would be better served by spending time with her so that she might teach him the English that was really needed to fit in. Learning by immersion, as Jesse said before! Jesse translated Jean's comment about the burp as a disapproving expression to underscore the impoliteness of a gesture or an act in public, especially among respectable folks.

The boy was picky, and he had put too much on his plate. He was about to discard the rest of his food when his mother spoke up, with an authoritative voice.

"I told you not to waste the food. You must finish your plate."

"But I am full," replied the boy.

"Why did you take more than you can eat?"

The boy stood still with his plate in the hand and avoided eye contact. He did not answer his mother's question and there was a moment of silence before the mother continued, "How many times do I have to tell you to think of the poor Africans?" And she ordered her son to finish his plate. The boy returned to the table with tears streaming down his face, and he sat quietly to resume eating. Meanwhile, everyone went on as if nothing happened, but Kovi was reflecting on what he'd just heard. "The poor Africans…? Where I came from, I did not recall any of us went to bed hungry. And thinking of the poor Africans will not get the wasted food to them. One should just make available what is needed and avoid wasteful excesses. Not all Africans are poor and some of them might be wealthier than many of the folks here…" Kovi was lost in his thoughts when he heard Steve announce, "Excuse me. I need to talk to someone about a dog." Then Steve left the living room. Kovi wanted to understand and again he turned to Jesse for help.

"Is that so urgent?" asked Kovi.

"Apparently so," replied Jesse.

"Son! He is just going to the toilet," said Jean from the other side of the room. Kovi kept quiet. In one evening, he had had a great Thanksgiving dinner and heard many useful expressions that he could not have learned in his English classes.

The next day, Kovi was happy to enjoy the leftovers of turkey and chitterlings before he took the train to Chicago, where he stayed with John's family.

Kovi stayed with John, his mother, two brothers, and a sister in a cozy apartment near the center of the city. They were tightly connected people of Italian descent with a great sense of family and friendship. John's mother, Silvia, integrated Kovi into the family as another one of her children. Each morning, everyone gathered around the kitchen table for a communal breakfast and Silvia packed sandwiches, snacks, and drinks for Kovi and John, who ventured around the city, especially to the museums that featured the work and achievements of the great physicist Enrico Fermi. In the evenings, they gathered religiously around a dinner that was carefully and diligently prepared by Silvia. She was happy to see her children well fed, and she had authority and commanded respect, often intervening to quell an argument between her sons before it got out of control.

She did not enjoy going to restaurants, particularly Italian ones. Instead, she preferred to make the meal herself, to her desire and taste. The quality of any meal at any Italian restaurant could not match that which she could make at home, so she found it pointless and a waste of money to dine out.

In Silvia's house, there was always food for any extra individual. Often, extended family members popped in unannounced and Silvia always had a meal ready to serve. Silvia reminded Kovi of his own mother in Africa, who always accommodated other folks who appeared unexpectedly at meal times. Often, Kovi and his siblings waited for a guest to leave before they had their meal when they believed there was not enough for another individual. But Kovi's mother was against that, especially when the guest was a child. She maintained that all people under her roof ought to be well fed, equally. She always estimated the quantity of food needed and if she determined that there was not enough, she disappeared for a moment to the neighbors' houses to borrow a few ingredients or to the market to buy more food items, and before Kovi knew it, there was enough for everyone. Silvia did likewise with a huge fridge full of reserves, whereas with Kovi's family, there was no fridge and, as a result, Kovi's mother had to step out to collect additional ingredients as needed at the moment.

Kovi never asked about Silvia's husband, who had died many years earlier, when the children were still young. She still raised four fine individuals by herself.

***

While Kovi pursued graduate studies in physics, Jesse and John went for degrees in religion and became influential pastors in a major congregation near Chicago. It was many years later when

Kovi saw Jesse and John again, when they attended a religious convention held a few hours away from where Kovi lived. Kovi took his family along to meet them, and they attended one of Jesse's sermons, which he delivered with emotion and passion. In that meeting, Kovi learned the sad news that Jamal, Jean, and Silvia had died years ago, and Steve moved to live closer to Jesse to help in his congregation. John's brothers and sister moved away from Chicago and were then scattered across the country, driven by the demands and constraints of their respective jobs. Kovi looked with excitement at the photographs of the families of Jesse and John, and he promised to bring his family to Chicago to visit them someday. Kovi left his old friends that day hoping to see them again soon.

***

Kovi saw Josh for the last time after the Thanksgiving holiday. Although they did not meet in person again, Josh and Kovi kept in contact. With encouragement from Kovi, Josh made a trip to Africa. He traveled there with a group from his church. They visited the people that they were helping through their charitable organization, and Josh did the game drives, so he finally saw the animals he'd dreamed of. While there, Josh, the accomplished handyman, built houses, schools, and wells for the people. He took on many young people as apprentices and trained them in carpentry and masonry. After his return, he called Kovi and narrated his experiences with excitement. The warm hospitality of the people there touched him. Josh ultimately became a frequent visitor to Africa, engaging in several philanthropic projects.

Chapter Three
Higher Education

When Kovi returned to the university after the trip to Gary and Chicago, the AAI informed him that his English had improved enough to start the master's degree. They gave him an airplane ticket to Ball State University, and he started the program after Christmas.

Kovi arrived at Muncie Indiana a few days before Christmas, and his host family met him at the airport. It was a Polish couple of respectable standing. They introduced themselves as Pawel and Liza Majeski. Pawel worked as a medical doctor at the university hospital and Liza was a great lawyer. Kovi stayed with them until he found an apartment.

Liza and Pawel had many types of exercise equipment in their basement. They had a treadmill, a bicycle, a weightlifting machine, and some other devices that were not familiar to Kovi. Every day, Liza and Pawel spent at least forty-five minutes in the basement doing their daily exercises in the mornings before they went to work or in the evenings after work. Occasionally, and weather permitting, they dressed warmly and went for long jogging sessions around the neighborhood. Liza and Pawel were fit and slim, and they looked as if there was not even an ounce of fat on their bodies.

The university had many international students. The locals hosted and helped many of these students. Kovi spent his first Christmas Day with his host family and a few other international students who were "stranded."

Extended family members of Pawel and Liza drove from as far away as Chicago for the occasion. The meal on Christmas Day was like what Kovi had on Thanksgiving Day at Jesse's house, except for the collard greens and the chitterlings, and with the addition of the cranberry sauce that Kovi could not stand with his meal. For Kovi, the sweet cranberry sauce ought to be a part of breakfast or dessert, not a condiment for a great turkey meal for which the spices and flavor of the broth should suffice. Kovi noticed that some international students avoided the sweet sauces whereas the other people enjoyed the meal with a significant addition of the sweets. People sat or stood around in small groups engaging in small talk, nothing dramatic as in Jesse's house.

Many times, Kovi had to tell the story of his journey from Africa to the USA. Some brave people insisted on guessing his home country from his story. They started with a wild guess, like "Let me see, your country… Is it in the center or the east of Africa?" and they studied Kovi's face to decide the correctness of their guess. If they sensed disapproval, they took another wild guess. Ultimately, they guessed West Africa and were pleased as if they correctly provided the question to a Jeopardy game answer. Some stopped at the correct guess of West Africa, uninterested in knowing more, maybe tired from having used more brain cells than they expected for the evening. Or, conceivably, they were satisfied with the erroneous thought that the country was "West Africa," and there was nothing more to learn. Others carried on guessing at Kovi's country of origin, and since they narrowed the region to West Africa, they had a better chance of success.

After the guests left that night and the extended family members went to their rooms, Kovi, Liza, and Pawel sat for a few more hours in the night to enjoy their great digestive liquors. That was when they told Kovi about Billie. They apologized to Kovi in case they appeared sad and subdued; they wanted Kovi to know that it was because they were still grieving for Billie, who had died several days earlier.

Billie was a great companion, a lifelong friend that was with them from the beginning. They did everything with Billie, but when they went on vacations, they sent Billie to stay with a friend of theirs, as they did not want Billie to stay in the house alone and lonely. As the story unfolded the sadness conquered Kovi, too, and the atmosphere grew somber, and it gradually dawned on Kovi that Billie was a dog.

Kovi excused himself since he was tired and needed to rest, and he went to his room shaking his head. In his village in Africa, people had many dogs, which appeared to belong to no one in particular. The dogs came and went and no one worried about feeding them. Surely the death of a dog did not trigger intense emotion, equal to or surpassing the death of a human being. Here, he was sharing the pain and sorrow of his hosts over the death of a dog that in its lifetime had received the most impressive medical attention and treatments. Kovi respected the feeling of his hosts, but he did not care much about Billie the Dog. The next day, Kovi reiterated his condolence to Liza and Pawel about the passing of their beloved Billie and prayed that they found comfort and joy with their other dog.

Kovi needed a haircut desperately. He had not cut his hair since he came to America, and his kinky hair grew thick and became difficult to comb. Pawel took Kovi to the barbershop that he used for his own haircuts. When they got there, Kovi's hair posed a great challenge to the most experienced barber, who had never cut the hair of a black man. They did not want to say, "Sorry sir, we don't know how to handle your type of hair. We do not have experience with that. Frankly, we have never cut the hair of a black man before and you are the first black person to come in here for a haircut." To Kovi, that would have been perfectly understandable with no offense taken. But they attempted to cut Kovi's hair and the task first fell on a young lady who was an apprentice barber.

She was a friendly lady; she talked to Kovi to put him at ease. But after several minutes, she poked a few holes in Kovi's hair, made no visible progress and gave up in frustration. They left Kovi there, and he looked in the mirror and worried that his hair was worse than when he came. The young lady came back with the chief barber who was the staff member with the most experience and skill. He introduced himself and informed Kovi that he was taking over the task. So, then he started to work on Kovi's hair and at each step commented on the hair and showed his apprentice what to do. A few other students of his came over to watch and learn from their great professor in action. In Kovi's hair, the chief barber found a golden and unexpected opportunity for education. When the lecture and demonstration were over, the barber professor was pleased with his work, but by their looks, the students were less impressed. Kovi looked in the mirror and could not contain his unhappiness when he saw that his hair was uneven across his head with many holes of various sizes.

Pawel stood there and watched with a look of disbelief; his great barbershop did not handle the hair of a black person. In the many years he had been using that barbershop for his own haircuts, he never saw a black customer. Black people got their haircuts somewhere else, but he had no clue where, and was surprised to realize that even the haircutting business was segregated. He promised to find the barbershops with the proper experience and knowledge of black people's hair, but for the time being Kovi had to live with a mess on his head.

A few days later, Kovi went through the university registration process and met a gentleman on campus. They were walking in opposite directions and as they got closer to each other, Kovi greeted the individual and said, "What's going down, bro?" The man stopped dead in his tracks, looked at Kovi, and replied.

"You ain't from here, are you? Why do you want to imitate people? 'What's going down, bro?' You ain't saying it right and you got an accent. Where're you from? Nigeria?"

"Close to Nigeria."

"What happened to your hair, man? Who did this to you? We got to fix you up, bro. You can't walk around like this!"

"My host family took me to the barbershop at the town center. They tried and did their best, but it still did not come out right. I am not happy with it myself. My host is looking for a different barbershop."

"The barbershop downtown? You saw any black dudes in there? Good Lord, have mercy! I will get you fixed up. My name is Hakeem. What's your name?"

"My name is Kovi. Thank you. Appreciated."

"You got a number I can call you at?"

"No, not yet but you may call my host. Here is his number."

"Okay. I will call you tomorrow. Tomorrow, bro!"

As he walked away, Kovi heard him when he said, "Shit! Why do they have to mess up the brother's hair like that? That ain't right, man. That ain't right." He said the word "shit" as though it contained at least three syllables, like "Shi-yee-ett!" Kovi practiced many times, but even with practice, he still could not curse so elegantly.

They took Kovi to a barbershop uptown where he received a large amount of attention. Folks expressed sympathy and disgust that someone messed up the hair of a fine-looking brother from the Motherland. An old gentleman took charge of cutting Kovi's hair, and as he was about to start, he said,

"The white dude wants a haircut, too?"

"No, I am fine. Just him," said Pawel.

"We can fix you up, man. We cut all kinds of hair here."

"Thank you. Maybe next time."

The barber took his time and during the entire time he worked on Kovi's hair, folks came in and went, and there were jokes, gossip, small talk, and laughs. When the barber finished, he marveled at his own achievement and stated confidently that Kovi looked so great that he would get a girlfriend in no time.

Kovi found a room in a house known as the Physics House near the Physics Department building where he took most of his courses.

The Physics House belonged to a senior physics professor. He rented the rooms in the house to graduate students, most of whom majored in physics, hence the name.

After taking the required courses, Kovi opted to do his master's thesis on theoretical physics related to solar energy applications, which he hoped might be valuable for energy needs in Africa.

To improve his skills in computing, Kovi took a few courses in the computer science department, where he impressed some with his different style of handling arithmetic. For instance, they marveled at how swiftly he carried out complicated divisions or square roots without using a calculator or a computing tool.

For extracurricular activity, Kovi got involved in the management of the African students' organization. The university had many African students from various countries, and there was interest, at the university and in the town, in showcasing a piece of African culture through a fashion show and a drumming session, annually. These activities required careful planning and preparation, and the African students came together voluntarily and self-organized into one of the most successful groups at the university.

The events organized by the African students always drew large crowds. During the fashion show, many people—not just African students—wore African clothes. They allowed volunteers to stand for a few moments before a crowd of spectators. Kovi wore the traditional outfits that his uncle, Théodore, a tailor, made for him before he came to America.

During the drumming session, people brought their musical instruments and freely partook in the play with a few experienced people who maintained the rhythm so that the noise still sounded like pleasant music. The crowd usually got involved in playing the drums and dancing. At the end of these events, many people approached Kovi and the other participants to offer praise and useful commentary on the different styles and designs of the items paraded. Among the interested people, were the academics, the learned folks and experts in aspects of African traditions or cultures. Some of these people spent time in Africa for research or charitable causes. The academics often shared insights from their observations or analyses, insights that the African students did not have or were pleasantly surprised to see that the outsiders had conceived. For example, they might comment on a particular musical instrument— its origin, how folks made it and the primary purposes for which they used it.

There was an African-American lady who formed an African dance group equipped with skillful drummers and dancers from all over. She traveled to many parts of Africa and learned many beats and dances from various regions and skillfully integrated them into her repertoire. At the beginning of each performance, she made a short speech to introduce the piece they were about to perform, where it originated from and how the locals in Africa used it. Since she showcased a variety of music and dances from different regions, there was always something she introduced that some African students did not know about; they had to come all the way to America to hear and see it for the first time. When she performed a piece from some particular place, African students from that region happily joined her troop and sang along and danced, and that increased the intensity of the good ambiance.

After one of these events, when most people left and there were just a few people around to clean up, the discussion focused on Kovi, himself. A group of African students approached him and wanted to have a word with him. Kovi was worried and thought it was a serious matter, although he could not figure out what he had done. They saw the look of worry in his face and assured him it was nothing serious, and they merely desired to have a friendly conversation.

The people had observed that Kovi had been at the university for several months, yet he did not have any girlfriend and, according to the information they gathered, he was a heterosexual. They wanted to know if his family jewels were dysfunctional or if there were some other issues. One member of the group started to talk and pretended to choose his words carefully. Everyone else kept quiet and avoided eye contact. Kovi listened intensely, and as he did, he noticed that everyone, including the speaker, could hardly contain the urge to laugh. When Kovi finally understood what the discussion was about, he too could not stop laughing. Kovi said he was a shy individual determined to focus on his studies so he could get fellowships to continue with his doctorate degree. Kovi got more and more defensive as the people listened to him attentively yet with looks of suspicion. After that conversation, they made a remarkable yet unsuccessful effort to get Kovi to loosen up and learn to balance leisure and studies.

Kovi thought the community of African students offered a replica of what he was accustomed to without the discomfort of exploring beyond that cultural bubble. So, Kovi again joined a non-denominational church where he hoped to meet new people, in particular, the American students, to increase his immersion in the new cultural setting.

Kovi made many new friends, some through the church. One of them was Jeff, who claimed that he had Native American blood — twenty-five percent. After many weeks, Jeff invited Kovi to spend a weekend with him at his parents' house, and one Friday afternoon, they made a three-hour drive there.

They arrived late in the afternoon in the spring, when the trees started to recover their leaves and attractive flowers cropped up everywhere. The house was isolated from the rest of the town and surrounded by tall trees except at the front, which connected to a long and steep gravel road flanked by well-aligned rows of trees. The end of the gravel road was a T-junction to the main road that in one direction led to the town within a few minutes, and in the other direction to a busy highway. Across from the intersection, there was an impressive yellowish-green meadow extending in both directions; its seemingly infinite extent was breathtaking.

The house itself was huge, though it did not appear so until one got inside. The vast living room floor was of a shiny golden-brown wood and at the center lay an exquisite carpet, around which was a carefully positioned matching set of living room furniture that comprised a sofa, a rocking recliner, a love seat, a center table, and a pair of end tables. They mounted a huge television into the wall, and it faced the main sofa. They arranged entire set by a large transparent glass door that offered a view onto the gravel road and the meadow beyond.

They decorated living room walls with paintings and the heads of game animals. A set of dimmable lights completed the picture of wealth and comfort. The kitchen, too, was large with floor tiles that matched the kitchen table in color, and equipped with a carefully selected matching set of appliances. The dining room was no less appealing, and at its center was a large table and twelve cushioned chairs that appeared to be priceless antique items. The bathroom Kovi used was spacious, squeaky-clean, and equipped with a sauna.

A slow country music song reverberated through the living room when Jeff introduced Kovi to the family. Jeff's grandmother, a short and chubby lady with white hair and about eighty years old, asked Kovi for permission to touch his hair. At that point, Jeff's father and mother excused themselves and left. Kovi looked at Jeff, who froze, dumbfounded, while the grandmother maintained a look of innocence and sincerity, patiently awaiting an answer. Kovi allowed her to touch his hair, and she took her time, went around his head and squeezed the hair gently. When she finished, she only offered one comment, "That's so lovely!" Kovi wondered why she wanted to do that and why Jeff's parents disappeared when the grandmother made the request. But he did not think further about it until he talked to Hakeem when he returned to the university.

Meanwhile, Jeff took Kovi downstairs to the basement to show him his father's gun collection. Kovi did not realize what Jeff meant by "gun collection" until they were in the basement and he was startled by what lay before his eyes. Guns everywhere! There were guns on the north wall, guns on the south wall, more guns to the west, and even more on the east wall. Guns! Guns! And different guns!

"Why does your father own so many guns?" asked Kovi.

"For hunting!"

"How many of these do you need to hunt? You have so many here that can supply an entire infantry!"

"He loves guns and collects them. Many people do, you know?"

"You mean others around here have basements loaded like this?"

"It is the right of the people, secured by the second amendment!"

"Oh! I'm not judging, Jeff. I am sincerely surprised by the need for so many per individual. I suppose if a foreign army ever invaded America, they may have to face so many heavily armed private citizens in town-to-town and house-to-house combat that the invaders might not win."

"It is not for that, Kovi! It's for the right to defend ourselves right here in our land."

"Defend against who? Fellow American citizens?"

"To protect the Constitution."

"I do not follow."

"A breach of the Constitution will face the objection of heavily armed citizens."

"I see. I am not sure that I agree, but I hear you."

Jeff's father came in, possibly to check what these two youngsters were doing in the basement. His beloved Jeff had come home with a friend that the father did not know. Then, Jeff took the dude into his basement full of guns and he did not know what might happen. But they were a lovely family, God-fearing, well-to-do, and decent folks who treated Kovi well that weekend.

On Monday morning, Kovi ran into Hakeem, who was excited to see him. He told Kovi that he was looking for him all weekend and asked where he'd been.

"I spent the weekend with Jeff's folks."

"What? You went there? Man, what was wrong with you? Next time, please ask me."

"Ask you what? For permission to go somewhere?"

"Well, yes! That place you went to is full of Ku Klux Klan people."

"I did not see any Ku Klux Klan people, and Jeff's family treated me well! Maybe I had the luck of the naïve."

"Maybe so man. Maybe so! Tell me what happened. Elaborate."

"The grandmother asked to touch my hair, and the basement was full of guns!"

"What? Wait. Wait. Wait. You let her touch your hair? Damn! I cannot believe you, Kovi. She rubbed your head for good luck!"

"Rubbed my head for good luck?"

"They used to consider it good luck to rub black people's heads. Besides that, you must not allow it because you are not some exotic animal."

"Oh! I see. Now, I understand what you mean."

"You do?"

"Yes. We have something similar in my village in Togo although the context is different."

Kovi said that in his ancestral village in Africa, there was no way on Earth he would let an old lady, mother or grandmother, touch his head, especially when supposedly, the woman was a witch. In the traditional belief of Kovi's people, a witch who rubbed someone's head would confiscate the victim's soul and death was imminent unless one initiated proper countermeasure.

***

Kovi told Hakeem about a childhood event, when he encountered a presumed witch. Kovi was about five or six years old when one afternoon he emerged from his grandmother Mawule's house and came face-to-face with a woman who kids in the village thought to be a witch. Kovi froze as they stared at each other for what appeared to Kovi like a long time. Although the "witch" did not touch him or rub his head, Kovi thought that if he stood there longer, the power of the witch would somehow consume him and he would die. Overwhelmed by that fear, Kovi ran in the opposite direction to Mawule at the village center and told her everything that happened. To make sure that Mawule reacted, Kovi embellished the story and added that the "witch" rubbed his head. When she heard that, Mawule stormed out of the marketplace furious and she went to confront the witch, "If something happens to this child, if he sneezes, develops a headache, fever, or stomachache, I will kill you with my bare hands." The lady attempted to explain that she had never touched Kovi. The more the lady explained, the angrier and louder Mawule became, and the commotion attracted the village folks, who gathered to watch. Kovi felt sad and to this day that was the one thing he regretted the most, to have falsely accused an innocent old lady.

There he was in America and at Jeff's house where an old lady touched his head. Inappropriate—highly inappropriate—but harmless in Kovi's view!

***

After a year at the university, Kovi saved enough money to buy a car, a used stick-shift sedan. Kovi did not know how to drive, let alone how to drive a stick shift, but it was a good bargain that Kovi did not want to miss. So Kovi bought the car, but it was still in the previous owner's driveway because Kovi could not drive and did not have a driver's license. Kovi asked one of his friends, André-Simon Le Beau, an African student, to fetch the car and park it at the Physics House.

Several months before he bought the car, Kovi had studied the driving code in anticipation of taking the driving test for the driver's license, and fellow physics graduate students were kind enough to take him often for driving practice sessions. When Kovi was comfortable maneuvering a car with an automatic transmission, André-Simon taught him how to drive a car with a manual transmission within a week.

Kovi went with André-Simon to the Department of Motor Vehicles, where he took and passed the driving test. They gave him a driver's license that day and he was pleased to drive by himself. By the time they left the Department of Motor Vehicles, snow mixed with rain was falling, and Kovi noticed that all the cars drifted and maintained large distances between each other. Kovi did not comprehend what was going on, and he took advantage of the large space between the cars and made his turn. Gosh! Kovi got a crash course that day about how to drive in dreadful weather when the snowy mix on the road created slippery and dangerous conditions.

***

After two years at Ball State University, Kovi graduated with the Masters of Science Degree in Physics, with honors. Several weeks after the graduation ceremony and all the farewell celebrations, Kovi loaded up his car with his few belongings and drove fifteen hours across many states to the east coast where he started the doctorate program in physics at the University of Virginia (UVA).

When Kovi arrived, he spent a few days with his new host family. Then, he started his graduate courses together with other international students. He had been admitted into the program with a teaching assistantship that covered tuition and fees and offered a monthly stipend. Kovi supervised laboratory experiments and demonstrations, and he marked exams and arranged tutorial sessions for medical and engineering students who needed to take some physics lessons to fulfill their course requirements. At the end of the term, the students filled out a survey to offer feedback on their instructors. Kovi and other assistant teachers saw the anonymous comments from their students.

For Kovi, negative comments centered on his accent, such as, "He has a heavy accent. I just cannot understand anything he says. I have to concentrate to understand what he is saying. It's such a drag. Please do something about him."

Kovi noticed that at the beginning of the term, his classes were full with enthusiastic students, but over time, progressively fewer students bothered to come.

In between their courses, teaching, and office hours, Kovi and the other graduate students discussed their homework and lectures. When the graduate students attended the lectures of an illustrious professor, they looked at each other at the end of the lectures, and all agreed they understood little. One professor often surveyed the perplexed looks on the faces of his students during his lectures, and under a barrage of questions, he said, "I am sure you will figure it out." He then continued his lecture unaware he had lost his students thirty minutes ago. In these moments, when Kovi understood a little from the lecture, not because of the professor's accent, he sympathized with his own students who had the arduous task of understanding the mumbo-jumbo expressed in his heavy accent first, and then comprehending the underlying physics message, next.

Kovi lived in an apartment complex with another graduate student named Xie, who came from Taiwan. They often walked together to the Physics Department and had many opportunities to discuss physics. One evening, Xie went to Kovi's apartment, and he sat on the sofa quietly for a while. He bent his head down and rested it on his left hand. Xie was usually talkative with a smile, but that day something dampened his jovial spirit. When he finally started to talk, he said that he had been walking alone and came across a group of young black folks, apparently students at the university. This group of people started calling him names, racially offensive ones. To avoid confrontation, Xie kept walking, he did not challenge them, and he acted as if he was not the one they were addressing. Kovi listened to him to the end, then felt compelled to apologize to Xie, although he had nothing to do with the incident. "We must set a good example of treating others—who are racially different—how we expect to be treated." Kovi told his friend.

From that day, the friendship between Kovi and Xie grew stronger, and they began discussing non-physics matters. Two men of different cultures and heritages, educated in different parts of the world, who competed fiercely in their graduate education, understood each other perfectly in their heavy accents. One day, they had a memorable conversation.

"Kovi, I have a question for you. Is it true that on average your people have bigger ones?"

"Bigger what?"

"I am sure you know what I mean."

"I've not seen any convincing scientific evidence for that."

"Well, what is your size?"

"Look at my shoes. They say there is a correlation."

"No. That cannot be. The assumption of correlation is not validated."

"Okay. I agree with you. Let's discuss our homework now. I looked at the problems and the first one seems to be the most difficult one. We will need to arrive at a Lagrangian with the correct interaction term first."

Reluctantly, Xie stopped talking, and he paced around the room in silence. Kovi said nothing further and after a few moments he attempted a smile. The two men started to laugh, and soon, the discussion changed to their homework problems. Xie never raised that subject again.

Xie got his doctorate degree, went back to Taiwan, and got married. He invited Kovi to the wedding, but Kovi could not go. Years later, when Kovi was in the region for a physics conference, he paid a visit to Xie, who had two kids. After a great traditional dinner, they were having a beer on the balcony when Kovi told his friend, "You have a wonderful family. You know what else I've heard? Size isn't happiness!"

Xie said nothing and continued sipping his beer with a smile. His wife thought she heard something, and she yelled to ask what they needed. Xie frankly responded, "Nothing. We are just wrapping up an unfinished conversation that we started way back in graduate school."

***

One day, Kovi got into his car and started the engine. He noticed that the car was running, but the key was still in his hand. It took him a while to realize that the key had broken in such a way that one piece was stuck in the ignition and the other piece was in his hand. He could start or stop the engine when he inserted the broken piece into the ignition carefully and turned the piece that was stuck. The maneuver required patience and was annoying. His host family arranged for him to see a repairman that they'd known and trusted for many years. He was an auto mechanic, a locksmith, or a combination thereof.

Kovi arrived for the appointment and had to wait for the repairman to finish the job. The broken piece of the key stuck in the ignition was to be taken out and a new spare key made. The repairman was a Caucasian man in his late twenties. He owned and ran the shop together with his wife, who handled the appointments, reception, and payments. The couple had a daughter who was about four or five years old, and that day the kid was at the reception desk with her mother.

Kovi was waiting at the reception while the gentleman worked on his car. The kid was playing and got her hands dirty while the mother was constantly on the telephone answering calls and booking appointments. She raised her head at some point and instructed her daughter to stop playing on the floor and getting her hands so dirty. At that moment, the father emerged from the shop and gave Kovi an assessment of the damage and a cost estimate of the repair. Then, he requested Kovi's approval before proceeding. Distracted by her husband and the necessity of updating an invoice, the lady's attention drifted away from her daughter, who then ignored her instructions and continued to play on the floor. Kovi butted in and told the kid that her mother said not to play on the floor and that her hands were dirty. The kid approached Kovi, pointed to the back of his palm and told Kovi he was dirty, too. Kovi said he was just a brown man and that he wasn't dirty. The palms of her hands were remarkably dirty. The kid did not understand that and insisted innocently on drawing a connection between her dirty hands and Kovi's complexion. Her parents overheard the discussion and disappeared in embarrassment. When the repairman finished the job, the parents reappeared. Before Kovi left, he asked them subtly to raise their wonderful daughter properly and offered his opinion that their daughter was just a kid whose development was highly influenced by what she heard and learned from adults.

Chapter Four
Grüezi Mitenand

Two years after he started the doctorate studies, when Kovi completed the course requirements, he passed the doctorate-qualifying exam and got a fellowship to start work on his dissertation. He worked with a professor who was preparing for one of his research experiments at the Paul Scherrer Institute (PSI) in the German-speaking part of Switzerland. The thesis advisor sent him there to collect the data needed for his dissertation.

He had gone there a few times on short visits, but this time he was to stay for eighteen months. The lengthy stay was enough for him to learn all the different aspects of the project, and to become the expert and the driving force toward the publication of the results, as expected from graduate students in experimental physics.

The project required in-depth knowledge in particle detectors, data acquisition and analysis—this could be fairly daunting. His professor assured him that only a few could achieve that level of knowledge in everything, and that it was only necessary to become an expert in a few things, to be a go-to and non-expendable member of the research team. Cynically, the professor commented, "If you take any project and arrange it into many small tasks, ultimately everyone involved would become an expert in something."

***

Kovi was to take the train from Zurich Airport, then change to a bus to go to PSI. By mistake, he got onto a train that went only to the city center main station, where he had to catch another train. At the main station, Kovi was late to notice that the train was going ahead to the train yard. He was not asleep. He just did not hear or understand the announcement.

He was not entirely sure on which platform to make his connection, so he approached a gentleman to ask for information. As Kovi started to greet the fellow in English, the man got loud and said a bunch of stuff in Swiss German that Kovi did not understand. The man walked away as Kovi stood there and did not understand what he did wrong. Fortunately for him, a lady who saw the interaction and felt sorry for Kovi stepped forward and helped him find the correct platform. Kovi climbed aboard the train, but could not find a seat. The train was full. Kovi dragged his bag from car to car and looked for a seat as the train left the station. He came into a car where there were many available and comfortable seats. Kovi sat happily and relaxed, and he was falling asleep after an overnight flight during which he was awake most of the time. Right at that moment, a lady dressed in uniform entered the car and announced, "*Grüezi Mitenand*. All tickets." When she arrived where Kovi was sitting, Kovi handed her his ticket. The lady looked at it and said something in Swiss German. When she realized that Kovi did not comprehend Swiss German, she switched into perfect English and explained to Kovi that he had purchased a second-class ticket, but he was sitting in first class. She ordered Kovi back through a series of cars into a second class.

Kovi became more and more exhausted when he arrived in a second-class car and still could not find a seat. As he walked down the aisle, he spotted a free seat finally, just across from the man he had approached earlier on the platform. Kovi hesitated awhile, but could gather his courage and took the seat. The man blew up again into a rage and yelled vehemently. Kovi did not understand what made him angry or what he was saying. Kovi just sat quietly, uncomfortable, and avoided eye contact. Now and then, the man looked at Kovi and said many things. There were no reactions from Kovi and that puzzled him. At the next stop, the man was still in a state of rage and continued to yell as he got off the train. Kovi stayed on the train. He got off a few stops later and changed to a bus to reach PSI. He spent the night at the on-site housing.

The next day, going to the cafeteria, people greeted Kovi and his colleagues with "Grüezi Mitenand." He noticed that if he was by himself, it was just "Grüezi," and the "Mitenand" applied to two or more persons. Kovi came to appreciate the polite and considerate nature of the greeting forms.

He found an apartment in Klingnau on the bank of the Aare River. He was the only person of color in the village and received extensive attention and respect once the village folks learned that Kovi was a scientist at the laboratory. Kovi learned when to say Grüezi, or Grüezi Mitenand, or other phrases for polite interactions, in perfect Swiss German. This helped improve his immersion in the new cultural environment and made his stay enjoyable.

***

One morning as he was going to the laboratory, a car exiting a parking lot hit Kovi gently. There was no harm, and the driver was apologetic. Kovi was in a state of a shock and had to go back to his apartment to change his pants, which had gotten dirty from the impact with the car tires. They encouraged Kovi to file a police report. So, he went to the police station with an English-German dictionary. The policeman spoke no English and Kovi knew only a rudimentary form of "High German." Here were two men with no common language and only a dictionary. Each took a turn to consult the dictionary and show the other what they meant to say. It was a pleasant exchange. Kovi filed the report to the great satisfaction of both men.

***

Kovi stayed there for eighteen months and completed the

experiment. He was to return to UVA to finish the analysis of the data and the dissertation. Before leaving Switzerland, he was to go to the town hall for a departure procedure. The fellow who handled his case wondered why Kovi was leaving. He asked Kovi in Swiss German if Switzerland was not good enough for him. Kovi struggled to explain the purpose of his presence and reasons for his departure. Satisfied that Switzerland had been good to Kovi, the gentleman said, "*Alles Gueti*!"

***

Kovi spent one night with a Swiss-German family in Bulach and the next day he took the bus to Zurich Airport. When he arrived at the airport, he noticed that he did not have his briefcase, which was where he had put his passport, wallet, and several personal documents. Losing his passport and wallet meant that he was a man with no identity. Had he left the briefcase on the bus? He did not recall. Maybe he'd left it at the house where he was staying. Kovi got into a taxi, with no money to pay the taxi driver at the end of the journey, to go back to where he spent the night. He knew that it was a risky move. What if no one was home? What was he going to do and how was he going to pay the taxi driver? To make matters worse, it was an expensive taxi ride.

During the ride, Kovi was on edge. He explained his worry about the lost briefcase to the taxi driver who did his best to go as fast as he could. When they finally arrived at the house, there was no one there as expected because the kids went to school and the adults went to work. Kovi knocked in vain while the taxi driver waited for payment with the meter still running.

In one of those magic moments when you see the hand of God, there appeared Christian, the man of the house. Christian had forgotten something and came back home for it. He looked at Kovi, who should have been on the flight somewhere over the English

Channel, and he knew that something was wrong. They searched the entire house and found no briefcase. The taxi driver waited. If they found the briefcase, he was to take Kovi back to the airport hoping Kovi might still catch a later flight. When there was no briefcase, Christian paid the taxi driver, as Kovi had no money. Christian did not go back to work that day, since Kovi sank into depression.

Togo did not have an embassy in Switzerland and it was difficult for him to get his passport replaced. He would likely have to go back to Togo with a special permit instead of the passport, but all the papers that established his identity were lost with the briefcase. He was, henceforth, a man with no money and no citizenship of any country, stuck in a place where he did not speak the local language well.

Even if he were to go back to his country, it was not obvious he could easily return to the USA to finish his research, since his entrance visa for the USA was pasted in the lost passport.

Kovi wished he were a citizen of a first-world country. Losing a passport should not be the destruction of one's future, if that were the case. He recalled that several months earlier, one of his colleagues, who was traveling to Switzerland for the same research project, had his passport stolen during transit through London, along with other personal items. His colleague appeared at the USA embassy in London, got a new passport the same day, and arrived at the laboratory later that evening. Maybe it was a temporary passport that his colleague got; Kovi did not recall. But still what a privilege, he thought, for citizens traveling abroad to get that level of service and special treatment from their government. In his case, after many years of high education, losing a passport threatened his entire future.

Christian suggested that they go check at the town hall where sometimes lost and found objects were taken. They were to go check there before Kovi started a police declaration of loss. So, they went to the town hall, and to the pleasant surprise of both men, his briefcase was there—Kovi did not expect to recover the briefcase. Christian only paid a fee of twenty Swiss francs to collect the briefcase. All the contents of the briefcase were there. They informed Kovi that a lady who waited at the bus stop where Kovi took the bus to the airport saw the briefcase on the bench there and took it to the town hall. Wow! Only in this wonderful country would one expect such a happy ending. Elsewhere, one might never see the briefcase again, or the unwanted contents might be tossed into nearby garbage dumpsters.

These days, they would consider a briefcase, left on a bench at a public bus stop, a bomb threat. The authorities would set up a security perimeter, and might destroy the briefcase.

***

Kovi boarded a flight the next day and returned to UVA. But, it was not the last time he lost his passport. It was to happen again in Switzerland, the second time, in the French-speaking part of the country. During his postdoctoral studies, Kovi went to Geneva, where he spent some time for a research project at CERN. One day, when he returned from a trip, a travel wallet that Kovi was wearing around his neck mysteriously disappeared somewhere between Geneva Airport and his apartment. The wallet had money, his credit cards, and passport. The unpleasant experience of the past was repeating—as did the happy ending. After a week of frustration and hopelessness, a bank teller called Kovi to inform him that a wallet had been left at the bank, in the same box where people make money deposits in envelopes during after-hours. The credit cards and the passport were still inside, but not the cash.

***

Years later, Kovi became a dual citizen and traveled with a passport from a first-world country. He spent much less time at consulates and embassies seeking travel visas, and the thought of losing his passport in a foreign country was not a nightmare. Until then, he continued to travel with a passport that could not be promptly and easily replaced, if lost.

Chapter Five
Family Visits

When Kovi finished the analysis of the data after his return to the USA, he wrote his dissertation and graduated with a PhD in physics.

Kovi could not afford the airfare for both of his parents to attend his graduation ceremony, so only Kodjo visited him for the occasion. Kodjo was proud, not only of his visit but also of his son's achievement as the first in the family to get a doctoral degree.

Kodjo saw the ceremony, during which Kovi and others appeared in sumptuous graduation regalia and Kovi received his doctorate diploma, which he later framed and hung in his apartment. Kodjo often teased his son that he went to school for many years and became a doctor, but he was in no position to cure any sick person. It was difficult for Kovi to clarify the distinction between a doctor as a medical doctor and a doctor as a PhD in physics. For Kodjo, a doctor received training to cure people, and Kovi was not "a real doctor that he expected," despite Kovi's many years of higher learning.

Many months later, Kovi and his father visited the White House, where Kodjo heard the story of where the name "America" came from. Kovi later remembered this when he was preparing for the test for naturalization as a citizen of the USA.

After their visit to the White House, they traveled by car to New York and stayed with Ashley who had since moved to Farmingdale. During the drive, it was getting dark, and it started to snow. Kodjo had not seen snow before and he asked Kovi what it was. Kovi struggled to explain why and how snow forms and falls. Kovi thought that he explained it well, but Kodjo could not relate to the explanation until the next day when they were standing at the edge of a cliff and looking over the Long Island Sound. Snow started falling all around them, and Kodjo stood immobile and watched intently saying nothing. Everything was looking white and only the bay was still resisting. Later, after his return to Africa, that was a sight Kodjo wished to see again, but he never got the chance.

In New York City, they did all the usual tourist attractions, culminating with panoramic views of the city from the tops of the famous skyscrapers. Kodjo's trip to America gave both men a chance for father-son bonding that they had missed for many years. Kovi wished his father could stay longer, but he could not exceed the maximum duration of stay on his visa, and Kodjo insisted on returning home because, he thought, his grandchildren were missing him. Before he returned to Africa, Kodjo told his son that the trip to the USA was the best and the most memorable one of his life.

***

Many years after graduation, Kovi moved to Wading River. Afi came for a visit. This was a remarkable and special journey for his mother. When she took the flight from Africa, with a changeover in Paris, she had limited mobility and was wheelchair bound, and in addition, she could not read or write French or English. There were worries in the family about her ability to make the journey. Kovi's siblings, in particular, were most worried about their mother and they were discouraging. But Afi was determined. She wanted to visit America to see for herself her son's new home and understand what kept him so busy that he no longer went back to visit often. She had not seen her son in many years and often complained that she did not know how much time she had left. As she was a disabled person needing help, her children arranged for her to be taken care of during the entire journey to America. Against the fears of everyone, she made a successful journey and Kovi met his mother at JFK Airport for a great reunion.

The day after Afi's arrival, they drove to the beach close to Kovi's place. She used a walking stick for a short walk from a parking lot. They were standing by a big rock on the beach, and she asked her son, "Are you not proud that I could make the journey alone?" Kovi was proud.

Afi stayed with Kovi for three months. That was a special period when Kovi spoke in his own language often and regained the full fluency that he once had. Afi showed him a few tricks to make great traditional meals.

During her visit, Kovi had to make a few trips outside the USA for research. These trips lasted a week at a time. During his absence, Afi stayed with Kovi's cousin, Ashley. The proximity of Ashley allowed for family get-togethers with the re-creation of the home atmosphere and ambiance that Kovi had not experienced in many years.

The day Afi was returning to Africa, Kovi and his mother took the same flight to Paris, where they went their separate ways. After a layover of a few hours, Afi continued to Africa. She arrived in the evening and her excited children met her at the airport. Kovi, meanwhile, took a different flight for a research experiment in physics at CERN.

Kovi had fond memories of his parents' visits. Occasionally, he looked at the photo albums and remembered a fun trip, a fight, or a disagreement. Kovi was always happy that his parents, at their advanced ages and with limited mobility, could visit America and experience a different culture. When they came and saw the different society in which their son settled, this provided a better understanding about life in a first-world country versus the day-to-day realities in a third-world country. Their visits generated stronger family bonds, for there were many jovial conversations during their visits.

***

A few years after Afi's visit, Kovi accepted an invitation to West Africa to lecture at a school of physics and he spent a few days with his family. Before he went to the airport for his return flight to the USA, Kovi went to a restaurant with one of his brothers, Koku Jean-Tonton.

It was an open-air restaurant, under a huge baobab tree, where Kovi used to dine often before he left the country for his graduate studies. The restaurant served meals only in the late afternoons and evenings, and it attracted people from all walks of life to enjoy food, music, leisure or business talks, and soccer matches on television. It specialized in a variety of African dishes from everywhere on the continent and created an international atmosphere where one could find someone from any place imaginable.

To cater to the foreigners, people did not put hot spices directly in the food as they do traditionally, but they served them on the side and they advised guests to use them with moderation.

They served the food in the buffet style, and Kovi and Koku were in line to take their shares. There was a lady in front of them who took a huge quantity of a hot pepper sauce against the advice of a waiter. She boasted about her experience with hot spicy food during her many travels to different places in Latin America, Asia, and Africa.

Kovi and Koku were enjoying their meals when suddenly she started screaming and running around hysterically like a headless chicken, grabbing and drinking every glass of water within her reach. Everyone turned around to look, and at first, no one knew what the problem was. A few members of her own party approached her to help, and they advised her to calm down. She sat on the floor with her mouth wide opened and tried to suck as much air in as possible to dampen the burning effect of the hot sauce on her tongue and throat. She was breathing heavily and fast. She moved her hands forward and backward in front of her chest, and her eyes were watering.

Some attempted to arrange a taxi to rush her to the hospital but, fortunately, with every passing second, she looked and felt better as the burn of the pepper subsided. When she was out of danger, the locals burst into a huge uncontrolled and contagious laugh and some people imitated her earlier hysterical moves while all the foreigners remained silent, still with looks of concern. The manager of the restaurant approached her and spoke. "I see that we had a bit of a scare and some excitement tonight. I hope that you are feeling better now. You know, folks here have been handling hot pepper from a young age. They put it directly into the food when they cook, not on the side, and there are no mild or medium seasonings. There is just hot. I understand that you've eaten hot food before, but when you come here, mind the hot and spicy food to avoid an unpleasant experience. Your meal today is free." The lady left with her party, embarrassed and apparently unhappy that the locals did not show more compassion.

Kovi avoided the hot sauce entirely and Koku teased him for being unable to handle it anymore after many years of not eating spicy food consistently. He replied to Koku that he could still handle it, but he did not want to worry about the three-pronged attack of the pepper during the long flight ahead. In the first attack, the mouth, the tongue, and the throat might be under siege, just like in the lady's case. In the second, the pepper might burn your stomach, and in the final attack, your rectum might be on fire. Sometimes, these three undesirable effects might overlap in time and culminate in a sorry and unbearable experience.

Kovi continued and said that he did not want to have to hog the toilet in the confined space of an airplane, thirty-five thousand feet above sea level somewhere over the Atlantic. Koku replied that he experienced no such effects, which proved Kovi had lost the ability to handle spicy food.

Kovi boarded his flight that night. He went down the aisle and arrived at his seat. There was the lady who had had the hot pepper attack earlier at the restaurant. She was not aware Kovi was a witness to her unpleasant experience with hot chili pepper.

"Hello. I think I am in the aisle seat," said Kovi with a smile.

"Oh! I am sorry. Give me a minute to gather my stuff and move to the window seat."

She had replied with a suggestive and coy smile, underneath somewhat slanted and brown eyeglasses that gave a beautiful face an irresistible attraction. She had a long and naturally dark hair, obviously well cared for and braided in a style that must have taken hours. She carried herself with a dignified allure that projected a confident and highly esteemed individual who was at ease with her charm and intelligence. When Kovi put away his carry-on luggage and sat comfortably, he continued.

"I am Kovi. What is your name?"

"Aisha! I am pleased to meet you."

"Likewise! What brought you to Togo?"

"I work for a church organization that is sponsoring a shelter for orphans."

"Orphans? Where?"

"We work with a local pastor and his church to find people in need. Then, we build them shelters where they stay until they finish school. I was in the center of the country for three weeks for the construction of a center there."

"It sounds like a great project. But now you are leaving?"

"Someone else came to replace me. Our agents will rotate like that until the center becomes operational. Then, two people will stay permanently for longer periods to help the pastor in the administration and finance."

"So, I assume you will come back."

"I am not sure yet, but I would love to!"

"It was your first time here? First time in Africa?"

"Yes, this was my first visit here. But I've been to other countries in Africa. We have different projects in many places."

"So how did you like your stay here?"

"It was great. The people are fine and friendly and the food is tasty. Except the hot pepper!"

Kovi tried not to laugh.

"The hot pepper whipped you?"

"Oh, my God, I thought I was dying. I was busy talking to my friend and not paying attention. I put a few of those round green ones into my mouth and started chewing. A few seconds later, it just hit all at once like a ton of bricks. I felt like my mouth was on fire and my tongue was burning."

"Yes, I was there. People were concerned."

"But why were the locals laughing? I did not like that. It was rude."

"They did not laugh until it became crystal clear that you would be fine. It was a potentially serious event that worked out well. So, people can release the stress and tension when there is no more danger. In my ancestral village, an event like that will earn you a nickname, like 'Aisha the one who cannot handle hot pepper' and folks might write a song about it. Teasing and making fun of you will continue for a long time after the event, lightheartedly and in fun."

"So, you are from here?"

"Yes, I am. Raised here until I went to the USA for more studies. I came to lecture at a school of physics, and now I am going back to the USA."

"Oh! That's great."

They continued talking through the meal service and exchanged contact information, as Kovi was interested in following the development of the orphanage. Kovi learned that Aisha was from the USA, a descendant of a white Caucasian man and a black African woman from Guinea. Her parents met in the USA when her mother was studying there and she grew up in a family that was engaged in many philanthropic projects in Africa and elsewhere.

At the airport in Paris, they said goodbye and started in different directions, but after a few moments, she turned around and said, "What?" To answer her question, Kovi smiled and said plainly, "I love to see you walk away!" She replied with a sassy "Thank you" and left.

Aisha took a connecting flight to Washington, DC, whereas Kovi continued to New York City after a short layover. On the way toward his connecting gate, Kovi looked forward to meeting Aisha, and a feeling of happiness and satisfaction overwhelmed him.

Chapter Six
Aisha

After his return to the USA, Kovi reconnected with Aisha and they maintained regular contact, although they did not see one another. After many discussions over the telephone, they carefully planned a trip around the country. It was to take several weeks, during which they would journey south, then west and north before they dropped off the rental car and took a flight back east.

Kovi started to drive before dawn—from Wading River—to fetch Aisha early at Rutgers University where she was studying for a master's degree. They arrived in the city of Lancaster, Pennsylvania, around midday. They wanted to spend a few days in the Amish Country before they continued south. They were following directions to their hotel in an Amish village, but they were not paying attention to where they were going. Kovi slowed down as their interest shifted toward the magnificent Amish countryside, farmlands, and the people they saw along the way in horse-drawn buggies.

After a while, they realized they were lost and Aisha, the designated navigator, looked for information using her smartphone. Kovi noticed that Aisha looked somewhat confused, stared intensely at her device, and was quiet for a while. Kovi wondered why she could not figure out where they were and tell him where to go and how long it would take to reach their hotel. Kovi kept on driving and since they were in a wonderful place and there was no rush, they did not care until hunger and exhaustion took the fun out of their leisurely drive.

"We should find the hotel soon or stop somewhere for lunch. I am feeling hungry and tired," said Kovi.

"Yes, definitely."

"Where are we?"

"In the middle of Intercourse!"

"Hey! Aisha, it is not the time for crude jokes."

"I am not joking. It says here we are in the middle of Intercourse."

"What?"

"Yup! We are right in the middle of Intercourse!"

Kovi turned toward Aisha. She showed him a map on her telephone, and on the map, they identified their location as Intercourse, Pennsylvania. Unconvinced, Kovi looked at the signs as he drove. He did not want to trust the electronic gadget that he thought had somehow misinformed them crudely. Then he saw the signpost, the undeniable confirmation he was looking for, and they were in the middle of Intercourse. Kovi and Aisha started to laugh and Kovi struggled to focus his attention on the drive while Aisha posted an update on social media about where they were. Soon, comments and reactions to the post started pouring in and there was one in particular that said, "Find a room!" To this comment, someone replied and wrote, "If you find yourself in the middle of Intercourse, you already had a room." But that was a highly subjective statement, and it did not take long before someone else wrote, "Not necessarily."

Kovi and Aisha rode in the Amish buggies, visited an Amish village museum and market, and learned about the communal life of the Amish people. In one store that sold many souvenir items, they found a sweater where on the front and the back was written respectively: "I love Intercourse" and "Pennsylvania." It was irresistible. Kovi bought that sweater. After the trip, he noticed various reactions on people's faces when he wore it. When they read what was on the sweater, they turned their heads and did not want to know more or pretended that they did not read what they read. Others showed disgust, shock, or bewilderment. Then there were the ones who smiled politely at Kovi as if they were saying, "Yes, I know where that place is. I've been there or I am planning to go there soon!" Finally, there were the ones who were curious and wanted to know more about the sweater, and Kovi explained that he bought it in Pennsylvania in a village called Intercourse.

They left Amish Country and continued south toward Washington, DC, where they spent a few nights at Aisha's parents' house. Kovi struggled to drive in the Capital City, especially around major intersections with different streets that converged in diagonal and rectangular patterns to confuse the novice driver into taking the roundabout repeatedly. Aisha drove while they were there. They visited the embassy of Togo and Kovi inquired about the requirements to renew his passport well before his future business travels. At the embassy, fellow citizens were pleased to see and know of Kovi. They took his details to keep in contact with him because, they said, they might call upon "people like him" for scientific projects for their country.

Aisha presented an overview of her philanthropic projects in West Africa, and she received enthusiastic encouragement and praise.

One day, they went to a restaurant that offered food only from Togo in a neighborhood of DC that had many restaurants featuring exotic dishes. The owner of the restaurant was also from Togo, so they spoke in their native language a while, and he told Kovi that he now had to up his game and cook the food to the standard Kovi expected back home. They served the food steaming hot and its aroma whetted Kovi's appetite. He started to eat and did not pay attention anymore to what Aisha was saying. They had cooked the food with pepper and the spices used in Togo.

When the owner had announced that he would cook the food to the expected standard, he was serious and determined to impress Kovi. The owner did just that, but Kovi warned Aisha not to eat the pepper-hot food to avoid the repeat of the worrisome pepper attack that Aisha experienced in Africa. To the disappointment of the owner, she had to wait for her food to be remade without pepper, and in the meantime, they got into a debate over the usage of hot pepper.

On the one hand, Aisha, who had become careful and avoided hot and spicy food since her unpleasant experience, maintained that it is far better to have the hot pepper, salt, and other seasonings on the side to give people the flexibility to season their meals to their taste and comfort. Kovi and the restaurant owner argued that cooking everything together conferred to the food an extra bit of good taste that one cannot achieve otherwise. They could not agree on a compromise, but they still enjoyed their meals.

Kovi and Aisha continued their journey south until they reached the Shenandoah Valley, stopping at the Warm Springs in Bath County, Virginia. That county offers hot or warm mineral springs used for therapeutic purposes or for relaxation in the calm setting of a valley bordered by the peaks and ridges of the Blue Ridge Mountains and the Appalachians. They spent the night in Warm Springs Virginia. Kovi and Aisha soaked in a warm spring to renew their strength for the rest of the journey ahead, which took them across the picturesque and breathtaking region into North Carolina and Tennessee. The next day in the evening, they reached Atlanta, Georgia, where they made another stop to visit with Kovi's cousin Ashley and her family, who had moved to the region near Atlanta after retirement. They stayed there for several days, and Kovi and Ashley caught up on the latest news and events in the ancestral village in Africa and to visit other family members in Atlanta. Then they continued their journey.

After many hours of driving, Kovi and Aisha saw a sign for a great steak house and stopped there. The menu consisted only of different types and sizes of steak, seasoned and marinated in various styles. Kovi and Aisha wished that they could come back there many times or find the same restaurant near where they lived so that they could sample the many options, especially the dried, aged steaks.

The restaurant was full of fellow Americans who appeared to enjoy their steaks cooked to their liking, with assorted vegetables on the side. Such great meals were accompanied with great imported wines.

The restaurant manager went from table-to-table and made small talk with his customers. He appeared delighted to hear them express their satisfaction. He boldly told customers that if, for any reason, they were not satisfied with their steaks, they would let them leave without paying for their meals. In the nineteen years he had been managing the restaurant, not a single customer had taken the option of the free meal. The staff and the cook paid so much attention to details and to customer satisfaction that people left large tips and the local meat eaters became regular customers.

One choice on the menu comprised a large, thick steak of one kilogram and there was a standing challenge that anyone who could eat that much steak by him- or herself in one sitting could walk away without paying. To avoid people taking too much time, there was the rule that the contestant had to finish the steak within ninety minutes of being served.

People were free to give detailed specifications regarding how to season and cook the huge steak. In fact, to raise the stakes, the contestants selected a bottle of wine and the entire meal, including the appetizers and the wine, became complementary if the contestant succeeded. However, they did not include desserts in the arrangement, for it was unlikely that someone could eat that much and still have any room for dessert.

They decorated the walls of the restaurant with the pictures of the determined individuals who had succeeded, but there was no information on the condition of these special people after they left the restaurant, i.e., whether they got sick or even survived after the gluttony.

Most people took the challenge just for the fun of it, and they were well aware they could not pull it off, but at least they took leftovers home to enjoy later. Kovi, too, rose to the challenge and Aisha massaged his machismo and ego, encouraging him to go for it, although she believed he was not capable of winning. Kovi tried hard and within the allotted time, and with a good bottle of wine, he consumed almost six hundred grams of the steak and went no further.

The next day, Kovi struggled to get going and felt sluggish. His stomach was heavy as though it still held a large, undigested quantity of meat. Aisha took charge of the driving and headed west, getting them to the outskirts of White Sands, New Mexico, in record time. There, they hiked in the searing heat through the impressive white sand dunes that extended as far as the eye could see. They marveled at the ecosystem that adapted to thrive in such a harsh environment. They were captivated by the sunset and the night sky, with its impressive moonrise over mountain slopes that appeared in the distance as giant silhouettes. The quiet natural setting, away from the noisy human activities, instilled a feeling of paradise on Earth. For a moment, it appeared as if they were the only two humans in such a paradise.

In the moonlight, Aisha's skin glowed and contrasted with her long, braided black hair, and her slender body took on a charming and angelic aura that Kovi found exceptionally beautiful and irresistible. Under the night light, Kovi's athletic build appeared more sharply defined and his shaved head grew shinier as he stared at Aisha with an intense look and a disarming smile. They faced each other and held hands as Kovi leaned forward and their lips got closer. They were silent and held the moment for a while. Their hearts beat faster as they squeezed each other's hands firmly. Aisha released one hand and placed it on the back of his head, caressing it gently while Kovi wrapped his hand around her waist and pulled her forward, and their lips connected in an engulfing kiss that seemed to last for eternity. They made passionate love until the wee hours and fell into a deep sleep for a long time, only to be awakened when the telephone rang and the receptionist asked if they were keeping the room for an extra night.

In the early evening, they arrived near Santa Fe and stopped at a restaurant on the bank of the Rio Grande. The restaurant was busy and for a long while they waited for the waiter. Impatient, Kovi went to the bar to order drinks. There were many people around the bar and some were seated while others stood, so Kovi waited behind a few people who appeared to have formed a queue. When he finally reached the counter, he was standing behind a gentleman and he tried to get the attention of the people behind the counter. The man Kovi stood behind sat comfortably and was staring intently at the television while occasionally sipping his drink. He wore a baseball hat over his thick black hair and his skin was of a distinctive yellowish-brown color. The man turned around and stared at Kovi for a while, but he did not speak while Kovi was still trying to get the attention of a waiter. The man turned around again and this time he spoke up.

"I dislike it when people stand behind my back."

"I'm just waiting to order drinks, sir," responded Kovi.

"It makes me feel jumpy."

"Well, many people stood in line behind your back a moment ago and you did not feel jumpy. When I came here, you suddenly feel jumpy. Don't worry, I am not here to steal your wallet."

"No. No. I am sorry, sir. That's not what I meant…"

The smile on Kovi's face faded rapidly, and he walked away from the man who was explaining why he felt jumpy when a black person stood behind him in a crowded bar.

Kovi returned in a state of anger and without the drinks and Aisha listened as he described the incident. Aisha thought it was not worth the anger and Kovi should have moved aside and placed his order, in which case they might quench their thirsts at the moment. Kovi maintained that the bar was so crowded that if he had moved aside, he might have stood behind another person who might also get jumpy. Aisha held Kovi's hands and advised him to relax and offered to go get the drinks. At that moment, the man approached their table and asked politely if he could sit with them for a moment. He apologized for the incident and offered them drinks. He appeared drunk, and he said a bunch of things about the histories of his and black people in America. He introduced himself as Bob, but Kovi insisted on knowing his real name and he said Puyama. He explained to Kovi and Aisha the meaning of his name, but under the influence of alcohol, they quickly forgot. After a great meal and many drinks later, Puyama invited Kovi and Aisha to a powwow and left.

Kovi and Aisha arrived at the powwow in late morning and saw a great gathering of the Native American people dressed in fine outfits in a large space. They were organized into concentric circles of dancers, drummers, spectators, and vendors. Between the announcements, chants, and dances, the many attendees walked around the circles to visit the vendors' booths where they sold food and various kinds of Native American pieces of art and souvenirs. Kovi and Aisha looked for Puyama among the elegantly dressed groups of people who took turns performing, but they could not identify him.

A group of young men performed a dance in which the pace of the drums quickened and the men followed along in rhythmic movements of their bodies until they bent down low and stretched their bodies up gradually. Among these men, Kovi noticed one who looked like Puyama, but Aisha was not sure.

Later, another group of people came into the dance arena and was introduced as a group from Mexico that had made the journey for the powwow. The master of ceremony announced that they would do a warriors' dance. This attracted a larger number of people and the ring of spectators dramatically increased. A female member of the group spoke in perfect English about the warriors' dance and their cultural heritage as a prelude to the expected performance.

When the dance finally began, a handsome and athletic looking fellow—wearing impressive decorative ornaments along his body from head to toe—led it. The drummers set a fast pace and the lead dancer covered the dancing arena with speed and agility. The elegant display of skills and talents mesmerized the crowd, and Kovi and Aisha stood in silence when they felt hands on their shoulders. It was Puyama, who had noticed them in the crowd. He looked magnificent in his native outfit. He informed them that his group had already performed but would do it again later in the day. They asked him for advice on souvenirs and while he was talking to Aisha, Kovi went to buy a dream catcher.

Kovi approached a young Native American lady at a booth and after a discussion he made his choice. He was ready to pay for it when his attention turned to a necklace he thought would look lovely on Aisha and he forgot completely the dream catcher. But there were many equally beautiful options, and he was not sure of the right one for Aisha. The young lady selling the items had dark hair similar to Aisha's, and she was of the same complexion and build, and Kovi asked her to wear the necklaces so that the one that looked best on her would be the one he would pick for Aisha. The lady wore the necklaces successively and looked in the mirror, and both commented on each necklace until they identified one that both agreed looked the best on her. At that moment, the young lady blushed and Kovi felt uncomfortable. Kovi paid and left promptly, embarrassed that his effort to buy the perfect gift for his woman triggered an attraction between him and another woman. He presented the necklace to Aisha who wore it promptly. She hugged and kissed him.

A short time later, Puyama had to rejoin his group of dancers. They informed him that they would stay until the next performance of his group and then leave. They planned to drive through the night. After handshakes and promises to maintain contacts, Puyama left. Kovi and Aisha waited excitedly to see him perform.

Kovi and Aisha continued their journey into Arizona, where they visited two things, namely the old city of Tombstone and the Grand Canyon. At Tombstone, they saw a reenactment of the famous gun battle at the O.K. Corral. They learned that the shoot-out lasted less than a minute and when the smoke cleared, one brave man was the only one standing, while the dead and injured lay on the ground. They went north from there and reached the Grand Canyon late at night. They had not booked a hotel room. The hotels in the area were full. They were too tired to drive until they found a motel with vacancies, so they resorted to sleeping in the car.

They were not aware that, although the place was hot during the day, it got cold at night. Kovi awoke several times during the night to turn on the engine and warm up the car. To save petrol, he turned on the engine, and when the car warmed up, he turned it off again and went back to sleep, only to wake sometime later as the car became cold again. Kovi did not have a good rest during the night and was grumpy in the morning, although Aisha slept soundly through the night.

They took leisurely drives around the area and stopped often at the edges of the canyon. Down below was the great Colorado River in the form of a giant blue-green snake. Above hovered majestic birds with large wingspans. In the far distance above, a sunset was in the making, and this attracted many people to watch the sun fading gradually into the canyon, leaving behind a radiant orange horizon.

They continued to travel west and reached Las Vegas, where they spent one night. The gambling activities that attracted people even from far away and gave life to a bustling city in the desert fascinated them. Aisha was tempted to try gambling as a fun and relaxing game, but Kovi was hesitant for fear of losing whatever he had or becoming addicted, and he convinced the disappointed Aisha to just watch the determined folks that came there to win-or-lose money.

Kovi told Aisha that in his experience, when he used to gamble in high school, he had good luck at the beginning with a winning streak that enticed him to continue playing, only to lose as the game continued until he lost everything. When it got to the stage of an addiction and he wanted to borrow money and continue after he lost everything, then he made a remarkable decision to quit gambling entirely. He was fearful that the old demons might resurface, and he decided not to tempt fate. "What was the point of going to Las Vegas and not playing even one game?" wondered Aisha, but she conceded to Kovi's reservations and they journeyed northeast and entered the state of Utah, where they drove through Provo to reach Salt Lake City by nightfall.

In Salt Lake City, Aisha met up with a friend of hers named Allison, who worked for the same church organization but did not travel to Africa. The head office of the church was in Utah and from there they managed their evangelical and philanthropic activities overseas. Aisha and Allison had spoken over the telephone several times, but that evening was the first time they met in person. Allison's father was a minister in the church, and he went to Africa many times to convert people to their faith. He was successful by offering the people concrete and immediate help in the form of a school, an infirmary, or an orphanage.

Kovi listened quietly while Aisha and Allison talked for a while to catch up on the many activities of the church. Allison, through her work at the head office, offered a broader perspective on the many activities of the organization while, on the contrary, Aisha possessed detailed practical information on the activities in the field. Allison was pleased to meet Kovi, as someone from a place where they carried out missionary work, and she asked for his impressions and comments on their activities. The blunt and honest Kovi did not hesitate to say that it was not right for a religious group or sect to lure people to the faith by offering them necessities. Also, he worried about the expansion and proliferation of American religious groups in Africa.

Kovi and Aisha had debated this topic in the past many times, but did not reach definitive conclusions. That evening, Kovi found himself in the same debate, but against two passionate young women of a remarkable argumentative talent characterized by large and coherent deluges of words that completely overshadowed Kovi's introverted demeanor. They did not reach any significant conclusions that night either, and Allison came to see Kovi as a quiet man who took the time to pay attention and listen carefully, and then expressed himself in a few thoughtful words that stressed his unwavering convictions. Kovi conceded that the various concrete aids the church organizations offered their local converts were useful.

They left Salt Lake City the next day and headed southeast into Colorado. They went through the picturesque region of Durango in the valley of the Rocky Mountains before they headed for Denver Airport, where they returned the rental car and boarded a flight to New York City.

They upgraded Kovi's airplane ticket to business class, and he exchanged his seat with Aisha, who, until then, had not flown in business class. Kovi went to his seat in economy class and put his carry-on in the overhead compartment after he took out a few things, which he threw on his seat. There was a lady beside him who became agitated that he was putting things there. She yelled that the seat was not a garbage dump and demanded that Kovi collect his things. Kovi looked at her, surprised, and told her politely that it was his own seat. The woman became quiet and embarrassed. During the flight, she became friendly and talkative, and she and Kovi conversed during the entire time. Kovi learned that her son was in the service abroad and came back briefly to the country, and she was traveling to Norfolk, Virginia, to meet up with him. She talked excitedly about the gifts she wrapped and the food she prepared for her son, whom she had not seen in a few years. She was a personable and friendly middle-aged lady different from the person with the unreasonable outburst of anger at the beginning of the flight.

***

In time, Kovi and Aisha's relationship matured. Kovi proposed and she accepted. Aisha's parents met Kovi several times and approved of the positive development, but they knew little of Kovi's family except for his cousin Ashley and her family. As Aisha later told Kovi, her mother asked her to tell her everything regarding how Kovi proposed.

"Come on, Aisha. Tell me. How did it happen? What did he say?"

"He did not say much. He took out a ring and asked for an engagement."

"How did he do it? Was he on his knees? Did he say something special? Tell me everything."

"I do not remember that he said something dramatic. He was not on his knees. He just took out a ring unexpectedly and said only a few words. In fact, he just talked as if he were discussing his physics experiments."

"Wow! Thank God you know he loves you. The man of few emotions!"

Kovi insisted on approaching the wedding in the traditional way, which comprised two steps.

In the first, he asked his cousin Ashley, her husband Keith, and his old friend Hakeem to stand as proxies for his parents and go with him to Aisha's parents and officially ask for her hand in marriage. They converged on Aisha's parents on the set date and her maternal uncles who had migrated years ago to the USA also took part. Aisha's uncles had never met Kovi, and the eldest one, who was the de facto master of ceremonies, asked to know who among Keith, Hakeem, and Kovi was the lucky man. Then, he asked Kovi and Aisha to leave the room and the deliberations began. After approximately two hours, they called them back in for the prayers and the blessings of the union, and a small celebration followed. Kovi and Aisha were officially engaged—it was the first step in the process of their traditional wedding.

A few weeks after their engagement ceremony, Kovi and Aisha moved to South Africa, where Kovi started a position as a visiting researcher.

Chapter Seven
Hatshepsut

Kovi got a long-term visa for South Africa, based on his exceptional skills. He felt proud to be identified as a talented person. Since they were not married yet, Aisha did not get the long-term visa as a member of Kovi's family. She relied on the ninety-day maximum stay for Americans and she stretched these ninety days over a few trips between her business travels to West Africa. They had to accept living far apart from each other, but fortunately, it was only within the first few months, and that was not severe enough to threaten the survival of their relationship.

When Aisha came in South Africa, they established a family ritual of meeting at home every Friday around 5:30 p.m. and kicking off the weekend with red wine, which they enjoyed on the veranda of their rented apartment. It was their sacred moment to reconnect and renew their bond and commitment. Even when they had a prior engagement, they found a moment to share a glass of wine.

They traveled around South Africa and fell in love with the area of the Drakensberg Mountains in the eastern part of the country, and they had their wedding there. After their marriage, Aisha's visa status changed to the long-term one, as Kovi's family member.

They planned the second step in the traditional wedding for several months and invited family and friends from everywhere. From the USA, besides Aisha's family, Ashley, Keith, and Hakeem came to South Africa for the wedding. Other family members from both sides came from West Africa and from France. Among them, on Kovi's side, were a nephew, a sister named Josiane Kayi, an uncle who was a Catholic priest and officially known as Monseigneur Cécile Le Grand, and a cousin Jean-Patrice from Paris. Kovi's parents were of advanced age and not in a good state of health to make the trip. When Kayi arrived in South Africa, she asked about the Zulus.

"Where are the Zulus? I want to see them."

"The Zulus?"

"The great people that we learned about in high school. I want to see the folks."

"Okay," responded Kovi. "I have Zulu friends and you will see a few of them at the wedding."

Monseigneur Le Grand teamed up with a local pastor and together they officiated the wedding ceremony. Jean-Patrice was in charge of photography, filming, and recording. The wedding took place in December during the southern summer and the day before, everyone gathered in Johannesburg and traveled in a convoy of five twelve-seater minivans to the Drakensberg, and there was a great ambiance of music and songs during the four-hour journey.

The venue was at a hotel set high on a mountain plateau surrounded by green mountain peaks. The hotel comprised a series of independent chalets constructed such that each of them had a spectacular view of the plateau and far beyond to the mountains.

The ceremony started that same evening when they arrived at the hotel and included performances by friends of the families in the Zulu and Tsonga traditions. Rapid and coordinated movements, which echoed the similar performance of the Mexicans during the powwow, characterized the Zulu dance. During the Tsonga dance, the music was of a rapid pace, and women old and young followed with quick and short steps synchronized with amazing agile vibrations of their bodies, especially around at the waist and the buttocks.

Hakeem spoke at the event that night and narrated the circumstances of when he and Kovi met and how he felt sorry for the young dude, from the "Motherland," with an ugly haircut, and how they maintained their close friendship through the years, although they did not see each other often. The wedding was the first time they'd seen each other since the engagement ceremony. He expressed gratitude for the opportunity to travel to Africa, which was a dream that he'd always wanted to realize. After the wedding, Hakeem made a tour of South Africa and visited the major national parks and the Cape Town area. Then he traveled toward "Africa North" and visited many countries, always jovial to have come to the "Motherland to see his brothers and sisters."

***

At the end of his trip, Hakeem went back to the USA and started a new position in Seattle as an aerospace engineer. A few years later, Kovi and his family visited him when Kovi went to a university there for a conference. Hakeem wasted no time before telling his wife and Aisha about how this naïve African student had gone unconcerned to Jeff's family's house in a region that Hakeem believed was full of Ku Klux Klan operatives, and how he came back alive. He shook his head with a disapproving look when Kovi told him that he would not mind going there again to pay Jeff a visit.

***

The celebration continued until late in the night and as people retired to their chalets, someone instructed jokingly that Kovi and Aisha must not consummate the marriage that night before they said, "I do." The joke continued when another person responded that they had already consummated it many times before they got to that stage. But the elders were serious and insisted that the couple must not sleep together that night and forced them to spend the night in different rooms.

The next day was the day of the official ceremony, arranged such that the "I do's" happened at twelve o'clock and twelve minutes and twelve seconds on the twelfth day of the twelfth month of the year for the best of luck to the newlyweds on their life journey together. They got the month, the day, and the hour right, but because of delays and unforeseen circumstances they did not get the minutes and the seconds right. Had they managed, it would have been a remarkable and an unbelievable feat.

That day, Kovi did not see Aisha until her father led her into the chapel. Since the early morning, two young ladies had worked hard to braid her hair in an intricate and exquisitely elegant way that required many hours of dedicated manual skills. She wore a wedding dress that seemed to cast a white net that flowed behind her as she stepped forward.

The men, including Kovi, wore a uniform that comprised suit pants with a white shirt and purple bow ties that coordinated with the women's dresses. Monseigneur Le Grand delivered his sermon in French with the translation of Jean-Patrice to English, and the local pastor spoke in Sotho with a supporting English translator. When they pronounced "I do's", and the newlyweds signed the wedding documents before the priest and the pastor and the witnesses, they exited the chapel and boarded a decorated Mercedes Benz that took them on a leisurely ride through the mountains and the valleys all the way to the nearest town, with a procession of cars full of happy people behind them. It was the happiest moment for Kovi and Aisha with family and friends present.

The next day, Kovi and Aisha wasted no time in starting their honeymoon on a secluded island of the Seychelles. They flew from Johannesburg to Victoria, and from there they took an internal flight to their final destination, which was a small island of the archipelago with a sandy beach and tropical flora of green tall trees with thick undergrowth. When they landed on the island, hotel staff met and escorted them to their chalet. Inside, they found on a table a courtesy bottle of Champagne chilled in a bucket of ice. They catered meals with rich daily varieties of dish and served to their specifications.

One day, after a late morning breakfast and while they were relaxing in the cool breeze under a shed, a massive turtle emerged from the ocean and made majestic and nonchalant moves on the beach. Many people gathered to watch and a few dared to rub its massive shell. The show lasted for a few minutes, after which the beautiful creature dove back into the water and vanished.

On that island, time had no meaning, as everything was available to the guests and personal troubles fizzled away in an apparent paradise distant from Earth. There, Kovi and Aisha learned about the game of "island hopping," and it consisted of going from island-to-island in an insatiable desire for good living. It was not surprising to hear people talking with excitement about the islands they planned to go to next or the ones they had previously visited. Among the visitors, Aisha and Kovi were of the few who did not have the resources to hop islands.

Kovi and Aisha's daughter was conceived in the warm waters of the Indian Ocean on a quiet and deserted beach under the blue sky of a sunny afternoon. They spent six nights on the fantastic island before they returned to the daily realities of ordinary life.

***

After they returned, Aisha got sick often, particularly in the mornings. When the pregnancy was confirmed, they did not stop the Friday-evening wine ritual, but Aisha did not drink anymore. Only Kovi enjoyed the wine and Aisha became jealous. She came up with the rule that every time Kovi opened a bottle he had to save one unopened bottle of the same type for Aisha until such a time when she could drink again. So, then Kovi started to save at least one bottle a week throughout the pregnancy, plus an extra six months during the breastfeeding period, and this amounted to an enviable collection of fine wine bottles that Aisha claimed only for herself. She always sought acknowledgment that these bottles were hers alone. Kovi had already consumed his and learned to not challenge her claim, but Aisha still shared them with him in their perpetual family ritual.

About three months into the pregnancy, Kovi accompanied Aisha for a prenatal ultrasound and when the doctor asked if they wished to know the sex of the baby, Aisha quickly responded affirmatively. The doctor informed them that it was a girl, and he explained how he concluded that from the video images of the fetus. Aisha claimed she knew it was a girl, and this led to an argument that often arose when they teased and challenged each other. Kovi maintained that she said nothing about her knowledge of the sex of the baby, and as soon as the doctor said it, suddenly, she declared she had prior knowledge. To Kovi, it was like the forecaster who interpreted her prediction after the fact, to suit current events.

When the due date of the baby passed, and the labor did not start, the doctor advised them to induce labor. They admitted Aisha to the hospital, and the doctor tried a drug that triggers uterus contractions, but at first, nothing happened. It seemed the baby appeared in no hurry to come out. Other women admitted at the same time had their babies faster, either through caesarean sections, stimulated, or spontaneously induced labor, and they could not believe that Aisha had not delivered yet. The doctor instructed the nurse to call him when the cervix dilated enough, so that he would come to oversee the delivery. After about thirty-three hours that seemed like an eternity of a tense and edgy feeling, it happened quickly, so quickly that the doctor missed the show.

When he came, he seemed disappointed to have been stuck in traffic and did not arrive in time. In his absence, the nurse took charge and talked to Aisha and encouraged her constantly. Kovi was there, overwhelmed and unsure about how he could help, and with one hand he caressed Aisha by her head and with the other hand, he held her by her hand.

"I can feel something," complained Aisha.

"Push!" responded the nurse after she quickly gathered the tools and equipment on a table just below where Aisha's legs and thighs were spread as wide as possible. Soon the baby's head emerged first; it was small and full of wet and curly black hair. "Give me one big push," encouraged the nurse.

Then the rest of the baby popped out, and as she came out, she was lying on the side with her hands folded on her chest. The nurse clamped the umbilical cord and instructed Kovi where to cut it. Aisha and the baby, named Hatshepsut, after the great Lady Pharaoh of Egypt, were fine. The extended family received the news with cheers. For Aisha and Kovi, a new chapter and a huge responsibility just began.

***

A few months later, they went to the American embassy to report the birth of an American citizen abroad. Beforehand, they had to submit an armada of papers, including the unabridged birth certificate of the child, to secure an appointment.

On the set date, Kovi and Aisha showed up at the embassy with the child, and the agent who treated the case was friendly and courteous, yet unyielding in his questioning to verify the parental relation to the child. He checked the dates stamped in Kovi and Aisha's passports to corroborate their answers to his questions regarding the timeline of events from the conception to the birth of the child. He wanted to prove that this child was theirs and duly born abroad to Aisha as an American citizen. After about thirty to forty-five minutes, he was convinced and a week later, Kovi and Aisha received the papers that cleared the way to apply for the USA passport for the child.

Kovi got his Green Card through Aisha as her immediate relative, although at the time it was conditional on evidence that their marriage was genuine, since they had been married for less than two years.

***

After their stay in South Africa, Kovi returned to the USA as a family man, thanks to his marriage and the birth of his daughter. Two years later, Kovi and Aisha applied to remove the conditions on Kovi's permanent residency status.

Chapter Eight
Citizen

It was late in June when Kovi became a naturalized USA citizen. He drove several hours to the venue to join many others in the ceremony making them citizens that day.

Kovi needed to catch a flight that same day for a research experiment at CERN. He surrendered his Green Card during the naturalization ceremony and it seemed impossible to get a new passport and leave the country in one day. A few days earlier, he tried the expedited application for a new passport and made an appointment for the day of the naturalization ceremony.

Unfortunately, by the time they completed the naturalization proceedings, his appointment time had passed. After he became a citizen, he called the passport center and they informed him that it was not possible to get the passport that day since he'd missed his appointment. They advised him to make a new appointment. To make matters worse, he could not travel with his foreign passport without a visa or the Green Card, but he needed to go on the trip.

Against advice, he drove a few hours to the passport center. When he arrived there, without the required appointment, he explained his case to an agent, and they made the passport for him, anyway. So, his gamble had paid off, but he was to come back two hours later to fetch the new passport. By then, it was two hours before his flight took off and he was still a few hours away from the airport. He could not make the flight. Kovi drove to the airport and thought that although he'd missed the flight, he might get re-booked for another flight the same day. At the check-in counter, he explained to an agent that he might have missed his flight. He was frantic, with sweat dripping all over his face because of the heat of June and the excitement and anxiety of the day.

"Relax," the agent told him. "There was a delay, and the flight has not departed yet. You are right on time!"

Everyone from the check-in counter to the security checkpoint and the boarding gate commented excitedly on the new passport, issued just a few hours ago to a man naturalized earlier that day and then catching a flight he'd almost missed.

Kovi narrated the events of that day to friends and colleagues many times with excitement. Never had luck smiled so brightly on him.

***

A week later, when he was at the boarding gate his return flight, his thoughts drifted to the other people in a waiting area. Some of these people must have been visitors for business, education, vacation, etc. Others like him were possibly citizens coming back home. Of these visitors, some would ultimately migrate. Kovi was thinking, "Nowadays, it's hard to be a foreigner everywhere. Aliens! They seem easy to blame for many problems. Cannot come here. Cannot stay there. No work for you!"

"The Homo sapiens originated in Africa and migrated to every corner of Earth for the same reasons—in the hope to find better survival opportunities. What might have happened if the Neanderthals had stood their ground and subdued the modern humans?" wondered Kovi.

Science had taught him that people are all the same kind. "What might happen if extraterrestrials beat the odds, traveling the vast intergalactic space to visit Earth? As in the movies, maybe then we would finally truly unite for the same cause against the true aliens. We might succeed, should we ever have to engage in that battle, for we have perfected on each other what we will have to do to the extraterrestrials. For now, as far as we know, in this vast universe, Earth is the only place we can all call home. No aliens, no foreigners!" These thoughts were going through his mind when he boarded the flight.

***

When he started to travel with a passport from a first-world country, Kovi thought he would go through borders more easily and enjoy more respect, but he found out later that even with such a passport, crossing borders was sometimes still unpleasant.

"Next!"

"Born in Gabon! You are coming from Gabon like that?"

"No, sir."

"Where are you going?"

"To do my work, sir."

"What kind of work do you do?"

"Research in particle physics."

"What?"

"Particle physics, sir."

"Where?"

"At CERN, sir."

"Oh! You have papers to prove that you are a particle physicist?"

"What? You do not expect me to do particle physics?"

"Sir, you are an alien from over there, it is not obvious."

"Alien? I see that we still have a long way to go!"

"You are definitely a special alien. I heard about the Higgs boson on television."

"Please drop it, sir. You are not making me feel any better."

"Have a good day. Next!"

Then when he came back home,

"Citizens and permanent residents over here. Aliens that way. Do not step over the line. Back, go back. Next!"

"How long were you out of the country, sir?"

"Three weeks."

"Doing what?"

"Research in particle physics."

"Particle physics, sir?"

"Yes."

"Welcome home."

"Thank you. Have a good day."

"Next!"

Kovi cleared immigration and collected his bag fast while the "aliens" were still queuing in long and boring lines with no possibility of amusing themselves with handy electronic gadgets. Kovi remembered he used to be an "alien." He had hated to be called and treated as an alien. After naturalization, he enjoyed the privilege of not being an alien, although anywhere else he traveled he was still one.

"Everyone that journeys outside her homeland is considered an alien somewhere else. It just depends whether one is in her own country or a foreign country," Kovi reckoned.

Chapter Nine
Plant Whisperer

When Kovi and his family returned from South Africa, Kovi became a "Plant Whisperer."

"Gardening, it's fun," Kovi thought, but he needed to get good at it. When he was a renter, it was the business of the landlord to keep up the property. He used to just come and go, and did not notice the beauty around the property or the neighborhood. It was his duty to report problems and issues in the house, not to maintain the property, but for his own comfort. He resented the fact that he had to throw money away to pay rent and did not have any claim or rights to the property, not even any tax deduction benefits. Then, he got lucky enough to buy his own house with Aisha.

When he became an owner, his outlook on the property changed. He remembered there was a clause somewhere in the deed stating that one pledges to take care of the property. Besides considering what was in the deed, he started noticing how people decorated their houses through the year in the different seasons. When he drove to work, he noticed the beautiful lawns along the way and imagined the amount of money spent through the seasons by the well-to-do decent citizens.

He realized how, in an advanced society, everything has become a specialized source of making money. There are those who can put food on the table for their families by just cutting trees. They came to his property with a set of skillful employees and equipment and removed many trees and their stumps in one working day. Every time he called for a service, many experts converged upon him and wanted to turn him into a lifelong customer. They tried to convince him that it was an easy monthly payment, which over many years would be a significant amount. There were many specialized services—for the lawn, the driveway, the boiler, termites, ticks, rodents, etc. The number of specialized expert services could be limitless, and each service provider offered the option of an extended payment plan, oblivious of the possibility that the owner might have many of them to worry about.

Sometimes, the service provider looked at him surprised, unable to understand why Kovi was thinking about the offer that he just described. Other providers adopted clever strategies, and Kovi assumed they were more successful at selling their products and services. They first sent a salesman with excellent interpersonal skills. The salesperson quickly learned the pronunciation of the customer's first name and was good at small talk with a few jokes and anecdotes interjected.

Depending on what they sold, they could tie the customer up for many hours, especially when the customer was stubborn and hesitant. Their actions and statements appeared rehearsed or choreographed in terms of what to do or say next if they sensed resistance. Most of them were not experts and had only superficial knowledge in the technical specifications of the products. But they learned or memorized enough essential details to project a good image. At the end of a somewhat lengthy interaction, if Kovi stood his ground and refused to buy anything, he might get a call several days later, and the provider might suggest sending someone else who magically had special offers at reduced costs that they wanted to run by Kovi. It was a strategy to not let a potential customer go to their competitors.

On one occasion, the salesman warned that Kovi might get the call, and if he did, he should insist they send him back—not someone else—so that he got the commission. He bitterly complained that he had traveled from afar, spent several hours with

Kovi already, and still had a few other customers to get to on that day. If Kovi ended up buying after they sent a different person, his effort would be a waste. But in this game of getting the best value for your money, Kovi couldn't care less about his wasted efforts. This must be a part of his job, a risk that he took, although Kovi understood his desperation since his income depended on the sales he made. Still, Kovi felt he should not buy from him before he got a few other estimates. If the provider sent another salesperson with a much better offer for the same service, Kovi did not care whether the person who came the second time was the same salesperson or not. Cynically, Kovi thought that since his income was a percentage of the sale, he possibly inflated all the figures that he was quoting, so it was reasonable to not commit without further investigation.

***

Kovi became fascinated by lawn designs with various plants and flowers. He saw neighbors with enviable lawns using expert lawn services. He thought he could excel at this at a reduced cost if he did it himself, and also, he would have the freedom to select what he planted while he gained knowledge about plants and their care. One time, he planted six Thuja Green Giants and six Spartan Junipers. He was slowly developing a new interest in life. Gardening! "It is fascinating what one can learn about flora", he thought. He instructed friends and family to know him henceforth as "The Plant Whisperer." To his chagrin, only two of the Thuja Giants and five Junipers survived, and each summer, he was in a battle against the crabgrass. He added another hobby, i.e., plant watching. He thought the struggles for survival are even more dramatic for plants. They come back in the spring. The vicious attack of the wild grass occurs in the summer. These are plants that live and die in a single season. They fight to sow their seeds for the next cycle. The fall with the late bloomers after the crabgrass has died away. The winter and the evergreens able to tough it out in subzero temperatures when most other plants look like skeletons. The onset of spring! Cut one plant and watch how the ecosystem changes. Be still and watch the flora. Plant and whisper to them. It is grounding. Kovi went mad about plants.

***

Toward the middle of June, Kovi lost the battle against crabgrass that proliferated quickly and took over his lawn. Around that time, he accepted an invitation to Jefferson Laboratory in Newport News Virginia, and that trip brought back many memories. He had lived and enjoyed a few good years there before. Yet, he could hardly remember how to drive back to where he used to live. There were so many new developments. The Patrick Henry Mall he often visited had become unrecognizable. He ran into folks whom he had not seen in many years, and he noticed that these people conserved their wonderful and jovial attitudes, unspoiled by the sheer stress of age. He was happy to be back in the area to give a lecture on a new topic that was the focus of his recent research work.

One afternoon, Kovi walked into a bar in Newport News. This bar must have been new for he did not recall it was there during his time. He had a delicious burger as he watched the world cup soccer games. The USA was playing against Ghana. Watching the game was emotional. In earlier editions of the world cup, Ghana caused the exit of the USA from the tournament. This time, a confident USA team faced Ghana and was determined to change the outcome. When Kovi joined the crowd, the USA was leading the score. He was enjoying the excellent burger, with half a liter of beer, on a hot day, surrounded by patriotic citizens. The regulation time was winding down slowly as Kovi's burger and beer were disappearing. He was losing hope.

Then, in one of those magic moments unique to soccer, one of those special moments that all soccer fans might relate to, with a display of agility and skills, Ghana found the way to equalize. Kovi cheered off his seat, and he was dancing. Then, he realized that he was the only one in the bar to cheer loudly, so loudly that he got a few dirty looks. He was feeling uneasy. As a show of his patriotism, Kovi yelled loudly, "I am an American, too." That seemed to defuse the tension. Everybody in the bar started laughing, and they invited Kovi to join a table. They watched the rest of the game together, commented and bet while they tossed down many glasses of beer, and each person took a turn to buy for everyone else.

Kovi supported the USA team and hoped that it went further in the tournament, to surprise all the big soccer powerhouses of Europe and South America. He was also rooting for the African teams, any of them. "One of these days, Africa will produce a soccer champ!" he said.

Africa had almost achieved that dream four years earlier, when Ghana, after it eliminated the USA, got the golden opportunity to put Africa in the semifinal for the first time. For all the people who rooted for Ghana, that was a tough loss. Kovi was traveling in Europe at the time and that game finished late in the night and Kovi could not sleep. After that night, he dreamed many times that Ghana won the game, and that Africa was in the semifinals with a chance to advance and win the ultimate game for the championship. So, here he was again, cheering and hoping for Ghana to realize the dream that many people had been holding.

The USA scored again, and they all cheered. When the game ended and Ghana lost the chance to advance, Kovi had with mixed emotions. It was perfectly understandable and commendable for the USA to turn the tide, and not to be eliminated in three consecutive world cups by the same team. The almighty USA, always sent home when they face Ghana? Not this time. "America must be great again!" And the USA team did just that in that game. Ghana did not create the miracle of four years ago and fell even shorter this time—

that was a disappointment for Kovi. Kovi left the bar and placed all his hope in the rest of African teams that were still in the tournament. Repeatedly, he tasted the bitter disappointment of their elimination. The great hope of an African champion was still a possibility—in his lifetime, he hoped.

After the soccer match between the USA and Ghana, Kovi remembered how they used to follow sport events in his ancestral village in Togo. In those days, the village did not have electricity or television, and to follow an important soccer match, in particular when the national team was playing, people congregated around shortwave radios powered by batteries, and they connected to the match through the voice and the emotion of reporters. The reporters were good at relaying the soccer matches live, and although people did not see the match, it was like they were present in the stadium and watching a live game.

People could feel the emotional state of the reporter through the tone or the pitch of his voice, and in a way the reporter had an important task to do, and that was to hold the attention of the people and make them hang on to the radio. The reporter relayed pieces of the match as follows.

"Koffi has the ball, and he dribbles past two defenders. Oh, my! Oh my! What exquisite dribbles! Now Koffi is being tightly marked. He finds an opening and releases the ball to Kossi on the left wing. Kossi is running fast, quick with the ball. What is Kossi going to do? He is getting near the goal, still on the left with the ball. The defense is regrouping and converging upon Kossi. Wow! Kossi kicks the ball over the defenders into the center. What an unbelievable pass to Kodjo, who stopped the ball dead at the center. Kodjo will shoot to the goal. Kodjo moves to left for space and he is about to shoot but the defense regroups again. They force Kodjo to move to the right and takes the shot on goal. It is going in and it looks a goal. Oh! The goalkeeper deflects the ball over the bar and it will be a corner kick from right. It looks like Mohamed will take the corner kick. All the defenders are at the center and Koffi and his attacking squad too. Mohamed kicks the ball, and it is coming. Everyone is moving around in front of the goal. There he is. Koku is jumping above everyone else. Koku is now above three defenders and his going to use his head. The goalkeeper is approaching fast to block, but Koku was faster and there is the header. Goal! Goal! Gooooooal! He did it again. That son of a bitch Koku equalized the score so late in the game. And folks, we are going into overtime. Don't go anywhere, it is going into overtime…"

People were overjoyed, disappointed, or saddened if it was their team that scored, missed an opportunity to score, or conceded a goal. The only times in the USA when Kovi experienced the same levels of excitement were when he watched live college football matches at his university in the Midwest. The atmosphere in the stadium reached a feverish pitch with all the cheerleading in between the game set pieces, and on the opportunities for touchdowns. When Kovi arrived in the USA, he did not at first like football because of the frequent stops of the game, followed by the changes of the squads depending on whether the imminent action was offensive or defensive. However, he enjoyed going to the stadium for live football games where, besides the game itself, the accompanying entertainment could sometimes propel the crowd into a transcendental state of joy and pleasure.

***

It was on a hot day in August when Kovi exhausted his vacation days for the year. He preferred to spend such a day being lazy out on the beach, but he had to go to work. "It's such a drag to spend such a fine day working," he said to himself. It was so hot that his brain could not work at its full strength. Constantly, he looked through the window and lost concentration, and thought about the summer fun that he should have instead. He thought it would still be hot enough when he left work at 5 p.m. to enjoy the beach. On the way home, the burning desire to quench his thirst overwhelmed him. So, Kovi made a quick stop at a bar close to home.

As he took a seat, the person close by attempted to draw him into a conversation. "Do you know what the secret of life is?" he asked Kovi. The man appeared to be drunk. Kovi replied, "No. For now, a cold beer is just fine."

The bartender gave Kovi a half liter mug of beer, a mug that was super cooled. Kovi's hand felt the cold at the touch of the mug, and the drink went down his throat and hit the spot on the way. A satisfying burp followed and Kovi was coming back to life. Meanwhile, the drunkard went around the room and posed the same question to anyone who cared enough to give him attention. Most people disengaged and ignored him once they noticed his drunken state. He waited a few seconds, and if he did not get any answer, he then staggered to the next table. With no introduction or greetings, he surprised folks with the same question. "Do you know what the secret of life is?" Some people, when confronted so abruptly, seriously started to think right there and then, as though they had never pondered these mysteries.

Kovi saw them stop sipping their drinks, and suddenly, they were in deep thoughts, as though the question hit a chord and brought to their consciousness a long-forgotten past event deeply hidden in their subconscious for many years. Lost in their thoughts, they did not notice that the drunkard had already moved on to another table.

Other folks jokingly posed the question back to him. "Do you?" When he got the attention he needed, he took a swallow of his drink, raised his glass in the air, and sang and danced around the table. In his euphoria, he asked ladies to dance with him, unmoved and undeterred by successive rejections. Then he continued to the next table, ignored and unnoticed by the fine people who were all trying to escape from the searing heat, until his uninvited question surprised them.

Kovi watched the scene unfold, and he realized that the drunkard always answered when people asked him his own question. "Do you?" But no one cared to notice. When he finally came back to where Kovi was sitting, Kovi had by then almost finished his drink, and turned to the man to carry on the conversation.

"Now, I will go home, take my bike, and ride into the park. Then, I will go down to the beach and dive into the bay. Later on, around eight p.m., my family and I will light the fire for a *braai* in the sunset," Kovi told him. The man smiled and said, "That, my friend, is a secret of life! It's what I should do on a day much like today. But I am just as happy with a drink and my favorite songs to which I let loose dancing. Maybe next time, I might join you."

***

Near the end of the summer, Puyama came for a visit with his family, and his daughter was about the same age as Hatshepsut. The kids got along well and learned Spanish and French from each other. The two families went to the Shinnecock Indian powwow organized annually in Suffolk county. Puyama was eager to get involved and perform with the dancers. He was still fit and agile and could bend down low while he shook his back and moved his feet to the music. He invited Kovi to join him and under the encouragement and pressure from the ladies, Kovi conceded and imitated Puyama's movements as best he could. After the dance they went around the shopping area, and on the advice of Puyama, Kovi bought a dream catcher that he later took to Africa unintentionally.

After Puyama and his family departed, Kovi and Aisha arranged for a babysitter for Hatshepsut on a Saturday evening when they went to see a musical performance in Port Jefferson. They were in line to collect their tickets when a man who appeared to be in his mid-forties approached Kovi with a smile. Kovi took a moment before he recognized the man as Sanjay, a colleague from graduate school when they were studying for their doctorate degrees. Sanjay, a graduate student from India, was a senior in the program when Kovi started and they did not have many opportunities to work closely together. Kovi remembered him being much younger during graduate school, and he too had a heavy accent, but that did not deter him from speaking fast and emphatically. He projected an aura of a senior graduate student who knew more than most others and this was clear when he became passionate in making his points.

At first, Sanjay seemed offended that Kovi did not recognize him right away, but that feeling evaporated when Kovi shook his hand with excitement and introduce him to Aisha. He smiled when Kovi remembered his name and said jokingly that he must have aged significantly and that was why Kovi did not know who he was. With that comment, Kovi realized he expected a reassuring statement that he did not look much different. Kovi then complimented his elegant look and added that he did not expect to run into him there after so many years.

In graduate school, when Sanjay learned that Kovi was going to New York City to visit his cousin Ashley, Sanjay asked Kovi to bring back a Sunday edition of the *New York Times*. Kovi did, but did not inquire why Sanjay wanted a Sunday newspaper from New York. A few months later, Sanjay graduated with the doctorate degree and Kovi did not see him again until they met at the theater. Sanjay informed Kovi that he had found a job in *Times* that Kovi brought to him and had been working on Wall Street for all these years, thanks to Kovi's newspaper!

As the show was about to start, they went to take their respective seats and Sanjay invited Kovi and Aisha for dinner on "the boat." Kovi thought there was a new restaurant in town set on a stationary boat in the harbor, and he did not know about it. On the scheduled date, when Kovi and Aisha arrived at the harbor, there was no such restaurant and they were looking around when a gentleman approached and asked if they were guests of Sanjay. They escorted them to a huge yacht of several stories. Sanjay was inside, relaxed and waiting for them.

Sanjay had amassed a fortune and built his own company in the hedge fund business with the mathematics and physics skills he gained in graduate school.

They equipped the yacht with a catering crew that catered only for four individuals, i.e., Sanjay, his friend, Kovi, and Aisha. There was also the navigation crew who, on the instructions of Sanjay, took them on a slow and leisurely ride of about four hours along the Long Island Sound in a magnificent sunset of vivid colors that transformed the sky and the surface of the water ahead into an inseparable and breathtaking colorful mist. They had a multicourse meal in a delightful atmosphere, accentuated by a slow music that coalesced with the sound of the boat as it dragged through the waves to produce a calm and soothing noise.

Sanjay gave them a tour of the boat. Besides the fine furniture, paintings, photographs, and imported carpets all packaged with a meticulous attention to details, there were large study rooms equipped with sophisticated computers, a library, living rooms, many bedrooms, and all this gave the impression of a floating mansion. Sanjay talked about the basic physics research that Kovi was doing and displayed a great knowledge of the current developments in the field. Although nostalgic that he did not carry on in the field for which he trained as a graduate student, he appeared content to use his physics education to make money. Kovi told him about the school of physics that he organized periodically in Africa and invited him to lecture to students about alternative careers they could consider with their physics training. Sanjay accepted the invitation and went further to donate private funds to support the school. A good training in fundamental physics may allow one to succeed in different career paths and Sanjay was a good example of such a success.

At the end of the lovely evening, Kovi told Aisha that he was seriously considering a career change, although later he did not take any concrete steps to make that happen.

***

When Aisha was pregnant and Kovi saved wine bottles for her until she could drink again, the number of wine bottles became large and that gave Kovi the idea to make a wine cellar, but at the time they were renting and did not have space for one. After they bought their own house, they transformed the basement into a wine cellar and filled it with great quality wine from various places. Kovi became a wine snob, and he installed a device in the basement to control the temperature to conserve the quality of their collection. He took invited guests to the cellar and proudly lectured them on the bottles that he selected to enjoy with dinner.

One weekend, his old friend Jeff from graduate school paid them a visit, and he took Jeff to the cellar. Kovi then compared their large collection of wine to the large collection of guns that he saw when he visited Jeff's family many years earlier. He teased Jeff and told him that unlike his father, who impressed Kovi with his large collection of guns, Kovi preferred to impress his guests with his good quality wine. He instructed Jeff to convince his father to remove all the guns from his basement and Kovi would come there and help them transform their basement into a great wine cellar. Jeff shook his head and said that would never happen as long as his father was alive.

Jeff then remarked that Kovi had gotten chubby and that his insatiable taste for good quality wine contributed to the excess weight. Kovi disagreed and stated that as long as one "hides the wine behind the starch," the contribution of wine to weight gain is negligible, but he did not offer any proof or evidence to support such a claim.

In the evening, Kovi opened a bottle from his finest collection reserved for only their distinguished guests, but Jeff preferred to stick to beer instead. Kovi challenged Jeff, saying that if he would have a glass of wine with lunch and dinner, by the time he returned home, Kovi would transform him into a wine snob. Kovi lost the bet that weekend, but he learned later that Jeff, too, transformed his basement into a cellar full of a fine assortment of great quality wines, instead of a basement full of guns.

***

Throughout the autumn of the election year, the presidential campaign was in full swing and was getting heated as the voting day approached rapidly. Kovi was looking forward to the day after the election. On Election Day, he planned to cast his vote and follow the results into the wee hours. He hoped his side won by a landslide. If they should lose, he would have to learn how to re-cork Champagne bottles.

On the big day, Kovi went to vote. As he got out of his car, he saw an old lady, frail looking, warmly dressed, and somewhat lost.

"Can I help you?"

"Yes. I do not really know where to go to vote. It's around here somewhere."

"Please come with me, I am going there too."

"Thanks, young man. So nice of you."

"I am not that young anymore. I used to be."

"I am one hundred and six! To me, you are a baby."

"A hundred and six? You look like you're in your seventies. What's the secret?"

"Regular exercise, at least three times a week, no less than forty-five minutes each. Two glasses of wine a day. Healthy eating and good sex."

"Wow!"

"You know, I voted in every election since the forties. Years ago, we voted to make history. We must do the same today. Let's vote for victory."

Kovi was not sure about the "we" that she mentioned. He voted and waited for her. He walked her back to her car.

"I live on Oak Street, around the cul-de-sac. Come by and bring your family. I make excellent pumpkin pie. Secret recipe. It's been in the family for generations. We must enjoy even if we lose. That's another secret of long living."

"Please give me the recipe."

"Not so fast, son. Not so fast. But thanks again. Nice talking to you. Enjoy your day."

"You too, Gran! We are coming for that pie!"

***

On a cold and snowy Thanksgiving night, Kovi and his family went to see the Old Lady of Oak Street. A few days earlier, Kovi drove to the City and got a deep-fried turkey for the occasion; it was seasoned with garlic and herbs, a flavor that he particularly liked. The old lady spent many hours preparing Italian food and her famous pie.

She had a cozy house, and it was full of great paintings and decorative items strategically arranged and squeaky clean. Kovi walked around the living room and stared at old pictures of her youth. She was an elegant lady who had handled herself with grace throughout her life, except in politics when she used ungracefully funny and trashy language to criticize her political opponents. She came over to Kovi, and with a somber face and a sad voice, she talked about the picture Kovi was observing.

She had been married for a long time and her beloved husband had died many years earlier. They had two children who were grown men with their own families and they lived elsewhere in the country. She did not get to see them much, and they were so busy that they hardly came back to visit her. They encouraged her to come and live with one of their families, but she always refused and cited the need to keep her independence.

Her living room led to a veranda with an enviable view over the Long Island Sound. From that vantage point, both the sunset and the sunrise over the bay must be stunning.

The old lady invited a friend of hers for the evening. By their own stories, both were politically active and engaged. When they talked about their efforts to change the minds of people who held different political views from theirs, her friend said, "I may not have convinced them, but they did not change me either."

They all gathered around the fireplace and the sound of the waves offered a constant and relaxing background noise. The food was delicious, and she bragged about her special recipes passed down in the family. She took a great pleasure in seeing other people enjoying her cooking. Several hours later, little of the food was left and there were many empty bottles.

It became a tradition for Kovi and his family to get together at the house of the Old Lady of Oak Street and enjoy her homemade pie after they had consumed much of the food and had many drinks. They listened to her and her friend bash their political opponents with funny and foul language.

***

On the New Year's Eve after their first Thanksgiving with the Old Lady, Kovi and his family returned home from a party and noticed that their heating unit broke down and the house was getting cold. It must have happened earlier in the day, but they found out only in the evening when it's harder to get it fixed right away. "It's such a drag to be in a cold house," said Kovi. After some time, the repairman arrived and was unsure about the problem, and looked around the boiler several times hesitantly.

"Is it serious?" asked Aisha.

"No, not at all. I will get it running again in forty-five minutes," he replied.

Two hours later, there was no visible progress, just an indecisive fellow unsure of the diagnosis and the fix. It was getting late and much colder, and they were getting worried.

"Do you know what's wrong?" asked Kovi.

"No, I am not sure. It could be the pump or the engine, maybe the fuel supply. Do you have enough fuel?" the repairman responded. Kovi looked at him with a grin, "Yes. We checked the fuel level before we called you; there is enough."

The repairman expected a quick fix like, "Hey, you ran out of fuel and did not even know. Always check the obvious first and that will save you money." When that did not work, he opened parts of the chamber, cleaned out some dirt, and greased up a few things. He hoped this was the fix, but the motor did not start. He was then confused with no ideas. All his actions were random, and nothing was planned.

Kovi told him, "The sound of the motor when you closed the fuel supply valve is the same as when the valve was open. That suggests that the fuel injection system is not working; that's why the motor shuts down for lack of enough fuel."

"You think so?"

"That is my guess from the observation."

"What kind of work do you do?"

"I am a physicist."

"Oh! You are a physicist. That's why!"

"For safety reasons, the unit will not come on because of lack of fuel. The safety switch will open to protect the motor. When you have a low fuel or no injection of fuel, the unit won't work. The thermostat will trigger the unit to generate heat, but the safety switch will prevent the engine from running until you find and fix the issues. Let's replace the pump." Kovi suggested.

He helped the repairman install a new pump a few hours after his arrival. The boiler was running again, and the repairman said, "You were right, it was the pump. I will still charge you for parts and labor, with a discount because of your help." Kovi was grateful they had heat again. Kovi paid him and before he left, the repairman tried to convince Kovi to become an engineer and go into a business partnership for him. Kovi thought about it for a moment. He could have fixed the heater himself; he just did not have the replacement pump handy, but the serviceman did. Kovi said he did nothing spectacular. He just applied the simple rule, "Always check the obvious first," and in this case, the fuel gauge and the sound of the motor.

They repaired the boiler just in time for the New Year.

Chapter Ten
Strange Creature from the Sea

On New Year's Day, Kovi was pacing around the living room drinking coffee and thinking about the "what ifs" of last year. "What if this? What if that?" He was thinking of a great New Year's resolution, "Hum… The baggage that we carry through life is self-imposed and drags us down. Get rid of it. Set yourself free."

He was pacing around the living room, holding the empty coffee cup. Kovi was thinking about which baggage to drop. This, he might need. That one has a sentimental value. The other has been in the family for generations. Another was a gift from a dear friend.

Kovi was pacing around the living room as he realized it's not so easy to let go.

He was pacing around the living room as he reflected on events of the earlier year which had ended on a high note. Kovi had received official confirmation of a high-profile professional promotion. "I've reached the exclusive club of the crème de la crème," he thought. Some people told him, "Oh, I thought you would have passed that threshold already, long ago." Not without embarrassment, Kovi replied, "I've noticed that in all human interactions, one reaches a point where competence and qualifications alone do no longer carry one further. One must add a measure of ass-kissing, among a few other social skills. And I am not a man known to be good at that, but I am learning fast."

Kovi paced around the living room as he thought about a great New Year's resolution. He finally found a good one, "Drop any unnecessary baggage and learn to kiss the right ass."

***

A few months later, in the spring, when Kovi noticed that he had already forgotten about his New Year's resolution, he wrote his thoughts and post them around the house as a constant reminder to put them into practice. On the next New Year's Day, he would want to see that he'd made good progress on his previous resolution. Kovi then sat in front of his computer and wanted to type quickly to transform his thoughts into written information. He found out that he could not type as quickly as usual because he'd recently cut a finger. Sloppy him. He then realized that when one cannot use a finger, the functions it performs, which are often taken for granted, become apparent. For, unconsciously, one wants to use the finger, but cannot because it hurts.

His finger was hurting and bleeding, but he ignored the pain. When the bleeding did not stop, Kovi ended up in the emergency room at the insistence of Aisha. He arrived at the hospital while he was still in pain and bleeding. After he completed the health insurance protocol, they wanted to find out if it was a deliberate, self-inflicted injury or if he was the victim of abuse. "No, no," he insisted. "It was an accident; I was working around the house and I cut myself unintentionally," Kovi protested, and he continued, "I'm in pain and bleeding. When I can see the doc?"

He waited for a while. During that time, a few nurses came into the room, to set up equipment, to clean the wound, or to ask further questions.

"Is your tetanus vaccination current?"

"Yes, I believe so," he replied.

"When last did you take it?" the nurse asked.

"About a year ago when I was planning a trip to Africa. I took the three-in-one vaccine, which, if I remember correctly, contains tetanus."

"Ah, okay, so you are good," said the nurse before she left the room.

He was in pain and anxiously waited for the doctor to come. He thought that at the reception desk they were seemingly still verifying his insurance or getting proper authorization from the insurance provider before he got the treatment needed. He hoped the process was quicker. They did not seem to be busy that Saturday morning. He might have bled to death just waiting alone in a room with no windows. He told himself the nurses were coming now and then with the primary purpose to check that he was still conscious. He was sure that they came in every so often to check that his condition did not worsen. Since everything took its normal course, there was no urgency. Maybe the nurses did all they could, and the rest must be in the hands of a qualified doctor. Probably, they did not have many such doctors on staff that day, and the one that should see him was still busy with another patient.

The doctor finally came and stitched up the wound quickly and skillfully. The doctor told Kovi, "You are lucky. You cut a vein, but the artery is still intact."

When Kovi was all fixed and about to leave, the doctor gave him a word of warning.

"You will not finish that project in your house today. What were you doing?"

Kovi did not have any lie prepared, and the question took him by surprise. He felt compelled to tell the truth because the doctor did an excellent job of stopping the bleeding and stitching up the wound. A sense of connection or closeness developed between the physician and the patient, and Kovi felt he could tell him what happened.

"I was slaughtering a chicken when the knife slipped and cut my finger."

The doctor looked at him incredulously.

"You were slaughtering a chicken?"

"Yes. It is a cultural ritual that I used to do, and which I have maintained."

The doctor stared at Kovi, speechless for a while, as though he just told him the strangest thing he ever heard.

"Slaughtering a chicken? Why don't you buy one from the grocery store?"

"One cannot use a dead chicken from the grocery store. Slaughtering one is the essence of the offering to divinity. The blood, as it pours out of the slaughtered animal, is an important part of the offering. You must cook the rest of the chicken, enjoy all of it with family or friends in one seating, and then burn the bones to complete the offering."

"Offering? To whom and for what?"

"To God! To pray or show thankfulness for something."

"But then, how come you cut yourself when you were doing such an important thing for your God?"

"You are right. That should not have happened. I definitely need to slaughter more chickens."

That made the doctor laugh.

"Be careful now. Please do not come back here with another cut. And pray for me while you slaughter more chickens."

Not able to use his finger, Kovi had an excuse to be lazy. Ouch! The anesthetic wore off, and he was feeling pain again. He needed a shot. A few shots! *Sodabi*, a hard liquor from West Africa would do right then, but he did not have any left. To get his mind off the pain, Kovi joined his family for a leisure drive to Montauk and a walk on the beach.

It was a pleasant afternoon in the spring. Occasionally, they threw small rocks on the water and competed to see who could make the rocks bounce off the surface of the water many more times than the others. This became a fun game and they paid attention to different criteria necessary for success—the shape of the rock, the weight of the rock, the speed and angle of the throw.

They searched around the beach for flat disk-shaped rocks that were likely to bounce off the surface of the water and threw the rocks horizontally so that the cross section of the disk touched the water to increase the chances of bouncing. To increase the probability of more bounces, they tried to throw the rocks, so that they did not twist or rotate in mid-air before contact with the water. Finally, the rock must have the right weight so that it got enough initial kinetic energy from the throw. A rock too heavy might be slow and just sink in the water on the first contact. The wind might twist or rotate a light rock by the time it reaches the water and such a rock will not bounce.

They took turns throwing, and they watched and cheered as they counted the number of bounces. Kovi's cut finger was on his right hand, but he threw the rocks with his left hand, which was his most comfortable one since he was born left-handed.

Kovi picked up a rock, and he was sure that it had a story to tell. It was smooth and shaped like a saucer and appeared like the right type that could bounce several times off the surface of the water. It was a beautiful rock and Kovi hesitated to throw it. He heard the rock telling him this: "It took millions of years for the waves to bring me to shore, where I've sat happily for millions more years. Compared to me, your existence has been ephemeral. You show up on this beach today, without regard and respect, you are eager to throw me back into the sea, and it will take me millions more years to come to shore again and I might look less interesting than I do now."

Kovi was thinking about what the rock had just told him when suddenly a strange creature crawled out of the bay. People gathered to watch.

"Daddy, is it a crab or a turtle?" asked Hatshepsut.

"I do not know. This is the first time I've seen this. The sea is full of strange creatures," replied Kovi.

"It looks like a shoe, maybe more like a horseshoe. Let's check if there is such a thing called horseshoe crab," said Aisha. With her electronic gadget, Aisha and Hatshepsut did a quick search and identified the creature as it crawled nonchalantly back into the water and disappeared. They continued the walk as the crowd dispersed. No more creatures came to shore. As for the rock, Kovi respected its wishes, and did not send it back into the water. He would take it home for safekeeping.

Before he knew it, Kovi left his family behind as he hiked briskly to the end of the island where the bay merged into the Atlantic Ocean at Montauk Point. There, he saw the seals and many of them were lying majestically on the rocks in the bay. They were relaxed and sunbathing. In the spring, the seals congregated on that spot, and depending on the day, one could see many or a few.

They used all the rocks that were protruding from the water. There were cases where what appeared as an alpha male or a dominant female occupied one large rock by him or herself. The seals did not mind sharing the rocks with large seagulls that flew and hovered over the bay and occasionally landed on the rocks for a while.

Folks stopped and stared for a long time in silence and some took pictures. It was serene and the only noises they heard were those of the waves or the seagulls. The seals lay content and motionless. Kovi did not dare throw any rocks in the water there. By many accounts, the seals often came out in large numbers that day, Easter Sunday.

***

Easter Sunday! A festive day back home in the ancestral village of Kovi. Fine people, elegantly dressed, congregated and there were food, drinks, laughs, music, and dance. People came from different places, even from faraway places in Ghana, Togo, Benin, Ivory Coast, Burkina Faso, Niger, Senegal, or Nigeria. Many from the village scattered to distant areas in Africa, and Easter was the time of the year when the village looked like a big family reunion. Folks were happy to see relatives and friends. Several days before Easter

Sunday, people bought clothes and went to see their favorite tailors. These professionals took many measurements of the client's body, and within a few days transformed the clothes into elegant dresses decorated to the specific instructions of the clients. One could see an entire family of eight or ten people—father, mother, kids, and cousins—that were all dressed in different tops and bottoms, but made from the same cloth, and they looked spiffy. It was a busy time for the tailors who, with their apprentices, worked long hours, day and night, to make sure that all orders were ready in time. Good Lord! A tailor must not forget or delay an order, for the client would miss the grand fashion show on Easter Sunday.

It was a time when the tailors made the most money from the volume of the orders, and they had so much work that the tailors themselves missed the show sometimes because they were pressed to work until late in the big day.

The Catholic folks went to church in the morning, and one of their own, a descendant of the founding fathers of the village led the catholic mass. He was a prince and a Catholic priest who worked for the Pope—Monseigneur Cécile Le Grand.

In the afternoon, after the heat of the day subsided, people converged on the village center for the traditional drumming session. The chief of the village and the elders arrived one by one, at their own time and leisure. As they came in and took their seats, they interrupted the music and skillful drummers played the drums to some particularly short beats that echoed and reflected the great nickname of the individual. It was important to acknowledge these great elders of honor who were the keepers of the laws and traditions.

The good ambiance continued until late at night. When the old folks retired, the younger crowd carried on the celebration until the early morning and they alternated between the different rhythms and styles of music from other parts of Africa, the Americas, Europe, and Asia.

At the end of the island, there stood Kovi, looking across the vast expanse of the mighty Atlantic Ocean, toward Africa. His ancestral village, Djéta, is across the Atlantic, by the Gulf of Guinea. On that Easter Sunday, the festive ambiance must be in full swing in Djéta.

He was remembering home, the place where his journey had started a long time ago, a place where options were scarce and the means were modest, a place of mostly a pedestrian life, a place where another day was a blessing, a place where smiles and laughs were easily offered regardless of daily struggles, and a place of simple living.

He could feel their vibes and he wondered if they picked up his. One of their own, stranded on the other side of the Atlantic, reminisced with only indifferent seals for company on Easter Sunday! He missed it. Easter Sunday in the village of his people!

***

Early one morning in the spring, Kovi was reflecting on his own life and thinking that there were moments when he felt he tried his best, given his limited means and abilities, yet he did not achieve his desired results. There were these moments when he got a great feeling that fame and fortune must be within reach, if only he could get there. When he thought that he'd made it, they just slipped away, although closer than before.

Tirelessly, he kept thinking that he was almost there, yet he never really reached. But what if he was almost there?

"Come on, let's make the extra mile. You've come too far to quit now," he encouraged himself. So, he gathered his courage, and tirelessly he continued. Yet, he never achieved fame and fortune.

"Hope is the greatest placebo in the human condition, often unjustified, yet nice to have," he reckoned.

***

As the summer approached and the weather warmed up, the number of people in the area where Kovi and Aisha lived increased and so did the noise from human activities. Occasional visitors—at the park and the beach—and the summer residents caused the noise. These residents often migrated to warmer regions of the country during the winter months. Kovi frequently took leisurely walks on the beach and occasionally engaged his neighbors in small talk along the way.

One day, he started from home and walked for about a mile up the hill to reach Smith Point Park. During the summer, the park was full of visitors, some of whom were camping. Opposite to the camping ground, there was a huge area for *braai*, behind which stood a children's playground where many children were at play under the constant concerned watch of adults. From a distance, the smell of the burning meat was appetizing. Other people were playing volleyball, or biking or jogging around the park. The ice-cream van came around with its distinctively familiar music and drew a great number of excited kids and adults.

From there, it was a short distance to the beach or to the beginning of the trail. Kovi had the choice to hike along the trail or go down to the beach. He'd hiked along that trail in the past; it was near the edge of a cliff and offered a great view over the bay. Since it was already late in the day, he went down to the beach and walk back home along the beach facing the sunset.

The beach was full of people. Some were swimming and others were fishing. The seagulls were also around and searched for food. When he stepped closer to them, they flew away, with acrobatic moves in the air over the water, and landed somewhere else on the beach.

As he continued walking, he saw isolated pockets on the beach not occupied by humans or seagulls. There, in the water near the shore, were myriad small fish just under the surface, perfectly aligned. They made fast, rhythmic, and sinusoidal movements. The scene was creepy until he realized that it was the fish.

A distance ahead, people started to gather, and of all them faced the sunset. Kovi looked across the bay and saw that the red ball was sitting on the water at the horizon. As it sank, rays of colors filled the sky. It was a view he enjoyed many times as he stood under the tree on his back lawn that overlooked the bay.

When he got closer to the people, the sun had just disappeared into the horizon and people started clapping and marveling at this awesome mystery. Kovi could not resist and he said loudly, "What are you clapping for, God?" Everybody laughed while Kovi continued the walk back home as he stared at the colorful radiant sky with the remnants of the mighty red ball.

After the sunset, Kovi sat in the backyard at home after supper. The sky became partially covered, and the moon was struggling to shine through the clouds. In the distance, he heard the frogs and the noises of the creatures of the night. He stared at the sky and marveled at the constellations of stars that were visible. "Who created this?" He wondered.

Scientists say there was a bang. A big bang! And billions of years later, here he was, an intelligent creature, on a small planet who was trying to make sense of it all.

"What banged?"

"What caused it to bang?"

"What happened before the bang?"

These were some questions that were going through his mind as he sat there in silence. "No one has answers to these questions," he thought. For the people of faith, it was the work of the Creator. Whatever the ultimate answer, that night he felt privileged that his kind is self-conscious and intelligent enough to understand it. That night, he got the true sense of how small human beings are. That night, he truly found peace.

The night was still young and a cool breeze through the trees was taking over from the heat of the day. As the darkness set in, Kovi saw his daughter approaching with a smile so sincere, so true, and offered so easily. "Let's go inside," Hatshepsut requested. They sat in the living room and sang songs that she knew better than Kovi. He stared at her and realized that her choices were always sharp and simple, whereas for him, only a few choices were simple. That's being an adult.

He saw his daughter, his new source of courage, the best of him to hold and the carriage to keep him going. The young lady might cry in one minute, but they were best friends again in the next. "Sharing is caring," that was the rule. But that rule only applied when Kovi had the goods and it was not a commutative rule at all. He looked at his daughter with a smile and thought that here was a young person with never a hard feeling and to whom forgiveness came so easily. He hoped that for one moment, he could escape the complications of adulthood.

"What is that white hair cropping up?" asked Hatshepsut.

"A sign of aging."

"What is that?"

"When you live long enough!"

"You do not seem happy about this white hair. You always pluck it out."

"Hey! That's a sensitive issue! People want to live long, yet look and stay young."

"I do not understand, Daddy. I will just have my milk now."

"Good idea. You will understand someday."

"You have that red drink again and you never give me any."

"The red drink is not good for you!"

"But the red drink is good for you? Does it help you stay young when you grow old?"

"Just have your milk and I will have my wine. Are we cool?"

"Yes, we are. I wish for many nights much like tonight when I can enjoy wine with you, Daddy."

"I do, too."

The wind picked up and they could hear the roaring of the waves and the movements of the tree branches. Not so long ago, Kovi was there during her birth. She was helpless and cried as her father cut the cord. Just a few years since then, she thought she knew a lot and offered arguments and rebuttals. In his head, Kovi could not stop these words repeating: "I do, too. I do hope for many more nights much like tonight. It's been a lovely ride so far."

***

In the early morning, Kovi enjoyed peace as the bay was calm and the sun started to rise. In the warmth of the house, with a coffee cup, there he stood and contemplated the view.

"So magnificent and impressive. What a mesmerizing place!"

"Daddy look, there is a fire in the sky. It is the first time that I've seen this," said Hatshepsut.

Repeatedly, he enjoyed that view, and he always took time to look, for he did not know when it could be the last look he would ever take. But sometimes, he needed to stop looking and to get ready for another trip far away. Hatshepsut followed him around to make sure that Kovi did not leave her.

"I must go now," said Kovi.

"I want to come with you."

"No, not today."

She burst into tears and hugged her father tightly, not wanting to let go, and she sobbed. They stood there and rocked gently as she came down slowly. "I must go now," Kovi repeated while trying to break out of the hug. It was so hard to walk away and Kovi did not turn around for he could not continue, with each step harder to take as she cried louder. Kovi heard her angel in his head, "Your daughter needs you, but there you go again pursuing the futilities of life. The time will come when you will need her, just a moment with her, and she will not be there as much as you hope. She will be busy on the futilities of her own life. Sadly, humans are condemned to such a journey, alone, in the pursuit of happiness."

***

It was on one of these quiet mornings that the telephone rang and broke Kovi's reflections. He picked up the telephone and heard a loud wailing in the background, and he knew that it was bad news. The voice at the other end of the line announced calmly, "Our father is dead!" During the telephone call, Kovi learned that when Kodjo sensed he was dying, he asked folks to forgive him for any wrong he might have done. He expressed regret for not having had one more chance to see Kovi again. After the telephone conversation, Kovi thought about his father. He remembered that they took Kodjo to the hospital several times, and each time when it looked like he would not come out alive, he somehow recovered. He became known at the hospital as "The man who even Death himself fears to take." The last time, they admitted Kovi's father for stomach cancer, which had not yet metastasized, although he had accumulated fluid around his lungs, which made it difficult for him to breathe. The doctors did a bunch of tests, assessed the condition, and performed a surgical operation to remove the cancerous cells. Kovi's father recovered and lived for many years with the cancer in remission. Kodjo's final visit to the hospital was because of a severe ulcer, and this time, he did not come out alive. Death did not fear him, and it was the checkmate or the end of the game so to speak. It seemed like death was watching him all these years, saying, "You are on my page, but not at the top of the list and I hope that you are spending well the time that you have. For when I finally get to you, I will not wait. I will not negotiate, and ready or not, you must go."

Chapter Eleven
Recording of Life

Kovi wished that it were possible to rewind life. Not to change anything. Not to relive it. Only as a spectator! Memory becomes hazy. "Did it actually happen as I recall? Nobody can tell you, so personal an experience!" thought Kovi.

Many years after Kovi left Africa to study in the USA, he learned about the last hours of his father's life. Kodjo regretted that he did not have one more chance to see his son. Had Kovi known he would never see Kodjo again, he would have told him how much of a positive influence he had on his life. Kovi also thought that they would have more chances.

Sometimes, Kovi felt his spirit, especially at difficult times when he lacked the courage to continue. Then Kovi remembered what Kodjo used to say, "In your path in life, you will arrive at crossroads where you must choose between the easy or the hard way. Success depends on making the right choice, given the circumstances of the moment. Take a chance even when it is meager."

"It is difficult to put into practice," thought Kovi.

Sometimes he found himself at the crossroads of life and he hesitated between the tough decisions to make. As far as he could, he looked down each path ahead, unsure of which one to take. His past choices and experiences were of no help and Kodjo was not around to give great advice. There was no option to turn back! Kovi knew that he must not linger.

"Fear and hope are useful when they drive us to excel. Fear in the choices we make and hope in that we still have choices. When your path has no more crossroads, surely you must have run out of luck," Kovi reckoned.

When he heard the news, Kovi booked a flight right away to be there for the burial. He traveled with his USA passport and planned to get the travel visa upon his arrival at the airport there. The agent that handled his visa application at the airport understood after he asked a few questions that Kovi was a native of the region, and the agent could not hide his disappointment regardless of Kovi's reason for needing a visa to come back to his native country. To be sure, he questioned Kovi about his dual citizenship. Kovi explained that he needed to come back urgently and did not have enough time to renew and travel with his native passport. The agent encouraged Kovi to keep his old passport current and said that it looked strange to have to ask for a visa with thirty to ninety days' maximum stay in his original country. Kovi should not have any restriction on the length of his stay or the legal activities that he could perform in his own country.

After the agent checked Kovi's vaccination records, he issued the visa. He told Kovi that the next time he came back he did not want to see him in the line of the foreigners who sought visas. Kovi assured him that he understood his point, and he preferred to enter his home country proudly with minimal and swift immigration protocols. After he collected his bag, Kovi met up with his brother, Koku Jean-Tonton, and sister, Josiane Kayi, and they all journeyed together to Djéta.

Jean-Tonton and Kayi prearranged a taxi that took them nonstop to the village about sixty kilometers away, and it was already dark when they started the journey. From the airport, the shortest path for them was to cross Lomé straight to the motorway that ran along the Atlantic coast. From there, they traveled east for about thirty-five minutes to Anèho where Kovi had attended middle and high schools long ago. Djéta, is just about twenty kilometers from Anèho, but on an unpaved road the journey took a much longer time. The last leg of the journey on the unpaved road was the most painful in a vehicle that did not seem to have any shock absorbers. It was an uncomfortable experience for Kovi.

The driver explained that the vehicle was his own. He'd bought it thirty-five years ago with money that he saved from doing odd jobs. He'd maintained the vehicle himself through the years, and now in the state of junk, it still ran well and he was the only one capable of fixing it when it broke down—he and his vehicle developed a symbiotic relationship. Kovi asked him why he did not save money to buy a replacement, and his answer was the economic downturn and the ten kids that he had to feed. He seemed to be a skillful and agile driver, and he did his best to maneuver around to avoid big potholes on the road.

After driving on that road many times, he developed a keen sense of how to handle his vehicle and the road even at night with no streetlights. When they finally arrived, he apologized and explained that if it were during the day, he would have navigated the road better to reduce the roughness of the ride.

Kovi was thankful that the uncomfortable ride was over and that the vehicle did not break down on the way. Kovi unpacked his bag quickly and noticed that the dream catcher that he'd bought at the powwow during the Puyama's' visit was in the bag. He recalled that just before he left the USA, Hatshepsut was playing with the dream catcher and she must have inserted it into his bag without his knowledge. He just hung the dream catcher on the wall behind his bed and did not think of it further.

***

It was the night of the wake when, at some point, Kovi fell into a deep sleep. He woke up sometime later, and he attempted to reconstruct a dream. He remembered it so vividly that he believed that it was because of the charm of the dream catcher, since Kovi usually forgot much of his dreams when he woke up. Kovi saw his deceased father surrounded by a veil or a white cloud. The deceased appeared visibly happy, said goodbye to Kovi, and started his journey into the afterlife, a journey that we must each take alone when our turn comes. Kovi saw him walk away, and he never looked back.

Kovi kept watching as the deceased appeared in some kind of courtroom. The presiding judge was elegantly dressed and commanded attention. Kovi noticed that there was a queue of defendants, all of whom were recently deceased, including the one who came to say goodbye to him in his sleep. It appeared to be the ultimate judgment and there were no defense lawyers and no prosecution team. The judge took a seat.

The defendant that was at the beginning of the queue stepped forward into the middle of the court, and they played a recording of an entire life. From birth to death, they showed the defendant the recording of a lifetime. They played for the defendant and tallied a list of the good and the bad. Further, they divided the list into the subcategories of the wrong done to self, the wrong done to others, and the good. They weighed each item on the list according to its importance or severity.

Kovi saw the deceased standing. He was astonished by various episodes in the recording. The judge asked the deceased to analyze the various events, weigh, mark, and categorize them into the prescribed list. Kovi kept looking. At each point of the analysis, the judge nodded at the defendant to encourage him to carry on. The defendant was eloquent and expressed disappointment at the many failures, harms, and hurts of the life that they asked him to analyze. He gave a rare praise to the things in the recording that were good and commendable and instead super-analyzed the bad. He pointed out each episode as one of the seven deadly sins and related them to the harms done to other people.

At the end of the proceedings, the judge retired to his chamber.

Kovi noticed that the defendant made a fist and shook it—he was proud that he had done a great job of categorizing all the good and bad.

The judge came back and told the defendant that the life he'd just analyzed was his own. The defendant did not believe him and at first rejected the accusation. Surely, he was not as bad as claimed. Or, he could not have done this or that. One by one, the judge refreshed his memories and took him back as a spectator to events in his own life. Soon, denial gave way to resistance, then vain and defensive justifications. The defendant claimed that he did not intend to do bad, that other people or circumstances pushed him, that he tried his best, and that it was his right to pursue happiness.

After a failed self-defense, he begged the judge for an opportunity to go back and learn to correct the wrong. He wished to make amends. "Well, no one goes back," the judge told him. "You each got one chance, only one. See what you did with yours?"

The defendant learned that there was a possibility of being sent back through reincarnation, not resuscitation. Given his basic issues, weaknesses, and shortcomings in his previous life, he was to go back as a poor man who later in life would become filthy rich. He must then learn to manage his wealth and get involved in philanthropic activities where he should give away much of his wealth. They believed that the next time he appeared in that courtroom, he should have corrected his wrongs, and purified his soul to gain acceptance into everlasting life. There was no right to appeal to this verdict.

The judge ordered away defendant and added him to the list of the souls that were waiting to come in the flesh and restart their journeys toward purification.

Before they dismissed him, the judge allowed him to make a final statement. He complained, saying that he wished to review the recording of his life while he was alive, so that he could take corrective actions before his death. The judge pointed out the array of services that are at the disposal of humans to guide them in their lifelong journeys: conscience, morals, religion, science, memory, human considerations, and free will. The defendant further complained that the pursuit of good living necessitates stepping on a few toes and/or occasionally stepping outside rules, norms, or laws. The judge showed him a clip of a life where the person lived a happy life while he abided by the rules and laws.

The judge reminded him that freedom comes with responsibilities and respect toward others, and that within those boundaries, there are still limitless possibilities for a happy life. He learned that happiness should just be a way of living, that the pursuit of it suggests something unattainable, that the goal of his reincarnation was not only the purification of the soul after death but also happiness of the flesh in life. He received free will to him toward that end.

Defendant after defendant stepped forward into the center of the courtroom, and they showed and asked to analyze the recording of a life. Each defendant appeared to be an expert and pointed out what was wrong, how things could have been handled better. Kovi was curious about the deceased who came to say goodbye to him in the dream.

As Kovi continued watching, defendants got different sentences, always to give them a chance to reincarnate into better humans. A few were pure and sent into an everlasting life of happiness, without the constraints and pitfalls of the flesh. There were some who had exhausted all the chances to return to flesh. Strangely, some become worse in their next incarnations. The judge sent sorry souls to hell for eternal pain and sorrow, or ordered them extinguished forever.

Kovi got scared when he recalled the gory details of the dream and started to do soul searching to understand the improvements he was to achieve in his current incarnation while pursuing happiness of the flesh within the boundaries of his free will.

**

The burial ceremony was a special and memorable event centered on tradition. It started with the gathering of the important people of the village in the ancestral house of the deceased. When all the relevant people were present, they slaughtered a goat, and a procession followed as the coffin was carried out.

Before they headed to the cemetery, they took coffin to the house of each important elder for an added ceremony, and finally to the village center. Special drumming, chants, and dancing—invoked only for grim and sad occasions—followed around the coffin. The drumming styles and the chants were special and passed down from generation to generation. Slowly, the gathering developed into such a festive event that one forgot it was still a sad moment. However, folks believed that the celebration was what the deceased would have wanted, i.e., the celebration of his or her life.

After a while, they carried the coffin toward the cemetery, followed by a huge crowd that continued to drum, chant, and dance unabated. As they lowered the coffin into the grave, the noise stopped and a few gave speeches. They said good and funny things about the deceased and no one dared to say anything bad. It was funny, Kovi thought, that some dead were perhaps bad people when they were alive, yet in death, they were all glorified. But then Kovi remembered his dream and believed that it was good for the living to remember and recount the good about the dead, particularly on his or her sendoff day. He reckoned that the deceased was probably already in the courtroom to face the judge.

Kovi was one person to speak at the cemetery. He was emotional as he recalled many of the sacrifices that Kodjo made for his education. The weird thing about that speech was that Kovi spoke in French. In order not to appear condescending or not to show disrespect for his own culture, Kovi asked the elders for permission to speak in French. After many years abroad with few opportunities to maintain good conversation skills in his native language, Kovi had lost his fluency. He could understand everything when other people spoke. Expressions, figures of speech, and other forms of communication particular to the language came back to him when he heard others using them, but he could no longer speak spontaneously and eloquently. It was unfortunate. Many years earlier, he'd gone to the USA unable to speak English fluently, and then he came back home as a stranger among his own people, unable to express himself in his native language with the speed and grace that he once possessed.

Kovi had become a changed man, a complicated man who absorbed bits of many cultures around the world with none that he could claim to be a hundred percent his own.

Folks stayed until the tomb was completely sealed off before they dispersed for more food, drinks, and dance to celebrate of the deceased's life.

***

Kovi learned later that they took a baby boy to one of the revered elders in the village soon after his birth, and the elder performed a religious ceremony to identify the dead person who incarnated as the baby boy. At the end of the ceremony, the elder identified the boy as the reincarnation of Kodjo, and gave him one of Kodjo's nicknames of power, "*Lanta pupu hayo hayo. Avu'ong do guidi, ldu o'ng gbin'ong!*" One may translate it as "A resilient and unbreakable person." And they initiated the boy in the religious order from which they selected the chiefs of the village.

Chapter Twelve
Ancestral Village

The day after the funeral, Kovi paid visits to the elders and family members in the village in a symbolic yet important gesture to secure the blessings and well wishes from his people for a safe return to the USA. The amount of blessing and good wishes increased if Kovi offered a small gift during the visit. A gift to the person visited generated joy and happiness. The elder or family member started the blessing by giving praise to God the Creator, then to each of the lesser gods, the protectors of the people, followed by the invocation of the great ancestors by their names of power, all the way back to the ancestors who came from Ghana and settled in the region, without forgetting to explain how the families were related and at which points in the lineage they branched out. Never did Kovi enjoy gifting.

Afi made sure that they omitted no elder or major family member when they went around the village, "Come on, son. Your aunt lives here. She heard that you came back and we must go see her. Make sure you give her something and do not forget to ask about her children, your cousins!"

Afi also instructed that her son must not eat or drink anything when offered during the visits—to avoid intentional poisoning because of envy or jealousy. She kept a constant and concerned watch over all the interactions of Kovi with others.

At the house of Kovi's aunt, Donsi, after the greeting protocol, which must be observed by each side so as not to offend anyone, they sat down. The aunt offered a libation before she started small talk about what Kovi had been doing all these years. Kovi remembered Donsi well. She had aged gracefully since the last time he saw her. She still looked healthy with good-looking white teeth, even though she had never used a modern toothpaste and toothbrush. Instead, she relied on a special tree trunk cut into narrow pieces. The villagers chewed upon a piece every morning to make a mesh and they used that to brush. Donsi was naturally slim and stayed slender through the years, and she had an enviable golden-brown skin tone from the use of coconut oil as lotion every day.

It was striking and impressive to see how beautiful and glamorous the women of the village became as they aged.

Donsi asked Kovi about his family and was disappointed to hear that he had only one child. She had eight children of her own and thought that something must be wrong to have only one child. Jokingly, she asked Kovi if the issue was with him, or if he needed more wives. It seemed strange to Donsi that a healthy adult in his prime had only one child, and the first advice Kovi received was that the next time he came to visit, he should bring the family; she wanted to see more kids. Kovi attempted to explain the limiting factors and constraints leading to having the single child—money, both parents working, high cost of daycare and schooling, lack of an extended family around, etc. To Donsi, and also to Afi, none of these were justifiable reasons, and both said, "Just have more kids and God will provide." At the insistence of both ladies, Kovi promised to come back for a visit in the not-too-distant future with a much larger family.

Donsi asked why Hatshepsut did not have a name according to tradition. The name of a newborn was not random, and it followed a conventional pattern that alternated between two consecutive generations and depended on whether the baby was a boy, a girl, the firstborn, second, third, etc., or a twin. As a result, a son could never have the same name as his father, no junior, but his name could be the same as that of his grandfather or of one of his granduncles.

In that culture, they considered cousins brothers or sisters and there were no such things as distant relations. It may happen that two individuals related to the Nete Brothers did not know each other, but if they met anywhere in the world, their names would let them know that they were both descendants of the four patriarchs. If they talked further, they would figure out the lineage and the relation.

Kovi was always proud of the traditional naming system that nowadays is being lost, as people have been using Christian names more often. He gave Hatshepsut a second name according to tradition.

Besides the name and a nickname, one may get a title depending on their standing in the family or society, or depending on their age. Kovi, being the firstborn in the family, had the privilege of being addressed by his title name by his younger siblings and cousins as a sign of appreciation and respect. Conversely, the title so conferred came with a responsibility toward the younger ones to set good examples as a role model and to help in case of need. The older ones were often the first to become comfortable financially and had the responsibility of helping the rest of the family. Kovi still enjoyed the title given upon him because he was the oldest, even when they were all grown men and women.

The other members of the family or the community, such as uncles and aunts, also had title names that by construction stated the relationship. For instance, an uncle older than Kovi's father had a title name that clarified that he was an uncle to Kovi and older than Kovi's father. An uncle who was younger than Kovi's father had another title name. As a sign of respect, they addressed people by their title names. Only older people called someone younger by their given name or nickname.

***

To explain how she was related to Kovi, Donsi started to recall the ancestral lineage. During the slave trade a few centuries back, there were four brothers known as the Nete Brothers who left their village, located somewhere in present day Ghana, to escape from being taken into slavery. They migrated during the 1600s along the Atlantic coast to found the village where Kovi came from. When the Nete Brothers settled in the area that became the village, there were some other folks there already who fled in the wake of the arrival of the new people, who were practicing strange customs. The Nete Brothers left behind their people, and through the years, they lost contact with their ancestral lineage. Ultimately, they lost their original language, too, and adopted the language of the region where they resettled. The brothers carried with them and passed down to their descendants the stories of their migration and some of their original customs. However, they lost all contacts and links with their people.

The Nete Brothers became the patriarchs of the four branches of the family and continued to reign among those of Ghanaian ancestry until the present day. The brothers brought with them some of their gods, one of which was a goddess positioned at the village center. At the entrance of the village stood another god that was the first line of defense. Any evil that passed the god at the entrance faced the goddess who came into action in protecting her people.

The goddess was a great defensive warrior that the sons and daughters of the village saw. Even in distant lands, when they were in difficult situations, she came to help them. The goddess appeared often as an unknown heavyset lady who did some extraordinary things—such as giving crucial advice—to avert imminent danger. All the people who experienced such moments, when they avoided or escaped potentially catastrophic events, always mentioned the appearance of the heavyset lady and related her to the goddess at the center of the village. However, for Kovi, such correlations were not straightforward.

As Donsi was telling the story of the people, Kovi remembered that when he was younger and growing up in the village, there was an annual ceremony organized in honor of the goddess. When that time came, descendants of the Nete Brothers went around the village and seized all chickens with pure white feathers for an offering to the goddess.

In Djéta, the chickens roamed around freely, but each family knew which belonged to whom. All the white feather chickens they collected were brought before the goddess and slaughtered, and they poured the blood over the head of the goddess. After the blood offering, the villagers cooked and enjoyed chickens in a feast of drumming and chanting, and the descendants of the Nete Brothers performed the warrior dance of the goddess.

Kovi learned that many years later, as the economic condition of the entire region became dire, when the people of the village learned the date of the offering to the goddess, they did not let their chickens roam freely on that day. Such a wonderful ceremony, which brought the people of the village together and each year renewed their ancestral bonds in a great awareness of communal life, was no longer observed with the great intensity and significance that once characterized it.

There was another god, the god of thunder, who took charge during thunderstorms and lightning to punish the wicked. In such weather, the bad elements of the society, i.e., the bad witches and sorcerers, were engaged in a great battle against the god of thunder. The bad sorcerers and witches recited incantations as the thunder roared and the god of thunder wanted to strike them with lightning strikes. Ultimately, the god prevailed; if death came to someone in such weather, the folks justified it retrospectively as the punishment for the evils that the individual might have committed. In that society, nothing remained unexplained. Luck or misfortune were intimately linked to the good or bad that an individual or her ancestors did, always as a lesson for the people to do well and treat each other with kindness.

Sometimes priests from different villages believed that their particular god was the one that inflicted the punishment and they claimed the body of the individual who died during the thunderstorm for more ceremonial purposes.

There was one such time when a great priest and his consorts traveled from another village to Kovi's village. The elders of Kovi's village did not agree to release the body and took offense that these people were coming from somewhere else to claim a body as retribution from their god. A great war of witchcraft and sorcery was looming, and they ordered all the kids to stay inside the homes. The atmosphere in the village grew tense as the people could hear the intimidating drumming and chanting of the visitors across the river.

Never had Kovi seen the people of the village come together to prepare for a war not fought with traditional weapons, rather with religious ceremonies and incantations.

Adults, dressed in dazzling religious costumes, came out from the houses and gathered at the village center. They made offerings to the god at the entrance of the village, and also to the god of the great river that the unwelcome visitors had to cross. They also invoked goddess at the center of the village. She was their last line of defense, to lead her people if the undesirables entered the village—like a defensive army against occupying invaders that must battle street-by-street and house-by-house.

Then there were the learned men and women of power—the witches and sorcerers—ready to use their great experience in the manipulation of the supernatural for the defense of the village. People recited incantations and talked to each other in a weird language that Kovi did not understand, for only people selected when they were infants on the orders of the gods and ordained after lengthy religious training learned to speak that language during special religious rites.

The villagers started a loud drumming session of their own, loud enough for the folks across the river to hear that they were in for a total war, if they dared cross the river. The folks brought special big and heavy drums to the village center, and these drums made creepy and far-reaching noises, not only to demoralize the invaders but also to call friendly villages for support and to alert the village people that had gone to markets and farms of the impending war.

The sun retreated behind the clouds and an eerie cool wind blew through the village. Lightning pierced the sky, and the thunder roared louder. The god of thunder heard the call of his subjects and if he was to strike that day, it was the undesirables who would be punished.

The village folks performed warrior chants and dances that dated back hundreds of years to the time when the Nete Brothers settled in the region and scared away the previous inhabitants. The visitors across the river realized that if they crossed, they would be doomed. They wised up and returned without the body. Kovi's village earned respect in the region as the first that stood up successfully to the revered priest, who had previously claimed bodies from intimidated villages.

***

Donsi explained to Kovi that recently, the people of the village had found the place where their ancestors came from in Ghana and reconnected with their people there. As it happened, an uncle of Kovi's, who was also a great traveler, was passing through a village in Ghana and he noticed that the people had similar customs and naming conventions—some names were almost exact matches with those of his own people. His uncle became curious, asked questions, and found out that the oral tradition of these people in Ghana contained an account of the Nete Brothers who had mysteriously disappeared, and these people did not know what happened to them. They learned that the brothers had fled east and founded a village full of their people, and that Kovi's uncle was one of them.

They organized meetings and visits on both sides, although the two communities now lay in two different countries. Kovi learned about the missing links in their cultural heritage and the aspects that changed during the centuries of separation. The naming convention for a newborn was one feature of the cultural heritage that survived between the two communities.

***

When they left Donsi's house, they headed toward the village center where Kovi paid respect to the goddess before they went to the river. Afi needed to go back to the house, but she was overprotective of her sons and she instructed Koku Jean-Tonton to stay with his brother. Kovi wanted to see the great river that was once the major source that sustained the village for centuries, and the river where he'd learned to swim and fish.

During the raining season, the river swelled over its banks and flooded the region, providing natural irrigation that led to great harvests with an abundance of food. During such seasons, the much bigger river brought many types of fish and crabs, and some of these crabs dwelled in the river while other species thrived in the bushes on the riverbanks. On particular nights of the year, during of the rainy season, there was an impressive migration of the crabs from the southern riverbank toward the Atlantic Ocean.

The rainy and dry seasons were punctual in their arrivals and durations, and the people of the village came to know the timing of the seasons well, planning their agricultural and fishing activities accordingly. Since they knew when the crabs made their journeys to the ocean, many people went hunting for crabs at night. There were so many of the crabs during the migration that one had to learn to just pick them by hand while they were crawling, without getting bitten. The trick was to grab by their forward legs, away from the pinchers, and hold them between the thumb and the index with the other fingers resting against their abdomen.

Before dawn, men returned from crab hunting with tons of crabs, and the people who did not go on the hunt took the shift of fishing during the day. There were many people in canoes and they cast nets in the river or checked the traps that they previously set, while others did fly-fishing.

The rainy season brought so much abundance that every household had plenty of everything. No Africans went hungry there; instead, they ate well and enjoyed the fresh bounty they got from the land. The people learned to dry the excess fish and to conserve the unused grains for periods of drought.

The rainy season also brought some nasty devils, including the proliferation of mosquitos that buzzed around people's eardrums in the evening, to announce their menacing presence. There was a tale that kids used to tell each other, a tale also passed down through the generations, "Mosquitos buzz around the ears because the grandmother of the ears was indebted to the grandmother of the mosquito. But then both grandmothers were dead and subsequently the mosquito came around asking the ears for payback by buzzing."

There were some mosquito repellents that helped in the evenings before bed, and at nights, people slept under mosquito nets. Unfortunately, sometimes in their sleep, people rolled against the net and thus offered the mosquitos a chance to bite them through the material. The sheer number of mosquitos meant that, ultimately, each person got bitten several times anyway, during the rainy seasons, and children were vulnerable.

Kovi and his cousins, all of whom lived together and slept in the same room on mats laid on the floor, got sick one after the other or sometimes simultaneously with malaria. There were some over-the-counter pills based on quinine that people took, and which helped sometimes, but in cases of complications, the village had a small infirmary for first aid. The poor nurse was constantly busy saving lives.

For major problems or emergencies, they transported patients to a town, less than an hour's drive away on unpaved roads, to an overcrowded hospital.

Some children, and even adults, succumbed to malaria-related complications during the rainy season, although a fraction of them might have survived had they received proper care in time. Some adults refused to see the nurse until after their conditions became desperate. Some preferred to treat themselves with traditional medicinal herbs that folks used systematically on different symptoms; though they worked brilliantly on some illnesses, they did not work on all.

One such traditional medicine was made from a green leafy vegetable that they crushed or ground and then boiled. Then, they consumed it early in the morning before eating anything. It was a dreadful drink that no kid looked forward to having because of its bitterness. The adults drank huge bowls while they closed their eyes to bear the unappetizing taste, and they urged the kids to drink after they showed them the example, trying to convince them that the cure lay in the bitterness of the taste. This traditional treatment worked fairly well for stomach related issues, and also as a periodic cleansing of the digestive tracks as it triggered about fifteen minutes later the urge for a massive bowel movement and a great feeling afterward. However, for malaria or other illnesses, this treatment was not effective.

There were two hospitals in the region, and both were far from the village because of traffic and the state of the roads. They built one hospital during the colonial period and it served many people through the years. After independence, the doctors at these hospitals were black citizens who studied medicine in Europe and went back home to serve their people. These doctors worked tirelessly for long hours every day to treat all the people automatically admitted, with no requirements of health insurance coverage, and they took only thirty minutes lunch break. God bless these doctors who accomplished miracles to save the lives of many people. Often, they worked with limited means, and learned to stretch resources to cover as many cases as possible. Kodjo was taken to one of these hospitals where he died.

Chapter Thirteen
Remembrance

Kovi and Koku boarded a canoe to cross to the other side of the river, and all the while Kovi kept remembering the old days when he was growing up in the village, and he thought about all the changes that had occurred.

The years when the rain brought abundance were long gone, maybe because the people were not allowing their white-feather chickens as offerings to the goddess anymore, or they somehow offended the gods of the river and the land.

One thing Kovi noticed—from the few trips he had made to Togo and telephone conversations with his folks—was that the seasons had changed; they became unpredictable with periods of excessive rain or droughts, so the people could not successfully predict when to plant crops. The river, too, came with fewer fish and the great migration of the crabs diminished. At least the area was not developed and conserved the country atmosphere that it always had.

Kovi and Koku conversed while they were crossing the river in a canoe, and Koku argued that the unpredictability of the seasons and the devastating impacts on the life of the people were presumably the results of global warming, not an offense to any god. He offered no concrete evidence except to point out that the greenhouse gas emissions of the people had not significantly changed for centuries, and compared to that of the people in first-world countries, including his own brother it was negligible.

These people lived locally in a global environment and were

paying the price of human activities elsewhere, Koku said, while he looked at Kovi for sympathy.

"I hear you, but it is a complex global issue that is facing all of humankind. Locally, our communities, country leaders, and policymakers also have responsibilities toward concerted solutions. And it is not obvious that the problems of our village can be exclusively linked to global warming, bro."

Kovi argued that several traditional values were no longer passed down to younger generations and observed because young folks were migrating to bigger cities. As a result, the village was losing its skillful workforce that could have applied the traditional knowledge and combined it with modern techniques to adapt to the changing environment and current realities to sustain the people.

"Well bro, if there are no opportunities here, young folks would go elsewhere. You, yourself, went to America and don't come back often because there isn't much for you to do here," Koku replied. On the other side of the river, the two walked a short distance toward the Atlantic coast, still arguing.

The coast was sandy and full of tall coconut trees, which, together with a slow wind that blew across the shore, provided refreshingly cool spots away from the heat of the day, and attracted a bunch of people to relax at the beach. The brothers stood there and stared at the blue water, and Kovi pointed his finger across in some direction and explained that over on the other side of the Atlantic was his new home in America. Kovi was telling Koku that it was the same great Atlantic Ocean between the two continents when a man approached them and introduced himself.

The gentleman, named Kouassi, was not happy that Kovi did not recognize him right away, and he felt compelled to remind Kovi that many years ago, he was the one who taught Kovi how to catch crabs.

***

That was a long time ago when as kids, they built traps from plywood in the form of rectangular boxes with bait and set the traps at the entrances of suspected crab holes in the bushes by the riverbanks. Eventually, the crab came out of the hole and entered the box and as it went for the bait, the box closed, trapping the crab. They went twice in the day, in the early morning before school and in the afternoon after school, to check the traps. Often there were crabs inside. Sometimes, the crabs were strong enough to push the door open with their pinchers and escape. To solve this problem, they piled mud on top of the open door, and when it shut, it became difficult for the crab to push it open.

Kovi was unsuccessful at building the traps and he was also not successful at identifying good holes that were likely to contain crabs. Often, Kovi came home empty-handed and in tears while other kids, including this fellow who had just introduced himself, were skillful at catching crabs.

As children, they were unforgiving to each other and teased the unsuccessful crab catchers to tears. Kovi remembered Kouassi fondly as an older cousin—since everybody in the village was related to others—who protected and taught him a few skills, not only how to catch crabs but also how to make fly-fishing equipment, build drums, and cut other people's hair perfectly with a pair of scissors and a comb.

Kovi only had the upper hand at school in solving mathematic problems and doing homework. Kovi took pleasure in explaining the homework problems and solutions to the people who performed the handy tasks better than he did.

When Kovi ran into Kouassi at the beach after they had not seen each other for many years, Kovi recalled how skilled Kouassi was and that made Kovi reflect on his clumsiness.

Kovi was born left-handed in a society where people used the left hand strictly for handling toilet paper. It was an offense to shake hands or offer food with the left hand. Anything that could be done with the right hand should be, to leave the left hand alone until one was in the bathroom. Kovi was yelled at and punished every time his natural inclination unconsciously led him to use his more comfortable left hand.

When he started school in the first grade, he was already writing well with his left hand until the teacher threatened that if he ever saw him write with the left hand again, he would eject him from the classroom. From that day, Kovi had to learn to write with his right hand and never wrote with his left hand again.

It was a surprise when Kovi went the USA and saw his English instructor write on the board with his left hand, and many American students at ease with their left hands.

Although they tried to beat the usage of his left hand out of him, Kovi grew up still more comfortable using his left hand for a few things, such as skipping stones. He reckoned that his clumsiness at hand skills when he was growing up resulted from the immense pressure put upon him to do most things with his uneasy right hand.

Kovi jokingly reminded Kouassi that he was the one who solved the homework math problems for the kids, even for the ones who were in higher grades than he was. The only time when Kovi could not help the other kids with math problems was during the exams at the end of the school year. During the exams, each pupil was on her own under the constant and watchful eyes of the teachers.

One exam that Kovi liked the most and excelled in was the mental calculus, when the teacher asked the pupils to raise their hands with their pens in the air while the teacher read the math problem, in French, only once. The pupils were to memorize the problem as it was being read. When the teacher finished, she gave the pupils twenty seconds to solve the problem in their heads, still holding their pens in the air. After these twenty seconds passed, the teacher gave ten seconds for the pupils to write the answer and raise their hands again. The mental calculus exams required a great deal of focus, concentration, and rapid understanding of the problem with an accurate mental computation of the arithmetic to get the right answers.

There was one exam that formed a part of the literary subjects that Kovi did not excel in and it was dictation. It was a process in which the teacher read a paragraph from a book or an excerpt of a political speech in French and the teacher asked the pupils to write what they heard him read. The teacher then collected all the papers of the pupils and marked them for spelling, punctuation, and grammar. There were no libraries and access to books was difficult, so the dictation was a way to encourage the early development of literary reading and writing skills.

The village had one public primary school up to the sixth grade, and there were two memorable events in those days.

To encourage the pupils to practice speaking French, at the end of the daily classes or at the end of the week on Friday afternoon, the teacher gave a necklace to a pupil. They called this necklace as the "signal."

If the pupil who received the necklace heard any other kids speaking any language other than French, he or she passed the necklace to that kid. The next day or on Monday morning, the teacher asked for the necklace, and the kid to whom he gave it said that he or she gave it to John. John then said that he passed it on to Peter, then Peter to Ruth, etc. All the kids who received the "signal" must not have practiced French and, instead, spoke their vernacular. The teacher asked to stand up as he called their names. Then, he punished for the offense, i.e., the usage of their own languages. This practice led to two problems.

First, as a show of camaraderie, the kid that received the signal from the teacher might not pass it on to anyone, even if she heard someone speak in his own language. The teacher expected a pupil to have spoken in a native language; he punished the defiant kid for not passing on the signal. Essentially, the teacher punished the last person to carry the signal.

The second issue was about the dispute in handing the signal over to someone that a kid heard speak in a language other than French. The other kid might argue or deny that she spoke in a different language and might refuse to take the signal, and it sometimes led to fights.

The other memorable event during their primary school years in the village was the punishment of the pupils who received the signal. The teacher tasked to go into the bushes and collect a sizable amount of wood for fire and cooking purposes.

Kovi was among the few that never received the signal from the teacher or other pupils. In retrospect, these practices were vestiges of the colonial era. Kovi and Kouassi recalled these times and laughed. Fortunately, they abolished these practices long ago.

As the three men were walking back from the beach, Kouassi reminded Kovi of an event from their childhood. Kovi must have been about six years old when a great celebration was in full swing at the village center.

Kovi and Kodjo arrived and were thrown forcibly into the middle to dance. In the build-up to the dance, the lead drum and a few essential musical instruments were used to keep the beat at a slow pace while people formed a large circle and moved their bodies and sang gently. Then, suddenly, the lead drummer increased the pace rapidly and loudly as the signal for the people in the ring to dance, and all the instruments echoed in unison as the music increased in intensity. The people then started to dance in an impressive coordination of the movements of their feet, backs, and hands. After a few minutes, the pace slowed again, and it was the turn of new people to come forward in the center for the next round of dance.

So, Kovi and Kodjo were dancing while the others were watching and laughing. Kodjo never explained to Kovi why they were laughing and Kovi learned much later that it was because he did not synchronize his moves to the music, and as a child he was imitating the adults without comprehension of the art and the complexity of the dance.

The day after Kovi's wild dance incident, Kovi accompanied a few people from the village to a farm of palm juice. To get the palm juice, first they cut down the palm tree and leave it for a few days. Then, they make an incision through the center to draw the juice via a tube connected to a jar. When not diluted with water, palm juice is naturally sweet and alcoholic. Kovi, as a child, was attracted to the juice, so he drank some of it and passed out drunk. A man had to carry Kovi over his shoulders back to the village. This event generated excitement.

Mawule was a flamboyant and successful business lady, and she was quick to speak her mind and tell it as it was. She was enraged that the adults let the kid consume an alcoholic beverage, and she was angry at this kid, Kodjo, and the grandfather Nete, too—though the latter two were nowhere near the scene and had nothing to do with it. In a rage, Mawule said, "The father, Nete, was drinking, the son, Kodjo, was drinking, and now the grandson Kovi, too, was drinking."

People gathered to listen to Mawule. Kodjo and Nete were not present. No one offered any comments. After a while, Mawule became quiet, and the crowd dispersed. It was a small place and any yelling or shouting drew a crowd of almost the entire village who gathered for the excitement as though it were a sport event like soccer. In the absence of soccer matches, other events such as the noise of Mawule provided excitement in the village. Only when the shouting turned to physical aggression or fistfights did the elders intervene to separate the belligerents who gave the people something to talk and laugh about for several days, and perhaps forever.

The people of the village were quick to assign nicknames to others, mostly to tease and make fun of them, based on someone's actions during a particular event. Kovi got a nickname based on the usage of his left hand. Every time they invoked his nickname, it was to remind, make fun of, or discourage him from using his left hand. Sometimes, the folks composed entirely new songs about situations and people's actions, and during the next village drumming sessions, they introduced these new songs, often to the amazement of the persons targeted.

The village folks took the harvested palm juice through a traditional distillation process to make a hard and transparent liquor called *Sodabi* that could then be flavored with tree trunks or roots to give it a distinctive aroma and taste. To test the purity of the alcohol, people poured a sample in a saucer and held a flame to it. If it caught fire and combusted rapidly, then that was a great sign that the liquor was not diluted with water.

They developed an annual game between the villages in the area to send a few representatives for a *Sodabi* drinking contest and the village of the last man standing was the winner. During the contest which drew large crowds of supporters and admirers, they asked the participants to take shots of *Sodabi* and the judges assessed their state, to decide if they were still sober enough to continue.

There was one time—Kovi was not an eyewitness to the event, but he swore it was true—when all the contestants gathered and the contest was to begin as soon as the elders arrived. The moderator asked for the people to be quiet, and as he started to introduce the contestants and the villages that they represented, a contestant that looked to be in his forties took out a half-liter bottle of *Sodabi* and tossed it down as a warm-up. People were bewildered, as the man was still sane and standing. His action so impressed the other contestants that they declined to challenge the man to the drinking contest. They declared the man the winner by default and to this day, his village hold the reputation of the best *Sodabi* drinkers in the region.

They also produced *Sodabi* from other sources, like fermented mangoes or bananas. Palm trees had to be cut down and destroyed to get the juice, and it took many years for palm trees to grow and mature. As the result, the palm trees were not being replaced at the rate at which they were being destroyed. Later, they developed a new technique to extract the palm juice without cutting down the trees.

The palm trees also offered a red palm oil through their nuts. Folks palm used the palm oil as cooking oil and as a flavor in some special dishes.

***

Kouassi suggested that they made a quick stop at the village supplier of *Sodabi* for a few shots. Afi had advised Kovi not to drink with the people in the village for fear of envy and jealousy that might lead to Kovi being poisoned. When Afi went around the village with Kovi to greet people, she meticulously examined and inspected anything offered, and with a disapproving look, she instructed her son about what to do. As a sign of welcome and respect, they offered visitors a glass of water first, some of which ought to be drunk and the rest used for a libation after a short prayer. It was a serious offense and an affront to refuse such a respectable gesture deeply engrained in the society.

As Kovi had lived abroad for so long, he'd lost his immunity to bacteria in the water. They advised him to drink only bottled water that he was carrying. Some could take offense that a prince of the village, after he traveled abroad, felt so superior that he did not accept water from his own people.

Afi always had a way to explain away any potentially embarrassing event and to defuse any tension to make sure that there was no resentment or any hard feelings. But she was not with them when they went for shots of *Sodabi* and Koku did not have the range and the finesse of their mother.

One thing that they all knew when they were growing up was

that, when offered a drink, the person offering must himself take a sip before the guest to prove that the drink was not poisoned. However, one could get clever and apply a poison in such a way that he took a sip and was not affected by the poison, and the unsuspecting guest thought that it was good to drink.

Kovi declined the proposal of *Sodabi* shots, and instead he proposed that they go to the farm for coconut milk, as he thought the likelihood of poisoning the coconut freshly taken from the tree was slim to nil.

To get to the coconut farm, Kovi, Koku, and Kouassi walked up the hill toward the primary school that they attended as children.

Kovi recalled how he used to walk that road every morning in school uniform together with many other kids. The kids had to all arrive by eight o'clock sharp and gather in the schoolyard perfectly arranged into groups, depending on their grades. They sang together the national anthem while the national flag was being raised, and after that followed some great songs of encouragement to study. Each school day, the classes started only after they performed that important protocol. The teachers always punished latecomers.

Before they went to school in the morning, the children and young adults fetched fresh water from a well in the village, and a few trips to the well were necessary to fill a barrel in the house—a barrel that was big enough to accommodate everyone taking their morning showers. Many people gathered at the well and each waited their turn to lower a small container down into the well, fill it, pull it out with the help of a system of pulleys, and transfer the water into buckets that the strong carried with their hands and others on their heads. A few iterations of getting water from the well were necessary to fill the barrels. The children got breaks only when it rained and the barrel was automatically filled with rainwater.

The morning showers were so refreshingly cold that they could fix even the most severe adult hangovers. When the children were ready for school, their parents distributed a few coins to be used to buy a breakfast on the way.

Many pupils congregated by the house of the lady who specialized in the making and selling of breakfast. The breakfast menu comprised rice and beans with a special tomato and pepper sauce made with coconut or red palm oils, and other local dishes. So early in the morning and with less than a penny, the pupils consumed large quantities of heavy meals that could sustain them for the entire day, even those who were less fortunate and had no options for lunch.

***

After they passed the school, the three men reached the coconut farm of Nete, and Kouassi and Koku climbed the trees to cut down the coconuts that were likely to have sweet juice. Kovi was no longer fit and able to climb the trees as he used to do, and was also no longer good at identifying the best coconuts to select, so he let the other two skillful men do the job.

The possession of coconut farms was a great source of revenue for the people, who through a traditional process, produced and sold coconut oil used for many purposes. Every three months, the people collected the coconuts that matured and sold them to others, either whole or after they made the coconut oil.

Kovi's grandparents possessed many coconut farms that were later divided among Kovi's parents and their siblings, and later Kovi and his brothers and sisters inherited coconut farms from their parents. To this day, Kovi still has his inherited farms managed by one of his brothers.

Over the years, some coconut trees produced fewer coconuts as they aged and that led to reduced revenues, so the people needed to plant new trees that took many years to mature and produce coconuts.

From the coconut farms, as they used to do as kids, the three men went for mangoes. It was the season for mangoes, and in such a season, one could collect succulent mangoes that had recently fallen or by just reaching out to pick them from the trees. There were so many mangoes to collect for free that they could afford to pick the best ones, and they sat in the shade of a mango tree and enjoyed a refreshing breeze away from the heat of day while they gorged on the tasty fruit.

They returned from the farms with coconuts and mangoes that they shared with the first villagers that they encountered on their way back to the river where people had gathered for the great traditional game.

They placed the game with a set of round beads, some of which they placed in a set of semi-spherical holes carved in polished wood. There were two contestants to play the game, and the winner was the person who gained the most beads from the side of his opponent according to a set of specific rules. Each opponent took turns playing, and the game involved high-level thinking, strategic moves, and forward anticipation of the opponent's next moves. The time to complete a game depended on the leisurely pace or the careful thought processes of the players. The games could attract many onlookers and admirers, and the villagers developed organized regional contests in the same spirit as the *Sodabi* drinking contests.

After they watched a few of the games, the three men went to the house of Kovi's parents. When they got inside the house, they found that a gentleman was there to see Afi and the two sat in the courtyard, conversing. The gentleman recognized Kovi and stood up to greet him excitedly. However, to his great disappointment, Kovi did not remember him and Afi had to intervene once again to subdue any offense, and she narrated an event that happened when Kovi was too young to remember.

The man, who was about twelve years old at the time of the event, was sent to Afi to collect a debt that she had promised to pay that day, and she was expecting someone to come and collect. When the boy arrived, Afi was not only busy washing the baby Kovi, but she was also cooking. As the food was burning, she handed the naked baby to the boy who sat down and waited for Afi to fetch the money for him. It was then that the baby Kovi defecated, and the baby smeared the boy's shorts and legs with baby shit.

This story, that not even the man remembered, made everyone laugh so hysterically that people from the neighboring houses came to find out what was so funny. As folks retold the story repeatedly, the hysterical laughs grew louder and attracted more and more people from the village.

It was an art among these people to take or invent a story and retell it with something new added to it to make it funnier. Eventually, it became difficult to tell which part of the story was real and which was just a tale. As for this story, no one else in the village recalled the event except Afi, who constantly refused to tell Kovi whether it truly happened as she originally narrated. Every time Kovi asked her, she responded with a smile, and preferred to let the uncertainty stay forever.

***

After the gentleman and Kouassi left, Afi and her sons talked about Kodjo. He was an auto mechanic by training for a few years in Lagos, when he lived there with a branch of the family that migrated to Nigeria. When Kovi got drunk after he consumed palm juice, Kodjo was working as a taxi driver. The vehicle that Kodjo was using for the taxi was a French Renault-4L that he bought with cash from the savings that he accumulated after many years in Central Africa where he worked for an oil company. They discovered oil and minerals in Gabon and that attracted oil companies from Europe and the USA and many African workers from different countries. Kovi and two of his siblings were born in Central Africa, and since they did not know the local languages of the people there, Kovi grew up using French until they moved back to their ancestral village when he was four years old.

From four to six years old, Kovi learned to speak Mina—the language of his people in the village—and he almost lost the French completely in the process until he started the first grade. Kodjo and his family might have stayed in Central Africa permanently, as Kodjo was well paid and the working conditions were good, according to what he later told Kovi. After some time, considering the political tensions and reactions to foreign workers, Kodjo left Gabon and took his family to Nigeria. The oil industry was booming in Nigeria, too, and since Kodjo had already spent some years training and they had family there, it was the place to go, although Kodjo was not fluent in English. However, they did not stay in Nigeria for long because the civil war broke out, and they moved to the ancestral village.

Besides starting the taxi service with his own vehicle—which was the first one ever bought by any descendant of the village people— Kodjo also opened a convenience store. Both businesses brought great relief to the villagers, who made daily trips to Anèho for provisions. Unfortunately, as time went on, the store did not do well, and it disintegrated slowly. At the front of the house remained some vestige of the shop that once flourished there, as a painful reminder of the long-gone good old days. The taxi service too did not do well over time because of the repair costs of the aging vehicle.

When the business failed, Kodjo needed to look for a job once again to feed his family. He found employment repairing transport vehicles for a national mining company, and he moved his entire family closer to his job, except Kovi. For several months before they moved there, Kodjo went there on Sunday nights and returned on Friday evenings and he was the only one who made the weekly trips while the rest of the family was still in the village. Kodjo had a Vespa motor bicycle that he used to travel solo at nights to and from his new place of work—by then, it had become too costly to maintain the Renault.

One night on his way to his workplace, a group of strong men intercepted him. They armed with guns and knives, most likely on a night hunting expedition. After they inspected and searched and questioned him, they did not harm him; they let him go. When he later told the story, people explained that his good fortune was directly linked to a good deed that he had performed recently.

There was a snake commonly found in the region, a python greenish-brown, and about a few meters long. It was not a poisonous snake and did not harm humans. As a result, folks associated this python with a god, therefore revered and not killed by humans.

In time, this animal learned to get close to and cozy with people, and they found it in people's houses, where it hid peacefully in various areas, including in the beds. It was not surprising to feel a strangely cold sensation with slow motions in the bed, and a close inspection exposed the python. When it was so discovered in human dwellings, it was respectfully and gently taken far back into the bushes and released unharmed. Kodjo had taken one of these pythons back to the bush a few days before his journey and that was why the python god protected him and he came away unharmed— so went the explanation.

The transition of Kodjo to a new job in a different village was the end of the shop and the taxi service.

Kovi, Koku and Afi continued conversing into the night and remembering the time when Kovi stayed with Mawule to finish primary school.

At the end of the sixth grade, the pupils had to pass the regional exams to enter to middle school. They gave the exams at a few specific places where pupils from many areas congregated for a few days to take the exams and waited for the announcement of the results. Kovi went to a neighboring village about ten kilometers away, where he stayed with relatives during the days of the exams. It was a time of great anxiety, as people waited for the results.

The day they announced the results, all the pupils gathered at the primary school in that village and waited for regional government officials to emerge after deliberations. After what felt like an incredibly long wait, the officials appeared late in the afternoon and it was already getting dark. They first announced the ten best pupils and the village and primary school that they were from, and then they called the names of all the other pupils who passed the exams, in alphabetical order. If your last name started with the letter "A" and you noticed that they were calling out the people whose last names started with "B," and you did not hear your name in the meantime, that was a sign you failed. All the pupils were standing there in the schoolyard and listening. Some cheered at the call of their names and some burst into tears at the realization that their names were skipped. Some hung on to the slim hope that maybe they called them, but they did not hear because of all the cheering and crying around and they desperately asked friends and fellow pupils if they heard their names.

When they finished with the announcements, they posted the results on a giant board, and the pupils who did not hear their names converged at the board for a definitive confirmation of their failure.

Kovi passed the exams, but with the disappointment that he was not among the best ten. Upon his return to his village, Kovi was excited and happy to inform Mawule, but she did not believe him. She insisted that it was too early for the teachers to finish with the marks and announce the results. She must have gotten confirmation from other people that Kovi told her the truth, because she never followed up to find out when the results should have been announced, and she only expressed pride that her grandson did well.

Adults were visibly proud and talked happily when their kids did well enough at school to pass regional or national exams. But it was always a well-measured expression of pride and happiness accompanied with praises to the elders, the gods, and God Almighty in order not to stir up envy and jealousy and attract the attention of witches and sorcerers. Some people's kids failed and the last thing they wanted to hear was someone bragging about the success of their kid. The envy and jealousy so generated sowed the seeds of evil intents and bad wishes that manifestly degraded the school performance of the child. Worse, an overt expression of a well-deserved happiness when others were not so fortunate could induce deep-seated resentment that might lead to a resentful person consulting a witch or sorcerer to hurt the child.

The year before Kovi took the exams, one of the best ten pupils of that year went back to her village after the exams, took ill, and died suddenly. Folks explained such an unfortunate event away as the work of a jealous person who envied the success of the pupil when other hopeful kids failed. Personal expression of success and happiness had to be well balanced against the expression of support and sympathy for the misfortune of others, to tame evil and enjoy the blessing and protection of the gods.

***

Afi and her sons had dinner together and talked further until late in the night. They shared many stories of Mawule, Kodjo and of the events in the village. The next day, it was time for Kovi and Afi to take a taxi to the village where Kodjo used to work for the mining company, and on the way, they passed through Anèho where Kovi attended middle and high schools.

Chapter Fourteen
Adopted Village

As they drove through Anèho, Kovi could not help but stare at everything they passed. It is a picturesque small town sandwiched between a river, a small lake, and the Atlantic. The ocean has been encroaching slowly on the coastal dwellings, perhaps because of the impact of climate change. They passed close to the house where Kovi had stayed with a family member during his first year in middle school, when he was thirteen years old.

During that time, Kovi, who had not yet made any friends and was missing life in the village, wanted to go back to Mawule's for the weekend, but he did not have money for a taxi. The determined Kovi walked barefoot along the highway by the Atlantic Ocean for about twenty kilometers to reach Mawule's house before dark. Much to his chagrin, Mawule never believed that he could make that journey alone, although she took good care to nurture back to life the exhausted and dehydrated child.

After a year, Kovi moved elsewhere in the town, closer to his junior high school, where he shared a rented room with another pupil. So, from about fourteen years old, Kovi lived away from his parents for schooling reasons, only returning home during breaks and major holidays.

As they continued to drive through the town, Kovi recalled that during his time there, the government commissioned a Dutch company that created an artificial beachfront, thus solving the annual flooding problem caused by the swelling of the lake and the river to the north during the rainy seasons.

From far away, they picked up the distinctive smell of a roasted pig. It was one of the local delicacies that Kovi used to enjoy fairly often, and though Afi did not care much for it, Kovi convinced her that they should stop for a taste.

The locals had slaughtered a pig, and without chopping it up, they removed the soft organs from the inside through an incision made in the abdomen. They then filled the inside with a special blend of local spices and stitched up the belly. Subsequently, they roasted the stuffed pig slowly in a clay oven for many hours, turning it as necessary. As it cooked, an aromatic flavor from the spices seeped into every part of the pig, blended into the meat, and gave it a special taste. The roasting pig dripped oil and fat into the oven and generated a smoke that diffused into the atmosphere and produced an appetizing smell.

Folks lined up and ordered sizable portions of the tasty meat and took seats right there around the oven to eat their roasted pig with Fufu, pap, and/or vegetable stew of their choice. With a meal that great, water was never the preferred drink, and there were many better choices from different beers sold in one-liter bottles, or an assortment of sweet drinks. Satiated adults dragged themselves slowly to midday naps or, in the evenings, headed toward the local suppliers for shots of *Sodabi*.

Kovi was enjoying the roasted pig that he had not had in many years living abroad. Afi never cared much for meat and was having one of the vegetable dishes that were exquisitely tasty in their own right. They made it with spinach, red palm oil, and some ground nuts similar to the cashew, and spiced with small, green, and rounded peppers that, when crushed, released a lovely smell that could make one drool. There were variants of the spinach stew. The one that Kovi particularly liked was like the one that Afi was having, but augmented with an impressive array of seafood—crab, jumbo shrimp, and smoked fish.

While they were eating, a lady came to sit beside them, and placed an order for food. Kovi had a vague recollection of the lady when he overheard her talk to a waiter and he was staring at her. She turned to look at Kovi and the two recognized each other instantly; they had attended together the middle school in Anèho for four years. There was a long moment of tight hugging and greetings that attracted the attention of Afi and a few others curious to know what they were excited about.

Kovi and the lady, named Delali, started the long greeting that people who know each other normally perform the first time when they meet again. This consists of a serious engagement of the two parties, who take all the time needed to ask about the wellness of the other and their families and what they have been up to since they last met. The greetings depend on how long ago they last saw each other—a few hours, a day, a week, or long ago.

Delali was short with dark skin and rotund with a generous behind, and as Kovi recalled, these were the features that she had when they were younger. She kept the same form and shape through the years, unchanged. She braided her hair in her favorite style that consisted of many subdivisions of the hair into small groups twisted into strands whose thicknesses and lengths depended on the original thickness and density of the hair. When completed, this styling of the hair, done only by the women, made the hair appear like the beginning of a small dreadlock.

Delali wore a traditional dress that comprised three richly decorated pieces made with vividly contrasting colors. The top piece was a short-sleeve shirt with a golden decorative pattern around the buttons and at the end of the sleeves and the collar. The bottom piece was pants tightened around the waist, not with a belt but with a single narrow cord inserted around the waistline and made from the same fabric. The lower extremities of the pants were also decorated with the same golden patterns.

The third piece of her dress was not needed, but only used by women to accentuate grace and elegance. It consisted of a single piece of cloth, like a large scarf, made of the same fabric, worn around the middle of the body, from just above the waist down to the buttocks. The bottom end of the third piece also carried the same golden decorative patterns and a series of different color beads. The entire dress fitted nicely on Delali, who carried herself elegantly in a jovial mood.

***

When Kovi and Delali started middle school, they were among the first wave of pupils to attend that school, which was just commissioned after many years of construction and preparation. They fondly remembered some of their teachers and friends. It was in the middle school when they started learning English as the second foreign language after French. Their English instructor was a fellow from Ghana, but of the same ethnic and linguistic background as they. During his lectures, he asked them to repeat after him phrases in English, and then he continued as follows.

"Who can say better?"

"Another one!"

"Only Kpakpo again?"

Kpakpo and Delali were among the best in the subjects grouped as the "letters", i.e. French, philosophy, and English. Kovi excelled in the mathematics-related subjects.

In middle school, all the subjects carried equal weight. They marked them on a scale where twenty was the maximum and ten out of twenty was the minimum passing grade. In the first year, when they tallied and averaged all the marks, Kovi was at the top of the pile, but as time went by, from the second year, Delali became the best, and she beat Kovi in all the subjects except mathematics. Kovi and Delali engaged in a fierce competition until their entrance in high school, when they had to declare their majors, and Delali majored in the letters whereas Kovi opted for the hard sciences. Their academic paths diverged from that point on.

Their mathematics instructor was a white American Peace Corps volunteer named Blaine who spoke French with a funny accent that often made the pupils laugh and he never understood what was funny. He was a great fellow, outgoing, often seen at lunchtime or in the evenings and he mixed with the locals and enjoyed African food at the open markets. The people were always pleased to see Blaine, and they made great efforts to put him at ease. They came to know exactly what Blaine wanted and at what time he arrived.

At first, they prepared his food separately with no hot spices. They introduced Blaine to spicy food gradually. By the time he was to return to the USA, he started to compete with the locals about who could sustain the spiciest food, and he often won.

Blaine was one of the most accessible instructors, and the pupils converged upon him and showed him game cards. On the back of each card was the picture of a great Western movie actor. His last name was the same as the last name of one the actors and the pupils often asked him if they were related. Blaine always told the pupils that he knew the actor or he was his brother or nephew, something like that, and the pupils went away impressed.

Years later when Kovi went to the USA, he found out that there was probably no connection between the famous actor and his former mathematics instructor.

Kovi thought that Blaine would be happy to learn that one of his former pupils ultimately made it to the USA for further learning and did all that he could to find Blaine in the USA. Kovi never found him, but he learned that Blaine was living in Asia and doing well there.

Blaine, the Peace Corps volunteer, was also the one who introduced the pupils to a different way of approaching problems in mathematics. Traditionally, solutions to math problems must show each step in the derivation with a box around each major analytical form. Only when one had solved the problem completely, would one proceed to the numerical applications by plugging in numbers. Blaine plugged in numbers at every step and argued that by doing so, one avoided flaws and propagations of mistakes by ensuring that the intermediary steps made sense. Gradually, the pupils came to appreciate his teaching methods.

The town had one small movie theater and many people, including Kovi, became addicted to Spaghetti Western or Indian movies. They showed these movies in black-and-white, once or twice a week, in the single theater with no roof, and if it rained, the show was interrupted with no refund or rescheduling.

The pupils who returned to the capital city on weekends to see their families had better chances of seeing these movies first. Come Monday mornings, they were excited to narrate to the other impressed and attentive pupils the entire movie scene by scene, as they unfolded, with the dialogue verbatim as though they wrote the scripts and acted in the movie.

Kovi waited anxiously for the movies to come to town and saved some money that his parents gave him for food to buy the movie tickets. It was fashionable among the pupils to talk about the great American Western movie actors, their projected machismo on screen, and their skills with guns that impressed many of the pupils.

The Bollywood movies were also greatly appreciated as the themes of friendship, family, love, betrayal, poverty, and life lessons projected through beautifully choreographed scenes of songs and dances.

When Delali and Kovi opted for different majors in high school, the two saw each other less and less, since they were in different classes with different requirements. Delali went to the university in Lomé and later got a scholarship for further learning in France. She returned to Togo as a respected professor in French and African literature at the high school they'd once attended together.

***

Delali asked Kovi a bunch of questions about life in America and listened attentively to his answers and comments. She only observed that Kovi ate well in the USA and looked fat and heavy compared to many years ago, when Kovi was skinny and known as the "slim guy who always wore long-sleeve shirts with the sleeves folded up."

Kovi and Afi finished eating, but they waited for Delali to finish her meal.

When it was time for Kovi and Afi to catch the taxi to continue their journey, they said goodbye to Delali, and Kovi and Delali exchanged information hoping to maintain regular contact.

At the taxi stand, Kovi and Afi located a taxi that went toward their village and waited for it to fill up. They were lucky to be the first ones to get into the taxi, so that they could choose their seats, but to be the first also meant that the wait could take a long time as the taxi did not leave until every seat was occupied. In fact, often the taxis were overcrowded. The front seats could accommodate the driver, his assistant, and one passenger sandwiched between the two. The assistant driver helped people get off along the way and helping others to get on as seats became available. The assistant driver also collected the payments and handled all transactions. He had a large amount of cash in his pocket from the many round trips that they had made since the early morning and he was careful to get all the cash out to give the proper change as he collected fares each time they stopped.

Kovi asked his mother to sit in front between the two men for more space and comfortable seating. Kovi sat in one backseat of the twelve-seater van, and unfortunately all the backseats had lost their cushions because of heavy usage without maintenance and replacements. During long journeys on unpaved roads with many potholes, one developed soreness at the buttocks, but at least Afi was fine in the front and that was most important.

When the taxi filled up and was ready to depart, Kovi found himself squeezed between two ladies with big asses and thighs that acted as much-needed shock absorbers in lateral displacements during sharp turns and sudden maneuvers to avoid potholes.

The taxi passed Glidji, a small village close to Anèho and much closer to Lyçée de Zébévi—the high school that Kovi attended after the four-year middle school program.

In Glidji, there is an annual ceremony around the beginning of the traditional New Year to predict what to expect in the year ahead. The ceremony involves the village folks and people from the surrounding areas; it draws a large crowd nationally, including reporters. During the ceremony, folks wait anxiously for many hours for a group of elders, priests, and princes who go to a sacred forest nearby to consult with the gods and come back with the gods' recommendations for the coming year.

In the old days, there were different predictions such as good harvesting and prosperity, drought and famine or war, and until the group returned, people held their breath, as they did not know what the coming year had in store for them. The predictions were correct and helped folks plan the year ahead more confidently. In time, however, the annual event attracted national attention and media coverage, and for reasons that were not clear to Kovi, year after year, they forecasted only a good hope and prosperity, and another great traditional rite decreased in significance.

Kovi used to walk with other pupils from that village to the high school, where all the pupils came from different middle schools in the region. Through the successively selective exams, the quality of the pupils improved at each higher level and that led to stiff competition, and for three years at the high school Kovi faced friendly competitions for the title of best pupil in his classes.

Kovi always maintained an edge in mathematics and physics, but there were other pupils who were equally good in the same subjects with the added advantage of excellent performances in the literary subjects.

One time, the English instructor shook her head and her voice became husky when she commented on Kovi's performance in an exam; she could not understand how he could be good in mathematics and physics and yet under-perform in the languages. Kovi, too, wondered about that and despite his best efforts, the languages, literature, and philosophy were not for him.

To level the field and stay competitive with the other pupils who were more rounded in all the subjects, Kovi had to outperform the rest significantly in mathematics, physics, and the natural sciences. He was not happy with this and as a competitive pupil, Kovi wanted to do well in all the subjects for direct comparison, subject by subject. So, he made remarkable efforts to study the literary subjects, but he only marginally improved his best average.

***

He was thinking about his high-school years when the taxi reached Anfoin. It is a small town where a huge weekly market attracted sellers and buyers from far away. They trade many goods in these weekly markets, from an impressive array of agricultural products to manufactured items and replacement parts for all kinds of machines and engines.

These markets look like a chaotic mess and were noisy, as sellers yell periodically and asynchronously to attract attention to their products. But, when one walks around the market, an internal and organized arrangement reveals itself, where they group together related items in different parts. Afi had sold freshly made bread in that market for many years when Kovi was in middle and high schools.

On the day of the market, Kovi took a taxi to meet Afi, and each week he looked forward to meeting his mother there. Kovi was always pleased to see his mother, who did a thorough examination of his appearance. She always thought he was not eating well enough and was too skinny. These were great moments with Afi, when for a few hours on that day of the week Kovi knew that his mother would spoil him.

Occasionally, Afi left him in charge to sell the bread with specific instructions about the prices of the various types and sizes of the bread while she went around to buy the items that she was to take back home to the village where Kodjo worked or to collect debts from people. When she returned, Kovi was happy to give Afi a detailed accounting of what he'd sold. She congratulated him, but always added that he must learn the art of attracting and keeping customers' attention to sell even more.

When the market was closing, she gave her son money, some food items that she bought, and a few of the unsold pieces of bread, and the two traveled in different directions until they met again the following week.

There was one time when Kovi had money only for a one-way taxi to meet Afi at the market, but he did not have enough for the return trip. He was sure that he would see her there, and that she would give him more than necessary for the return. When he got to the market, Afi was not there, and Kovi thought that she was just delayed, so he went around many times hoping the next time he came back around she would be there.

Some hours later, as the market was closing, the disappointed and fatigued Kovi needed to take a taxi back, but he did not have enough for the fare. He might have walked, for the distance was just about the same as the distance between the town where he was going to school and Mawule's house in the ancestral village. But in this case, he expected Afi to feed him when he saw her but that did not happen. He was hungry by the time the market was closing and much of the journey on foot would have been during the night. So, Kovi did something bold; he got into a taxi and calculated where he should get off and pay that distance with the few coins that he had and complete the rest of the journey on foot.

Unfortunately, the taxi waited longer to fill up. By the time they reached the place where he should get off, it was already night and that scared Kovi. So, he stayed in the taxi longer until he could see the streetlights of the town ahead. The taxi driver's eyes turned red, and he grew frantic when he noticed that Kovi underpaid him for the ride. He insisted that Kovi was hiding money and playing with him. He threatened to beat up Kovi if he did not cough up the rest of the money at once. When Kovi honestly did not have more money, the driver was even more enraged. Kovi was getting off on the way to town, which meant less revenue for the taxi driver, as the likelihood of getting another customer before the taxi reached the town center was slim after dark. The driver argued that he could have gotten another passenger who needed a ride from the market all the way to the town center and would have been able to pay the full fare.

Fortunately for Kovi, a gentleman in the taxi intervened and offered to pay the fare on the behalf of Kovi. The gentleman noticed that it was strange for someone to get off at that place and he talked to Kovi. When he heard Kovi's story, that he did not see his mother at the market as expected, he asked Kovi to get back into the taxi all the way to the final destination where the gentleman paid both fares.

The following week, Kovi borrowed money and went to the market again, where he saw Afi, and when she heard the story, she gave praises to the Lord and explained to her son that the gentleman who helped him must have been an angel. "Always watch out for them angels, disguised in the flesh and sent to help," she often said.

***

Kovi and Afi got off the taxi at Anfoin and they went around the flea market to buy a djembe that Kovi wanted to take back to America. The seller quoted a price for the djembe that Kovi wanted and Kovi laughed, as the price was ridiculously too high. Kovi explained to the seller that he was a native of the region and that the seller should give him the price for local people, not for tourists or foreigners. To this, the seller replied that Kovi might well be a native of the region, but for sure he did not look like he had been living there for a significant amount of time. Afi smiled at the observation and from that point on took charge of all purchasing transactions.

The local sellers had the uncanny ability to size up the people as they approached and adjusted the prices accordingly to systematic thresholds for their customers. In the flea markets such as that one, one needed the art of small talk and negotiation to be successful in selling at the highest price possible or buying at a reasonable or reduced price. The first price quoted by the seller was inflated and the buyer had to negotiate the price down to the compromise of both parties.

Some people went to the market as early as possible because of the practice that, to avoid bad luck for the rest of the day, sellers did not let the first customer go without buying something from them. So, the first customer had the advantage in negotiating the price down to the level where the seller might even concede a loss that he ultimately recuperated through later customers before the market closed.

After they bought the drum, Kovi and Afi boarded another taxi and continued their journey to Hahotoé—the village where Kovi's father had worked. They reached the village in the evening, to the excitement of family and friends.

Hahotoé is in the interior of Togo, about fifty kilometers north from the Atlantic coast. After supper, a gentleman who called himself Idriss came to the house and met Kovi for the first time. Idriss had been a colleague of Kodjo's in the auto mechanic department of the same company. He commented on how much Kovi took after Kodjo and talked a great deal about the work that they used to perform together and what good friends they were. Idriss became emotional when he narrated the story about how Kodjo stood by him during a difficult time.

Idriss was from a group of people that came from the northern part of Togo and settled in the village to work at the company. He did not understand the local language of the native villagers and got into a dispute about the ownership of a piece of land that he purchased to build a house. Idriss had to appear in the village court where they carried out the proceedings in the local language. He asked Kodjo to accompany him and speak on his behalf. So, then Kovi's father took the stage and explained the case eloquently in favor of his friend and colleague for several minutes. When Kodjo finished talking, the presiding local judge exclaimed, "Who is this northerner who speaks our language so well?" Idriss won the case. He explained to Kovi that in that village, should the northerners be thrown out or persecuted, he believed Kodjo would have been the one in front to defend them. Kodjo was from the south, but the northerners, too, considered him one of them.

When Kodjo moved his family to that village closer to his work, for the first several years they lived in a rented house shared with the owner. The areas around the village swelled with new developments and construction of new houses, as more and more people converged on that village from different regions of the country.

During school breaks, Kovi and his friends went to hunt for rabbits around the area. There were many wild rabbits, and they caused problems by eating much of the planted crops. These rabbits were great sprinters, and it was impossible to catch them by running after them or using rudimentary tools that consisted of pieces of tree branches that Kovi and his friends carried with them. To level the odds, Kovi and the gang located the rabbit holes and guessed at the connected pairs of the holes to know where the rabbits might enter or exit, then a few of them waited at the holes while the others made a noise and stomped on the ground to force the rabbit out. The scared rabbit emerged from the hole like a fast projectile and the person guarding the hole had to be alert to hit the rabbit hard with a stick as it came out. Unfortunately, sometimes they missed, and the rabbit regained the upper hand and covered a huge distance in a short time, running out of reach. Kovi and his friends argued and yelled at each other for a while because the rabbit escaped, and after a moment, they continued the hunt and rotated the persons that guarded the holes. They came back to the village after many hours away with at least one rabbit that they then roasted and enjoyed.

Kodjo looked at the bush meat with disdain, although he allowed the rest of the family to enjoy it, and nobody understood why he could not appreciate the fresh-tasting meat from the wild. Then one day, the great smell of the roasted meat was too much for Kodjo to resist, so he asked for a portion, then more and more until he became an ardent consumer and he enjoyed the roasted rabbit more than anyone. He looked forward to it each time they went hunting.

When Kovi did not go rabbit hunting, he went to the farm with Kodjo and the siblings and cousins who were living with them. Kodjo purchased a farm not too far from the village and they prepared it to have it ready to plant crops at the beginning of the rainy season. They removed the bad grass and the weeds with a traditional tool that one had to apply—in a bending position difficult to sustain for a long time—to the ground to yank off the weeds.

The process was slow and painful because of the uncomfortable position, the slowness to cover sizable ground, and the heat of the day that became unbearable as early as nine o'clock in the morning. It normally took several days to get the farm ready and then they went back after the first arrival of the rains to plant the crops that comprised maize, cassava, yam, and beans. After that, they returned to the farm infrequently just to check on the growth.

They harvested corn first, three months later, and they did this in two stages, as preferred. First, they collected succulent corn. Then, they harvested the rest when the corn dried. Kovi counted ten different food items made from corn: popcorn, boiled corn, grilled corn, fermented corn farina *pap*, unfermented corn farina *pap*, corn farina mush, steamed corn bread, bran-free corn flour *pap*, sweet corn galette, and corn dough. They used cassava leaves as green leafy vegetable. They also used cassava root and yam in a variety of dishes. Different beans completed the abundance and variation in the basic subsistence dishes.

During the expansion of the village, Kodjo bought two pieces of land, on one of which he constructed a house, and the family moved there. It was an entirely new community of the village that developed over time and was full of the nonlocals who migrated there for work. Close-by were quarters built specifically for managers and elite workers, most of whom were French citizens, and it was the only area equipped with electricity, tap water, and plumbing for many years. During the day, they allowed Kovi and the villagers to go there for walks, to have drinks at the bar, or to use the swimming pool and the tennis court. On some evenings, there was a possibility of going to a nightclub or the movies.

For many years when Kovi was in the USA, he had to make plans to telephone folks back home. On the agreed day and time, the entire family went to the house of a family friend in that area who had a telephone and Kovi called his family there. There was no other way for him to call his family, since there was no landline in their house, and this was before they extended electricity to the rest of the village, and before the proliferation of cellular telephones.

They discovered phosphate in the region of Hahotoé, and in cooperation with the French, the central government established a national company for the extraction and exportation of the mineral. The company used an elite workforce from France supported by qualified local skilled workers, and one of them was Kodjo. Some benefits for working there included one month of paid vacation, financial allocations for the number of children under eighteen years old in the family, and an enviable retirement package that sustained Kovi's family when Kodjo retired and a fraction of which passed to Afi when Kodjo died.

***

The day after Kovi and Afi returned from the ancestral village in the early morning around six o'clock, a strange, high-pitched distressed noise of a pig awakened Kovi. The noise went on for a while until Kovi came out and investigate. Just beyond the front porch lay two huge testicles removed from the pig in a castration process. This was a common practice done to pigs and goats to stop their pungent smells before they slaughtered them a few days later. Folks believed that castration not only eliminated the smell but also made the meat tender and soft.

The poor pig must have realized that, beyond the trauma he must have experienced in the castration process and his inability to mate, they would roast soon. They slaughtered the castrated pig the day before Kovi departed and the entire family enjoyed it with the extended family and friends in honor of Kovi's return to the USA.

A few hours after they castrated the pig, following breakfast, Koku asked Kovi to slaughter a chicken as he used to do when they were younger. Kovi hesitated, although even in the USA, Kovi had continued the tradition of slaughtering chickens. His brother teased him that he was out of practice and showed him how to do it quickly, remove the feathers, and cut up the animal into small pieces used to prepare a great meal.

Kovi and Koku ate together that day from the same plate and recalled fondly the protocols around lunch and dinner. Only breakfast was a personal interaction with the meal, in the sense that the kids received money each morning and they were free to buy anything that they wanted and enjoyed it freely at their own leisure.

At lunch and dinner, the children of various ages ate from the same bowl and used their fingers from the right hand. There could be four or five children, and all sat and shared the same plate, and it was some kind of race to eat at a faster pace than the others to make sure that one ate enough by the time they finished the meal. The people that ate together dipped their fingers into a mush of cornstarch freshly served from the pot to carve small pieces that they twisted in their hand to round it up and subsequently dipped it into a hot sauce. Then, they put the combination of the *pap* and the sauce in their mouths to enjoy, and they repeated the process as fast as possible.

There were three places where they might feel the heat of the freshly prepared meals. First, as they inserted their fingers in the hot *pap*, they might feel the heat, but when they saw that other children stoically resisted the pain, no one cried or complained, for they would waste valuable time to eat their share. Second, as they dipped the rounded *pap* from their hands into the hot sauce, they might also experience another source of heat from the sauce. Third, when they inserted the ball of *pap* smeared with the tasty sauce into their mouths, they might still experience an additional heat from the spicy sauce as their brains processed two signals, namely the great taste of the food and the heat of what they were chewing.

Depending on the sauce, they added small quantities of fish or meat, for the people who ate together to share. Sometimes, some children got clever and ate much larger portions of the fish or meat from the sauce before the rest knew it. Their mother then offered her share of the fish or the meat to appease the unhappy children and to avoid conflicts. Eventually, they found a solution to this problem, and it consisted of the division of any pieces of fish or meat among themselves before they started eating.

Only the much larger children and the adults had the privilege to eat from their own plates.

Kodjo never finished his plate, not because he did not enjoy the meal but because the responsible adults always left a sizable portion of their food for the children who cleaned up afterward. So then when their father called out that he had finished eating, it was with a great excitement that the children picked up his plates, for there was still extra food for them leftover.

On some occasions, when Kovi was with Kodjo or Afi alone, for example during travels, he got the privilege of sharing meals with the adults with great satisfaction and a feeling of love. During those times, it was like the roles were reversed and his mother or father ate slowly and waited for their child to eat well and be satiated before the adult ate the rest.

Kovi and Koku laughed at the moments when, as children, it almost came to fistfights over the unfair shares of the meat or the fish in the hot sauce.

Chapter Fifteen
Family Greetings

After the meal, Kovi and Koku took a taxi to Lomé where they were to go around greeting family members.

It was a forty-five-minute straight drive, but in a taxi that constantly stopped for passengers, the journey could take twice as long. Compared to the time when Kovi was there for university, the city seemed to have doubled both its area and population density. Entire regions along the motorway that used to be bushes and farmlands had evolved into bustling suburbs. Kovi had trouble recognizing various places. He remembered the football stadium and the university grounds as they were driving by and he could identify the university dormitory where he used to stay.

***

One of Kovi's uncles, Vincent, worked as a custodian at the university and was responsible for the men's dormitories, so he protected and supported his nephew, making sure that Kovi got all the supplies he needed.

Shared bathrooms and toilets were available on each floor of the multistory building, which only had stairs, and there were daily cleaners.

In the mornings, a bunch of naked young men took showers in one big bathroom where they had installed a few rows of several showers. The peak time for showers was around seven o'clock, when often one might have to wait for a slot to free up. Afterward, students headed toward the cafeteria for breakfast before classes began.

The university officials paired the students randomly into the dormitories, and Kovi shared a room with a student from the north of Togo who was majoring in philosophy, and the two became good friends.

During the weekends, after studying, it was a fun time and Kovi and his roommate went to parties, sometimes crashing them. One time during a party, a moderator posed a question and the person who answered correctly got a prize. The question was, "A woman had three sons, but each son had two brothers. How many kids did the woman have?"

Some people, including Kovi's roommate, raised their hand quickly and gave "six" or "nine" as the answer. Others wanted more information and clarifications and asked if they were to assume the brothers of each son were from the same lady because they argued it was plausible that each son—or some of them—might have a different father who might have kids with other women, and those kids, assuming they were males, were technically brothers of some sons in the traditional sense. The moderator explained that not complicated but people got perplexed why the answer was not "six" or "nine."

When the commotion died down and no one still gave the correct answer, Kovi raised his hand and said that the answer was "three." The moderator asked Kovi to elaborate and explain. Kovi explained that the lady had three sons and if you took any of the sons, then the other two were his brothers. So, there were just three sons. Kovi impressed some people, and he got two bottles of beer for himself and his roommate.

The weekend parties were great celebrations that attracted beautifully dressed young men and women, all of whom were impressive dancers. People were eager to show the latest trending moves and their own acrobatic inventions. Some people had complete knowledge of the dances appropriate for the music from the Caribbean, Latin America, Arabia, and different African countries. Traditional music from Togo that varied according to the different regions and ethnic groups was also part of the mix.

Kovi was not among the great dancers and was often one step behind the people who were up-to-date on all the latest moves. The most impressive male dancers were more confident and outgoing, and as a result, they were more successful with the young ladies, who were all great dancers and enjoyed dancing with the best.

The shy and intimidated individuals—who had nothing new to impress the others with or were too clumsy to move with grace and talent on the dance floor—formed a concentric ring around the dancing floor. These sorry individuals stood in the ring to watch the others with envy and dared not step on the floor to show outdated moves or the same repetitive moves to all the music. So, then all the nerds, subdued by the talents of their peers, resorted to watching, talking, and drinking until Monday morning, when they got their chance to shine in the classrooms.

Some students were excellent at sports and the most popular ones were soccer and basketball.

In soccer, besides the national league, there were teams at every level of society and people organized leisure tournaments. At the university, students majoring in the sciences might play against the ones in literature and each team took the field in their elegant jerseys, cheered on by excited fans without degeneration into hooliganism.

Kovi was not one of the good players in soccer or basketball and thus restricted himself to being a supporter or a great commentator of the games.

***

Kovi and Koku got out of the taxi at the last stop in the biggest market in the country, a market that spanned over several city blocks and was bounded only in the south by the Atlantic Ocean. In that market, they traded a variety of goods. The market attracted merchants from far beyond the boundaries of Togo. Some items sold were cheap imitations; one usually carried out thorough and careful checks before making payments.

Koku had lost his wedding ring and Kovi offered to buy him a replacement and, by chance, they saw a young man who sold many things including wristwatches and wedding rings. The man swore on his grandmother's grave that the rings were of eighteen-carat gold, and he scratched or set fire to the rings to convince them. He was convincing. Although Kovi and Koku were still hesitant, they bought the ring anyway at the insistence of Kovi—Three days later, the great looking and seemingly golden ring turned black, to the embarrassment of Kovi.

Close to where they were in the market was the stand of a younger sister of Mawule, who specialized in the sale of live chickens; they stopped there to greet her. Their visit surprised her. She smiled when she saw Kovi. As they were about to leave, she shook Kovi's hand. In the exchange, she slipped some paper money into his hand. She added that it was just a small gift for them to buy snacks on the way home. Kovi protested and said that he was then in the financial position to help and planned to come by her house later. But she insisted. As Kovi recalled, when they were younger, sometimes they found reasons to go see her in the market, and she always gave them money for snacks. She maintained that kind and loving gesture even during economic hardships.

They could hear cheering noises coming from the beach so they investigated at the insistence of Kovi. It was then late in the afternoon and the heat of the day gave way to a cool breeze that usually attracted many folks to the beach. Some were swimming or playing volleyball or other games while others were chitchatting while walking leisurely. Some, the great learners, sat comfortably under coconut trees to recite poems or read and reflect on excerpts from famous literary works of great philosophers.

The beach volleyball was the attraction of that afternoon. It was a fierce and serious contest between two teams from different neighborhoods of the city, supported by their fans, whose cheers echoed far into the market. The brothers watched the games for a while, then they removed their shoes and rolled up their trousers to walk close to the water where the big waves splashed cold water onto their feet.

From where they were, they could see the great port, where heavy ships docked to unload and pick up provisions at the service of not only Togo but also the landlocked nations deep in the interior of Africa. This then made the highway that ran along the beach busy with heavy trucks that delivered the goods to the port or took them from there to the final destinations.

The brothers walked back to the market to take a taxi to their uncle's house, and along the way, Kovi noticed that trades in the big market were under the control of three groups of people, namely the Nana Benz, the Lebanese, and other West African nationals.

The Nana Benz is a special class of ladies with a keen sense for success in business. In the local language, the word "Nana" is a respectful title conferred to a mother, a grandmother, or to a lady old enough to be one. These "Nana" became successful at trading many fabrics, a commodity essential to make different types and styles of clothes. Apparently, many of them possess a chauffeur and a Mercedes Benz, the vehicle of class and luxury, hence people called them Nana Benz.

The Lebanese controlled the major retail department or convenience stores and car dealerships. There were huge used car dealerships associated with—or close to—the big market, and the used vehicles came mostly from Europe, clear because of the sign "D" for Deutschland, "F" for France, "GB" for Great Britain, "I" for Italy, or "CH" for Switzerland on them.

The Nigerians, the Ghanaians, and others from the regional countries appeared to control fabricated goods, from shoes to other clothing items, musical instruments, decorative items, ornaments, etc.

***

Kovi and Koku reached the house of their uncle, Théodore, in the evening to the excitement of everyone. Some cousins were teenagers when Kovi was at the university, and they recognized each other right away. Others were small or not even born when Kovi left to study in the USA; these were then teenagers or young adults with a vague or no recollection of Kovi.

The next day, Koku pulled out a piece of paper on which their mother gave instructions about the family members whom they must absolutely visit while in the city, to avoid any disappointment and resentment. To forget or overlook someone important might cause an offense from the fact that Kovi was in town but did not bother to pay a visit. Sometimes, the offense might linger for many years, and the offender might not know.

Koku and Kovi paid a visit to each person on the list according to the instruction of Afi, and everywhere they went they welcomed and fed them with joy. Many were happy to share their knowledge of the USA and they commented on specific events in a recent USA history or about some famous actress or athlete. They saw the latest movies or watched the latest music videos, although sometimes there were several month delays before they released pieces of entertainment in Togo.

One endearing quality of the African people is the burning desire to stay abreast of the news, local and international. In the mornings and in the evenings, people listen to the news through the different media of television, shortwave radio, and nowadays the social media with the increasing danger of fake news. People everywhere, even in the remote villages, can converse and comment on major events, such as the American or French presidential elections, and debate knowledgeably about how such events may affect them locally.

Other news came up about the personal lives or activities of famous individuals, the news that one might find in the tabloids or in reality shows in the USA, the news that Kovi did not follow much, and people noticed that Kovi was not current on this information.

Some people wanted to tie up Kovi for many hours and ask questions and listen carefully, eager to find out about the things Kovi did and experienced in these many years of his great learning abroad. Others were proud to introduce Kovi to their neighbors and friends as their brother who lives in America, to the amusement of some of their guests, who looked at Kovi intensely and sized him up to convince themselves whether this dude had gone somewhere farther than a neighboring country.

When Kovi and Koku arrived at the house of their uncle, Monseigneur Cécile Le Grand, he was taking the healthy midday nap. A younger priest, who was his assistant, realized that Kovi might not come back before he returned to the USA, and reluctantly agreed to wake up the senior priest. Monseigneur Cécile came and talked to his nephews for a long time over cool drink.

***

Many years ago, before Kovi was born, Monseigneur Cécile and his cousin Kodjo were selected to attend a school for priesthood after they finished primary school. On the agreed-upon date, a French priest was to meet them in Djéta and take them to a boarding school for years of training, at the end of which they would anoint them to work for the Pope. When the big day came, Cécile was at the rendezvous, but Kovi's father did not pitch up. The French priest then declared that if Kovi's father was not honest enough to respect his engagements, then he was not good enough to be a priest. It turned out, as Cécile claimed, to the hysterical laughter of all of them there, that Kovi's father was busy courting Kovi's mother and forgot about the rendezvous. Nine months later… Voilà! Kovi was born. When he heard the story, Kovi wished Kodjo were still alive, to tease him about this great piece of information he did not tell his son.

Cécile went to Rome for many years to work for the Pope. They stationed him in many countries to minister to people and convert souls to the faith before he returned to Togo in the advanced years of his life.

When the Pope made a tour through many countries in the region, Cécile was living abroad and was not a part of the esteemed local clergymen who hosted the Pope.

The Pope's visit was a spectacular event that drew a large crowd of worshipers, believers, and onlookers to the airport and along the roads of the cortege, all the way to the national cathedral where the Pope delivered a nationally televised Mass.

Kovi was in the city at the time of the Pope's visit, and all the other adults where he was staying went to the airport while Kovi stayed home to watch the event on television.

The Pope was only in the country for a short time, but the visit generated excitement and it was as if for a few days after the visit, people were kinder and friendlier to each other.

***

Cécile told an anecdote that was noteworthy. The priest was in Geneva for business. He suddenly fell ill, and they rushed him to the emergency ward at a hospital there. The doctor that treated him, upon noticing his name, spoke to him in Ewe, their common African language. When the priest realized that while far away from home he got sick and was unexpectedly being treated by a doctor from his ethnic group, he was so happy that he automatically recovered. Cécile remembered the name of the doctor who treated him and, coincidentally, the doctor was an old friend of Kovi at the university. Even more strangely, both the doctor and Kovi were in Switzerland,

and Kovi visited the doctor in Geneva around the time when the priest got sick there. The Lord works in mysterious ways. Monseigneur Cécile Le Grand was saved by one of his nephew's old friends! Kovi later narrated the story to his friend, the medical doctor, who was a great believer in Jesus Christ, and he gave praises to the Lord.

Kovi told his uncle that he somehow followed his steps, not into the priesthood, but into another career dictated by the disciplines in which he excelled at school. Like it happened for his uncle, Cécile, Kovi's career drove him away from home for many years. When asked whether he would ever return just like his uncle did, Kovi observed a moment of reflection and said he was not sure, but he tried to help his people as best as he could.

Before they left, Cécile asked about Kovi's cousin, Ashley, who had been in the USA for quite a while. It was the same cousin who was instrumental in helping during Afi's visit to the USA.

Kovi said that Ashley and her family were doing well, sent warm greetings, and were looking forward to seeing him soon. The priest complained that, because of poor health, he did not consider traveling soon and if anyone wished to see him, they would have to come there. He reminded Kovi that they had met at four different places around the world, in Geneva, New York City, Paris, and Johannesburg.

When Kovi went to Switzerland for the second time and lived in Geneva, he met Cécile there during one of the priest's missions. Later, the priest came to the USA after another mission in Canada and spent several days with Kovi and Ashley and her family. After that, Kovi saw his uncle in Paris at Jean-Patrice's place during a business trip when Kovi transited through Paris. Their most recent meeting outside Togo was in Johannesburg during Kovi and Aisha's wedding.

Koku praised the Lord to hear for the first time that these two had had opportunities to see each other during their separate journeys.

Also, Koku heard about the incident when the priest saved their cousin Ashley from an unpleasant event that might have turned ugly.

Ashley, who was a naturalized American citizen, traveled Togo with her husband, Keith, who was a charismatic African-American fellow. Keith served in Vietnam and later became a policeman in New York City for many years. He always used to tell Kovi that "If you can make it in New York City, you can make it anywhere," and he knew the city like the back of his hand. When Ashley and Keith traveled to Togo, they did not realize that they needed travel visas and things went from bad to worse on their arrival at the airport.

There was no possibility of getting the visa at the airport on arrival. Keith, the macho American dude, refused to pay the heavy fine that they levied against them for their arrival without travel visas and got into an altercation with the border policemen, who were heavily armed military men. Ashley could not advise and contain her flamboyant husband. She realized that they were in grave danger by challenging military men who, by then, were trying to subdue Keith and take him away.

The guards seized their American passports and Keith kept asking his passport and argued that, as an American, he would not surrender his passport to any authority other than the government of his country.

To make matters worse, Keith did not speak French well and the military men could not understand his demands, expressed in English. Both sides got increasingly frustrated, and in the middle was Ashley, an American citizen and also one of their own who had returned to visit family, and she was crying. Keith stood his ground and refused to be led away or taken somewhere else. He told the military men that if they wanted to kill him, they had to do it right there.

It shocked the military men to see a civilian challenge their authority so publicly and so boldly, and this enraged them even further. People held their breaths and did not know how it would end. Ashley was still crying.

A family member who was there to meet them called Cécile and told him to get to the airport quickly, as his niece and her husband were in grave danger in a standoff with armed military men. Monseigneur Cécile Le Grand put on his full regalia and arrived at the scene as fast as he could. Surely, the military would not shoot a Catholic priest.

Cécile used his influence as a monseigneur and requested that his niece and her husband be released into his custody and promised he would resolve the issue in the morning. The military men conceded. However, Keith still demanded the return of his passport and insisted he would not surrender it to them, but the priest advised him to forget about his cherished American passport, that he would sort it out later, and the priority of the moment was to save his life. The priest got them out of danger that night. The next day, the priest contacted the authorities and paid a fee to recover the passports.

***

When Kovi and Koku finished visiting all the people on their mother's list, they were to return to the village with some provisions purchased at the big market.

On their return journey, their taxi passed by Collège Protestant de Lomé—the private high school where Kovi taught for two years after he finished the bachelor degree at the university. He was twenty-two years old at the time and the people to whom he was teaching mathematics and physics were just a few years younger than he.

The principal of the high school was also the Minister of Education. He was a senior physicist who did studies and research in the USA for many years before he returned to serve his country.

Kovi was an excellent student with a great desire for graduate school, but he was not a trained instructor. While he was teaching there, Kovi was also looking for scholarships to pursue higher education abroad. Many of the instructors were much older than Kovi and some had families and children about Kovi's age. Out of respect, Kovi felt subdued amid these career instructors who had been in the teaching profession for many years and appeared to be more of the generation of his own parents.

There was one instructor in particular, a fellow from Madagascar, well educated in France. He possessed amazing technical skills in physics experiments and demonstrations. Kovi teamed up with his Malagasy colleague to develop a concerted physics program in both theory and experiment for all the three levels in the high-school system. Kovi taught three courses in physics per semester—one for each high-school grade. The pupils in his classes were majoring in the literary subjects. His colleague supported the theoretical courses with the experimentation and instrumentation.

Kovi rented a room in a house within walking distance from the high school, and one day as he went work, he ran into one of his former instructors from middle school. The instructor praised Kovi for his academic progress; at twenty-two, Kovi was teaching at a prestigious and private high school while he, his former instructor, was still teaching in a public middle school.

Kovi also gave tutorials and practice sessions during the weekends and in the evenings to make extra bucks. By that time, Kovi's salary was comparable to that of Kodjo, who had been working much longer for many years and was supporting a huge family.

Young and with more money than when he was a student at the university, Kovi was free and at ease to enjoy the city life. He took a series of dancing lessons to improve his chances and confidence on the dance floor during parties and celebrations.

He also took regular English speaking and comprehension lessons at the American Institute associated with the USA Embassy, and in the process met another student who was also taking English lessons to prepare for his planned departure to the USA for more studies. The two became lifelong friends and leaned on each other in the USA.

The American Institute and the French Culture Center provided valuable educational and research resources to students and instructors. Kovi trained for and took the Test of English as a Foreign Language, TOEFL, and the Graduate Record Examination, GRE General and Subject tests at the American Institute, first as practice tests, then later for the official results. They forwarded these results to the prospective universities where he hoped to continue his education.

At the end of his first year as a high-school teacher, Kovi was among the instructors that the government called upon to grade the high-school final exams that determined the pupils eligible to continue on to university. The authorities asked Kovi to appear in Atakpamé, town several hours away in the interior of Togo. Atakpamé was a center to host the national exams. Kovi joined other teachers there to supervise the examination, grade the papers, and publicize the results, all within a period of a few weeks.

Four years earlier, Kovi was a pupil who took the exams to get the privilege to go university, but then he was on the other side of the table to test the performances of the pupils and decide who passed or failed.

That trip was the farthest he traveled in his own country. He rejoiced for the opportunity to see another part of the country during the first official trip that his work covered in full.

Atakpamé was bigger than Anèho where he attended high school and its people spoke a different native language. Kovi noticed that as one traveled farther into the interior, the flora progressively changed from the dense green foliage into savanna, while the land itself became hilly and more mountainous, with the highest peak at about one thousand meters. Also, the deeper inland one got, the more diversity there was in the distinct languages, not dialects, and more cultural contrasts clear in the variations of the traditional practices.

He had already met, befriended, and learned from many of his country folks from the north at the university, but it was the first time that he traveled north and experienced the greater cultural diversities among his people.

Kovi returned from the trip and supported a proposal for official group travels for pupils and instructors for educational purposes. In the high school where he was teaching, they organized two such trips.

The first trip took a group of pupils with some instructors east along the coast and eventually north into the interior to reach Abomey. They traveled in a single huge bus in good condition with a capacity of fifty to sixty people. The drive along the coastal highway was comfortable and the entire ride was pleasant in the bus equipped with air conditioning and cushioned seats. It was a successful and instructive trip for all the participants to visit the remnants of the great kingdom of Dahomey and to meet the locals and hear from them the accounts of their ancestral history that Kovi and others had learned from history books.

The other trip which happened a few months later, took a similar group of people west all the way to the Castle of Cape Coast. There, they heard the vivid and touching accounts of the harsh and inhumane conditions during which many went through the door of no return in the difficult times of slavery.

The gentleman who took them on the tour around the castle grew increasingly emotional and his eyes became reddish and full of tears as he narrated the story along the way. This was his regular job and he had narrated the events many times, yet as he told the story, he and the tourists could not help the heart-wrenching feeling with the images of the horrors that the slaves experienced. The mood grew grim as Kovi and his group followed along and occasionally they looked at each other in silence. When the tour finished, the excitement that had carried them on the trip gave way to sad internal reflections that crystalized in their minds the palpable reality of the historical accounts of the slave trade that they learned from history classes. Not too far from there is the origin of Kovi's ancestry, the place that the Nete Brothers left behind when they fled east to evade capture by slave traders. Although at the time of the trip, Kovi did not know this.

It was during his second year as a teacher in the high school that Kovi increased his efforts to find a scholarship for himself and his friend he met at the American Institute, as they had similar objectives.

When he learned that they offered him a scholarship to go to the USA, Kovi increased his English proficiency preparation, studied harder for the TOEFL and the GRE, and made official translations of his academic records into English. Although he won the scholarship, he needed to apply to a university in the program. The results and the officially translated transcripts were necessary for the application.

The AAI took responsibility over applications to various universities depending on the student's major and the student could not depart until they admitted her into at least one university. Kovi won the scholarship based on his academic record in French and, to a large extent, on the direct recommendation of the Minister of Education who was also the principal of the high school where Kovi was teaching.

When Kovi got word that he was admitted to Ball State University in the USA, his parents were happy and the news spread quickly in the city. Many people approached Kovi to get advice about how he had achieved that feat. But Kovi did nothing—instead, it was the minister, without whom the scholarship might never have materialized. Kovi was good enough to qualify for it, yes, but well connected enough to get it, no!

As a part of the departure procedure, at the instructed time, Kovi went to the government agency responsible for arranging his air ticket. When he got there, the government agent asked him about his final destination in the USA. Kovi responded that it was Indianapolis. The agent looked at him incredulously and completely baffled, yet he wrote "Indiana Police!" Kovi was to be purchased an airplane ticket to "Indiana Police!" Kovi noticed the mistake and contained the urge to laugh, for that could have cost him the entire scholarship. He protested politely and gave the correct spelling of Indianapolis. Later, they arranged his ticket only to New York City. The AAI took care of the ticket to Saint Louis Missouri and informed him when he arrived in New York City.

They set Kovi's departure date in August during the great summer break. By that time, he'd finished his second year of teaching at the high school, both the courses and the grading of the university entrance exams normally scheduled in June. For the exams that year, the authorities asked him to stay in the capital city, although he would have preferred to go to a different location in the interior for another opportunity to see more of Togo. His high school did well that year in terms of their percentage of pupils that passed the national exams major by major and overall, and in their rankings compared to the pupils from other high schools.

They organized a farewell party for Kovi at the high school after the excitement or disappointment of the results of the exams. Many parents of the pupils attended to pay their respect to the young teacher that they heard about from their children. Kovi had improved his teaching skills quickly and was well appreciated by colleagues, pupils, and their parents so much that most deplored his upcoming departure, though all agreed he was too young to engage so early and permanently in the teaching profession. All wished him well on his journey for higher learning in America and looked forward to seeing him successful.

The religious community where Kovi exercised his faith also organized a party in honor of his departure. Here, the "party" was a serious prayer session followed by an organized lunch, during which Kovi received advice from everyone. Suddenly, there were fellow members of the faith who seemed to have gained great knowledge and experience in living abroad and they offered free advice to Kovi, who listened politely and thanked every one of them.

Others offered more prayers after the prayer session, long prayers that started with the invocation of God Almighty in all His glorious forms, followed by an acknowledgment of the itemized list of the blessings that He had given them and finally the request for more blessings and protection expressed in many impressive phrases and forms.

There was a proliferation of religious groups and sects in the country, a fraction of which came from America in various denominations, others driven by charismatic, self-appointed messengers and disciples of Jesus Christ. Many people in Kovi's entourage, family or friend, was an active member of a religious group, and each eloquently expressed the reasons for their choice of a particular group over all others. Some groups were well organized and disciplined, which must have instilled a sense of righteousness with intolerance of others and an aggressive style of recruiting new converts. After the farewell parties, Kovi completed his English lessons and got all his travel documents sorted, then he went to spend a few weeks with his parents in the village before his departure.

**

When Kovi and Koku passed the high school where he had worked, Kovi did not say a word during the rest of the taxi ride. He was reflecting on his time at the high school and he did not notice when the taxi reached Hahotoé. Koku informed him that they had arrived and he should get out of the taxi. Their excited mother, who wanted a detailed report on family and friends in the city, especially the ones she'd instructed them to visit, greeted them at the gate of the house.

Chapter Sixteen
Another Departure

They sat under the gazebo and assured Afi that they relayed correctly her greetings and well wishes to everyone, who in return expressed the same, and some even sent gifts. They were just about done talking when an old man and his son who looked like he was in his early twenties walked in and wished to talk to Kovi.

The old man was distressed. He hoped Kovi could help his son get a visa to go to America. The son had a maternal uncle there, and he supplied a letter of invitation with bank account details to prove that he had housing and financial resources to support his nephew during the visit. The young man had collected the list of other required documents, filled out the application form, and got an appointment for the visa interview. On the day of the appointment, he showed up at the American Embassy in the capital city and paid a huge visa application fee with money that the father borrowed. At the embassy, the agent who was processing the visa applications that day asked him four questions.

"The person that you want to visit there, what does he do?"

"He works at so and so and here are his papers."

"And you, what do you do?"

"I am a student at the university here, majoring in so and so."

"Do you have a wife?"

"No sir, I do not."

"Do you have a kid?"

"No sir, I do not."

The agent ended the interview, informed the young man that he did not qualify for a visa and handed him a piece of paper. The visa fee was nonrefundable and lost in a brief interview. The father showed Kovi the piece of paper that they gave his son at the end of the interview. The paper suggested that the applicant did not show he had something significant to tie him to the country, significant enough to make him return at the end of his stay in America. "What must he do? Do they want him to father a kid without being married? He's just a young man and has no means to support a family! Should he get married and show that he will come back to his wife?" the father asked, in a state of anger.

When the father was calm, he reminded Kovi that Kodjo had gone to America to visit his son there, and that was great news in the entire village. Surely, Kovi must have done something more or different for Kodjo to get the visa, so the old man was expecting Kovi to help. Kovi looked at all the papers they had spent several months compiling and saw that everything required for the visa application was in order. Technically, on paper and according to all the documents requested, the young man appeared qualified to get the visa.

Kovi explained to them that with Kodjo's visit to America, Kodjo was a retired old man with two houses. He was a husband with many children and grandchildren, and the owner of coconut farms. Kovi's father did not care to move to the USA. He was settled happily in his ways, and he only wished to see his son more often. Compared to this young man, Kodjo did not have the profile of someone who was likely to go to the USA and settle there illegally. The old man walked away in a rage and complained that he still had to pay the debt of the visa fee.

About one year later, Kovi received a call from the young man, who eventually got the visa and went to the USA to visit his uncle. Jokingly, Kovi asked him how he managed it, whether he'd impregnated a young woman and got a child. The man just laughed and never answered the question.

Early the next morning, Koku got a call from a lawyer who summoned the entire family to appear at her office for the will that Kodjo prepared. Kovi sent a message to their half-brother in Djéta, and on the agreed date, they all went to the lawyer who read the will in the presence of the siblings who could come.

Kodjo divided his properties equally among his children, male and female, regardless of their social and economic standings. He left the two houses collectively to his wife and children as family dwellings.

At the time of his death, Kodjo had no debt and only maintained a small savings in a bank. Kovi and his siblings tried to claim the savings, but with no success. The bank manager informed them that only the beneficiary could collect the money and he must appear at the bank in person or through a third party with detailed instructions in a notarized letter, or do a bank transfer. The family never collected that small savings which, converted into USA dollars, amounted to little.

The news of the will quickly spread to Djéta. Kodjo was clever enough to prepare a will before his death—that impressed many people. Some reckoned it was the first time someone did such a thing in the village. It was Kovi and some siblings who convinced their father to prepare the will to avoid disputes that often arose among family members over the fair sharing of inheritances after the death of someone.

Some believed that the last child of a person who might not have benefited much from the deceased's possessions compared to the older children, or who might still be too young to be financially independent, should receive more of the inheritance, or the division should be inversely proportional to the ages of the descendants. Others might step forward with arguments to claim a particular piece of the inheritance before they divided the rest according to a plan that should be discussed and agreed to by everyone concerned. In the absence of a will, different claims and expectations invariably led to fights. Sometimes, the chief of the village and the elders intervened, and after long and arduous consultations and negotiations, implemented a final and irrevocable inheritance division scheme.

With Kovi's family, after many tough discussions, their father agreed to the will and carried through with the process, thus avoiding any potential problems after his death.

***

It was in those days that Kovi realized another potential problem, when a fellow from the village stepped forward to claim that his father did not sell the lands on which Kodjo built a house. To make matters worse, Kodjo did not have the papers as proof of the sale. However, he had built on the land and lived there for a long time with his family.

For many years when Kovi's family was living there, the plaintiff's father was alive and did not challenge Kodjo. At the time when the plaintiff challenged the ownership of the land, his own father was also dead. Ultimately, the case went to the regional court, and the judge collected all the depositions and the testimonies of the people who were still alive and were witnesses to the sale a long time ago. In addition, the judge made a trip to Hahotoé to see the land in dispute.

After he reviewed the evidence collected, the judge issued a written judgment of several pages wherein he first stated all the facts, his observations, and the depositions from both sides, and he made a final ruling in favor of Kovi's family. The written judgment henceforth served as proof of ownership of the land.

The judge said there were two crucial pieces of evidence that settled the case favorably for Kovi's family. First was the fact that the plaintiff's father lived for at least ten years close to the house and never pressed charges about his land, and second, the eyewitness testimonies of the elders, not related to either party, who witnessed the sale and the payments. The judge ordered the plaintiff to reimburse the other party for the costs associated with the case, but after discussions, Kovi and his family decided not to insist.

When they resolved all the issues associated with the funeral, Kovi and his siblings divided among themselves the rest of their father's belongings, which mainly comprised clothing items, traditional outfits, and kente cloth. Kovi brought some of his inheritance back to the USA and used it when the weather was appropriate, in remembrance of his father.

***

The time came for Kovi to return to the USA, and the family gathered for a meal that Afi prepared meticulously for hours. Afterward, she talked to Kovi for a while and reminded him to keep watch for angels on his path. She requested that Kovi should not be away too long, and not to come back only when there were sad events such as funerals. She complained that she might not see him again, though they often talked by telephone, and that the next time he came back might be for her funeral.

Guilt-ridden and conflicted, Kovi proposed that she should to the USA to visit him again. She first welcomed seeing Aisha and Hatshepsut, whom, up to that time, she had not met in person, but she then complained that she could not make such a long voyage alone. Kovi sensed that she was open to another visit to America, but overwhelmed with the fear of not being able to make the journey by herself. He reminded his mother that she made the journey alone during her first visit, and he informed her that they would start the process to renew her passport.

That same day, Kovi left Hahotoé to go to his uncle's house in Lomé. Later that night, he would take his flight to New York City via Paris.

Kovi arrived at the house of his uncle, Théodore, in the afternoon to find an old friend from middle and high schools, Abdel, waiting for him. Abdel, the man who never went to university, had great talents in painting and drawing, and he became successful. Abdel possessed art galleries in the big market and around the city where he collected and sold, not just his own work, but also many pieces produced by artisans in the region. He traded many things, including traditional music instruments, sculptures of clay or wood, cloth items, garments, paintings, and drawings. Most of his clients were international visitors looking for gifts and souvenirs, and ready to pay the prices appropriate for their economic standings.

By local standards, Abdel was a rich man who had combined skills and clever business strategies to achieve success. He gave Kovi a big hug and commented on his weight gain since the last time he'd seen him, which was when they took the university entrance exams and he failed. Their paths diverged from that point. Kovi continued to the university while he retook the same exams a few more times and failed year after year until he gave up.

Abdel then experimented with odd jobs and saved money from what he had, no matter how small an amount, until one day when he could launch a small art store, and at first, he attempted to sell his own products. Then, there he was, a man who did not complete the high-school degree, a rich and comfortable man who understood how to use his skills to make money, and who was planning to extend his business beyond the confines of Togo.

***

Kovi remembered Abdel as a charismatic and courageous pupil when they were in school. There was one time when Abdel and Kovi boarded the regional train going toward Anèho. They did not buy any train tickets and expected that there wouldn't be any ticket checks until they reached their destination. It was not the first time they did that, and they usually got away with it. When they saw the ticket controller enter the car, they escaped into the next car before the controller arrived where they were sitting. Sometimes, as they continued the game, going from car-to-car, they eventually ran into another controller and found themselves sandwiched. They then looked for the closest toilet and locked themselves in there until the train stopped.

They were hiding in the toilet when someone was knocking desperately to use the toilet and no one knew why it was locked. The two controllers who were checking tickets in opposite directions met where the person was still knocking on the door and they tried to help. They confirmed that they had checked and serviced all the cars before the train left the capital city. They were sure the toilet was not locked purposefully because it was not usable. Perhaps the door mechanically jammed, they thought, and they advised the person to head to another toilet located a few cars away.

While they were giving directions to another toilet, they heard coughing noises coming from the locked toilet. When the boys realized that their little game was over and feared they would call the police in at the next stop, Kovi insisted they open the door, but Abdel refused. He argued it was better to open the door at the next stop, to have a better chance to escape as people got on or off the train. After a heated argument the controllers could hear, Kovi opened the door to see that the incident had attracted spectators. Unable to produce tickets or to buy them right then with a fine, and because they had resisted direct instructions from the controllers, they tied Kovi and Abdel to the seats and passengers volunteered to keep a watch on them until they handed them to the police at the next stop.

Kovi was crying and scared at the thought that he was going into custody of the police, the authoritative men and women in uniform that no one dared to mess around with, while Abdel sat relaxed and unimpressed. Kovi pleaded desperately with the controllers and said it was the first time that this happened, their parents had not given them money, they had already journeyed for some time before they boarded the train.

People looked at Kovi with disgust, unmoved by what he was saying, whereas a sense of respect and appreciation developed for Abdel who sat quietly, dignified, and resigned to what would happen.

The next stop was a small town with no police station and the train would not wait until the police arrived, so they threw Kovi and his friend off the train there. They continued the rest of the journey on foot along the train tracks and they were arguing and yelling at each other.

***

Kovi and Abdel were drinking beer and talking and laughing about their adventures during their school years when Abdel got a call from one of his suppliers and had to leave. Abdel excused himself and expressed the desire that they see each other more often.

As Abdel was leaving, Kovi's uncle, Théodore, a younger brother of Kovi's father and one people who had played a tremendous role in Kovi's journey to the USA, arrived home. A tailor by profession, he had owned a shop in the center of the city and he trained many of his cousins and nephews in the same profession. He had many apprentices who did the actual work while he took customers' orders and measurements. He ensured that the products were ready on time and according to specifications. He was so good that he always had many orders and was constantly busy. Often, having recognized Kovi's last name, clients of his uncle approached Kovi and praised his uncle's work. When Kovi was leaving for America the first time, his uncle commissioned a suit for him. He bought the fabric himself after careful examination and choice, took measurements of Kovi's body, and made the suit himself without using his apprentices. On the day of his departure, Kovi looked elegant in his tailor-made suit.

**

Théodore decorated his living room with many lovely art pieces and pictures of Nete and Mawule on the walls. Kovi was staring at the pictures while he waited for his uncle. As he was looking intensely at the pictures, funny memories came back to him, of the time when Kovi was attending primary school in Djéta.

One cloudy day, Kovi went fly-fishing. The Lord blessed him that day, and he caught many types of big fish. Kovi was excited to relate his fishing experience to his grandparents who, after they verified that he caught the fish himself, congratulated him profusely. While Mawule went back to her shop at the village center, Kovi and Nete cleaned up the fish and removed the scales and intestines, and smoked the fish. When the fish was on the fire, Kovi went to fetch water from the well while Nete was to watch and turning the fish over the fire, as necessary. Kovi came back to find Nete soundly asleep and cats and goats had eaten ninety percent of the fish. It was a disappointment for Kovi. His entire day's effort was a waste. Mawule was mad at both her husband and her grandson for making her change the dinner plan that day.

In another incident, Kovi was in the first grade and preparing for the first time for the end-of-year exams to qualify to move to the next grade. A bunch of other kids older than Kovi got the idea that they needed magic or supernatural intervention to help them pass the exams. After discussions, they agreed that Kovi must lead them to go see Nete—a revered man with a great gift, a fortuneteller with the intuition and the power to work in the extra dimensions, and when he did so, he could influence the course of events for a better outcome. There were other gifted elders. Another one was a granduncle of Kovi. By the touch of his hands, with gentle and frequent massages, he could treat an array of illnesses, including inflammations and broken bones.

The kids thought that if the old man saw his own grandchild among them, he might help, so they approached Nete. After he listened attentively to the kids, he gave them a list of items to bring back, saying that he would perform a great ceremony to help all of them pass the exams.

Kovi, innocent and naïve, asked his mother to help him collect the required items. There was one particular item on the list that shocked Afi and made her furious at Nete, a responsible adult who should have known better than to ask children for such things. Afi vehemently forbade Kovi from going through with the ceremony, and she encouraged him to study and assured him that she would have a word with Nete, herself. Kovi passed the exams at the top of the class and realized, as his mother had told him, that he did not need any magic. Later, Kovi forgot the exact items of the list that Nete requested, so he did not recall what was in that list that made his mother furious.

***

Kovi was staring at the pictures on the wall, and he was thinking fondly of his grandparents when his uncle walked in and turned on the music. Like many people, Théodore enjoyed reggae music from Jamaica and from the new emerging talents from Ivory Coast and South Africa, Congolese music, French soundtracks, merengue, zouk, R&B, and country music. Kovi sat with his uncle in the living room and they talked while the lovely music echoed in the background, and his uncle spoke.

"How many children do you have now?"

"One, just one."

"How many wives do you have?"

"Only one."

"You are old enough to have more wives. And only one child?

That is crazy! Well, the only question is, can you take care of them? If you can, why not have more?"

"Uncle, nowadays, it is expensive to raise kids properly."

"It has never been easy nor simple, but having only one child is crazy."

"Uncle, how would you feel if you had one wife, and she possessed all the resources to afford a second husband?"

On that question, he looked at his nephew speechless for a while, as though he was reflecting on it, before replying.

"Just have more kids with your only wife. The Lord will provide! The next time you visit me, I want to see a bigger family."

After chatting to Théodore, with Kovi and Koku headed toward the house of their other uncle, Vincent, the one who was a custodian at the university and had helped Kovi while he was there.

Vincent clarified details about how they had reconnected with their ancestral line in modern day Ghana after some three hundred and fifty years. Kovi listened carefully with great interest and planned to go there one day to see for himself the place and the people that his forefathers had left behind centuries ago.

Finally, it was time to go to the airport and Kovi arrived there with an escort of siblings and cousins. It was the same airport where Kovi left the country for the first time many years earlier. The place looked like it had not transformed since then.

To his pleasant surprise, Abdel was waiting for him at the airport. Abdel presented Kovi with a few drawings and paintings that he commissioned himself, as a gift by which to remember him, for, as he said, it might be a long time before they met again. The paintings and the drawings were crafted meticulously and depicted the events on the train when they locked themselves in the toilet to avoid the ticket controllers. Kovi smiled and shook his hands. Then Abdel excused himself to attend to a client.

After he checked in and got his boarding pass, Kovi stayed outside and conversed with his siblings until it was time to go. They waved goodbye to each other, as they had many years ago, except then everyone was much older and most were there with their respective families. He went through passport control. Then, he was sitting happily, relaxed, and waited for boarding. After a long day of running from place to place to see family, the moment had come for him to rest. A short time later, he heard his name being called. They took him to the baggage area where they pulled out his luggage in front of him and opened it. Upon a thorough search, they took out a few bottles of *Sodabi* that his mother had wrapped. Apparently, it was just over the limit in terms of the volume or the number of bottles allowed. They would let it go, but in return they expected him to "make a gesture."

There, people understood the expression, "to make a gesture." Before Kovi left his siblings to go through passport control, he gave them all the remaining money he had, namely unused Swiss francs, USA dollars, and West African francs. He had only his credit cards still in his possession, and he was not expecting to still have to make yet another "gesture."

Kovi opened his wallet to show that he truly had zero cash left, but still there was a moment of waiting to see which side would blink first while the airplane was already boarding. After a moment, they must have realized that Kovi was not bluffing, and he did not have any cash—since boarding had started some time ago and the departure was on time, anyone with cash would have caved in already so as not to miss the flight. Reluctantly, they closed the bag and sent it off to the plane and let Kovi board the flight to Paris. He planned for a long layover in Paris to have enough time to visit with his cousin Jean-Patrice.

Kovi emerged from Charles de Gaulle Airport and met up with Jean-Patrice, who was waiting for him. They greeted each other warmly with hugs. Jean-Patrice was the son of his paternal aunt. Traditionally, the paternal aunt was a revered figure in the development of a child, one as important as the biological mother.

Folks saw such an aunt as the maternal manifestation of the father side and an important role model who could assume all the paternal authority in the father's absence.

***

Years ago, there was a dispute between one of Kodjo's aunts and Kodjo's mother regarding the ownership of a piece of land. Kovi's father must have been about fifteen years old. The two most important women in Kodjo's life were bitterly fighting. The case eventually went to the village court. Apparently, Kovi's father had witnessed the sale of the land in dispute. The elders called upon him to testify during the court proceedings. The fifteen-year-old young man, who was raised by these two great women and was close to both of them, had to testify on the behalf of one mother against the other. It was a heavy burden for the teenager who, after the judgment, still had to live with both women. Kovi's father testified to support his biological mother against his paternal mother and spent many years trying to mend the damaged relations.

Children from these mothers grew up together and become as close as brothers and/or sisters.

***

They drove to Jean-Patrice's house in a suburb of Paris, where Kovi took out all the items given to him for Jean-Patrice and his family. In anticipation of Kovi's arrival, Jean-Patrice had alerted other family members in the region, and they converged on the house with their families. More African food was prepared and enjoyed in a communal spirit.

Later in the afternoon, Kovi accompanied Jean-Patrice to a birthday celebration where the ambiance was distinctly African, including much of the music and the dances that were traditionally

African, and gave the impression that Kovi was still in Africa. Kovi noticed that these expatriates, who were away from their places of origin for a long time, maintained something of their cultural heritage and, occasionally expressed it with pride and happiness.

Kovi remembered his African cultural background well and could still articulate it in discussions and debates, but he lost much of its practice through the years when he lived abroad, whereas Jean-Patrice endeavored to maintain and practice their cultural heritage beyond the mere fancy intellectual articulation of it.

When it came time to go back to the airport, Jean-Patrice drove Kovi. During the ride, they spoke little. They said goodbye many times with a touch of sadness in their faces and voices, since they did not get to see each other as often as they wanted.

Kovi waved his hands as he walked toward the security checkpoint and passport control and disappeared into the crowd. He walked past the boutiques and the shops strategically placed to attract the attention of passengers.

He found his boarding gate, and while he was waiting for the boarding time, Kovi walked around in the terminal and stared at the various jumbo jets, all of which he had taken during his many business travels.

Sometimes, to amuse himself, he read about the airplane he was about to take to learn about its technical specifications, the year since the plane first entered service, the companies using it in their fleets, and its direct competitors from the giant jumbo jet makers. He was fascinated by the elegance of the landings and the takeoffs, and one time, he noticed two almost simultaneous takeoffs at a major airport.

The airplane that he took that day was one of the big jumbo jets, for which the boarding process alone can take up to an hour with long queues of people in the economy class.

He boarded the flight and was unlucky enough to sit beside a huge man whose body overflowed from his seat to encroach on Kovi's space. He greeted his new neighbor of the eight-hour flight politely as he squeezed himself into the tight and uncomfortable seat and passed out exhausted while the man was attempting to make small talk.

Upon his return, Kovi received a letter mailed a few months earlier from Africa. He noticed right away the handwriting of Kodjo. Kovi recalled that Kodjo had asked him whether he received his letter, but Kovi had not. They did not speak much about the letter, and then Kodjo took ill and died. There was the letter. It had arrived finally, but Kodjo was no longer in the flesh. Kovi decided not to open it and Aisha did not understand.

"Why don't you want to open the letter? Aren't you curious to know about the last letter your father wrote you?" asked Aisha.

"I do want to know. But the pain is still too vivid."

"What are you going to do?"

"I will wait."

"For what?"

"To keep his memory alive with me."

"I do not follow."

"As long as I do not open it, I know that he has a message for me. His spirit is still present."

Aisha noticed that Kovi's eyes became reddish, and he was struggling to contain the tears. After Kovi left Africa, Kodjo always wrote him a letter. One each month without fail! They were handwritten letters of several pages to tell his son everything about life back home and the latest news in the village. Kodjo had elegant handwriting, and he arranged his sentences in an elegant prose in French with a meticulous attention to punctuation. There were hardly any mistakes in his letters and he handwrote each of them in one session, carefully, without the need to make any further corrections.

Kovi always read his father's letters with excitement for the elegance of the prose, although many of them carried sad messages such as deaths in the village or nasty family quarrels. Kovi wouldn't be getting any more letters from Kodjo and the last one he received, he did not want to open.

"If I were you, I would open the letter. Then, I would go back and read all the letters you kept. That is my way of keeping his memory," said Aisha.

"Yes, yes. But I will not open this one until I am ready. When I do finally open it, it will be like he is speaking to me fresh on that day."

"Maybe in that letter, your father is telling or giving you a clue to some treasure he knew of or hid somewhere. You might miss out on something important," insisted Aisha.

"Maybe so. If Papa Kodjo had any such information, he would have told me long ago. Good try, Aisha."

So Kovi kept the letter in a safe in their house, and to this day he has not opened it… yet.

Chapter Seventeen
The Skinny Elephant Versus the Fat Donkey

Upon his return to the USA, Kovi needed to make a few repairs in their family house before he left again, this time on business travels. Kovi went into a store to buy something to fix a burned area in the house—an electrical discharge had caused a fire. It burned a part of the wooden board upon which they mounted the circuit and darkened the wall around. Luckily, the wire did not spread.

The cashier greeted him politely and Kovi described what he was looking to buy. After a few exchanges, Kovi showed the spelling of the material recommended for the job. He had written the information on the front page of a research paper he was reading. The cashier recognized what Kovi was looking for, but then he focused his attention on the synopsis of Kovi's research paper. Kovi again asked him if the store carried the material, to refocus his attention on the task at hand. As he led Kovi to the aisle to get the material, he wanted to know if Kovi was a doctor. He asked twice to be sure. Kovi assured him he was and carried out research in physics. He asked whether Kovi worked at the "Laboratory." Kovi replied affirmatively and the cashier became even more curious.

He wanted know whether people at the Lab were still working on turning water into energy. Kovi told him there are hydroelectric power plants for that, and a dam is often required, which they did not have at the Lab. The man insisted he was not talking about hydroelectric power plants. Kovi did his best to explain to him that another option to turn water into energy could consist of extracting hydrogen from the water, then using the extracted hydrogen as fuel.

Kovi continued and told him that he was not involved in or aware of such a research activity at the Lab and could not comment on its economic viability. The man was skeptical and thought what physicists were doing there must be a secret. He also assumed the physicist Kovi was not willing to tell the truth.

They got the material Kovi needed and the cashier was pleased to explain the differences between the various incarnations of the same product and the ranges of their applicability and added his personal experience and recommendations. Here was one area where he knew much more than the physicist. He took a vested interest in helping beyond what he normally did for any other customer.

On the way back to the checkout counter, Kovi talked about an international effort to show how to harness energy based on nuclear fusion, just like the way the sun works! Kovi explained the process that happens in the sun to generate energy in form of heat, and said if humans can reproduce that efficiently on Earth, we will have a cleaner source of energy than the one based on nuclear fission. The man stopped and wondered aloud about fusion versus fission and drew Kovi into a whole lecture on the subject.

Meanwhile, customers approached and asked him for help and each time he pretended he was already busy in helping another customer. He was particularly interested in the progress on a fusion-based energy source. Kovi told him that using the sun as our model, we must adhere to the requirements or conditions that all come together to allow the sun to harness fusion energy efficiently. The man wanted to know more about these conditions and wondered about the source of fuel to power an efficient nuclear fusion power plant on Earth.

"There are many ongoing studies," Kovi said. "Oceans might offer an inexhaustible reserve of heavy water based on the chemical element deuterium as a good ingredient of the fuel source." The cashier's eyes lit up at "heavy water," and obviously he wanted to know more. When he sensed Kovi's impatience, he let him go with his final recommendation, "Pour the material into something, and with a brush, try to cover the burned area. Well, you are a doctor. You will figure it out. We should go fishing some time, and you can tell me more. What you guys do over there is fascinating. Who pays for all that stuff?"

Kovi was already leaving, and he did not answer the question, and that was to dominate their conversations during their many fishing expeditions to come…

***

When Kovi finished with the repairs in his house, he embarked on a series of business travels.

During one of these trips, he visited CERN. In the evenings, Kovi and colleagues gathered in the lab's cafeteria. There, he often bumped into folks not seen in a while, and people expected small talk. Those who dined off-site ultimately converged on the same cafeteria. It was mainly the same crowd of those who visited for a week for meetings and discussions.

Occasionally, their local friends and colleagues joined them for quick drinks before they went home. In good weather, they sat around just outside the cafeteria, and on one side, in the distance, there stood the Alps with Mont Blanc covered by snow, and on the other side were the Jura mountains.

Some of them spent their entire visits in a small triangular loop of the office building, the on-site hotel, and the cafeteria. It was relaxing and useful to gather in the cafeteria and engage friends and colleagues that one rarely saw. The discussions centered on the physics topics that brought them there in the first place, although many were about catching up and joking. It was an international setting with many physicists and engineers.

On one such an evening, after a meal and many drinks, the discussion turned to the status of funding for physics research. There was among them a nice, elegant, and well-spoken fellow from India. He possessed great physics knowledge and experience because of a long career in physics teaching and research at many institutes around the world. He also appeared well read with an in-depth knowledge of current world affairs. He commanded a great deal of attention when he talked. He was a great listener, always careful to allow others to talk while he drank wine and grinned after each sip. He was careful when he talked, always taking a few moments between sentences, not to think about what to say next, rather how to put it gently. He was a slender fellow, somewhat short, well-coiffed with obviously a great deal of care put into his moustache and beard. He commented on the status of shrinking research funding for particle physics in first-world countries versus in his own country, "If the elephant loses weight, he would still be bigger than the donkey." Kovi thought the real issue was how many shared the skinny elephant versus how many for the donkey, and how the pieces were carved. But shy and intimidated, Kovi dared not offer any comments. The gentleman had moved on to a different topic by the time Kovi gathered his thoughts.

Many hours later, as the cafeteria was closing, they got enough drinks to sustain them a few hours longer. All the while, some folks joined the group and others left. Some, when they finished preparing for the next day, came to the cafeteria for a moment of relaxation before they retired for the night. Others swept into the ambience and hung around until late before they left to finish preparation for the next day. The crowd dispersed when there were no more drinks left.

That night, the elegant fellow had already left, and as the rest was walking back toward the hotel, Kovi posed a question to the group, "Folks, what do you say? What is the state of funding for physics research in your country? Do you say it is becoming a skinny elephant or a fat donkey?" Most agreed that it was becoming more like a skinny donkey.

***

At the end of the week, Kovi paid for his stay, exited the reception, and left his bag just outside the reception area. His taxi was prearranged and expected to be there in forty-five minutes. Time for coffee! Thirty-five minutes later, Kovi emerged from the cafeteria, just in time to see that firefighters had established a security perimeter. Fire trucks and firefighters blocked all accesses. From a distance, he saw his bag. He must fetch it, for the taxi was coming any moment.

"No access allowed!" the fireman ordered.

"I must fetch my bag. My taxi is imminent."

"That is your bag, sir?" the fireman asked in a tone of concern.

"Yes, that is my bag."

"Okay, go talk to the boss over there."

Kovi approached the fire marshal. He was on the telephone. He leaned toward him inquisitively.

"I need to get my bag, sir. My taxi will be here any minute," said Kovi.

The marshal put the call on hold.

"Is that your bag?"

"Yes, it is mine."

"Are you sure that is your bag?"

"Absolutely!"

He turned back to his telephone conversation. "Okay! The situation is under control. No more worries. See you." Then he turned toward Kovi and instructed, "Come with me." Slowly, they walked side by side toward the bag.

Still oblivious, Kovi asked him, "What is going on, sir? A fire?" The fire marshal was angry, "You left your bag over there. It is abandoned. Someone could have placed a bomb!" Then, the loaded reality started to weigh on Kovi. A moment of silence followed as they approached the bag. "Check that this is your bag," he instructed.

While Kovi was checking the bag, a colleague appeared.

"So, it's you who caused all the alarm? We had to evacuate the building."

Embarrassed and his head down and shaking, Kovi must have murmured something unintelligible. His colleague waited for no clarification and the fire marshal noticed the total embarrassment of Kovi, and he attempted a recovery. "No worries! It happens; all is fine." Then, his ordered his firefighters to disengage.

The taxi was still not there. Kovi went back to the reception to inquire. Before he even reached the desk, the young receptionist yelled.

"Sir, you are the one who caused all this problem this morning."

"I am sorry. I should have left my bag with you."

"Yes sir, we have a safe. Your taxi will be here in two minutes. Safe journey!"

As Kovi was coming out, he met another colleague. "Is that your bag that caused us to evacuate the building?" In the exchange, Kovi learned that his colleague was on the night shift, and had gone to bed just a few hours ago, only to be awakened by the firefighters and ordered to evacuate the building. As he went away, the man offered a statement of sympathy, "These guys truly overreacted."

The taxi arrived! "

Where are you going?"

"To the airport, please."

At the check-in counter, the lady told him,

"Sir, the first leg of your journey will be in business class."

"Thanks. And the rest?" Kovi asked.

"You will find out in Amsterdam. Here are your boarding passes. Safe journey!"

In an astonishing stroke of luck, in Amsterdam, Kovi approached the transfer desk and a well-dressed gentleman there greeted him with good news.

"Sir, we have a different seat for you. It is on the upper deck, business class."

The long travel day had barely started for Kovi, and it already was eventful! The event with the unattended bag might follow Kovi home. He could imagine the gossip. "Do you know what happened with Kovi's bag?" "Did you hear that they had to evacuate some building because Kovi left a bag?" etc., etc.

Scientists' business travels are normally in economy class. Yet that day, after the unpleasant incident with the firefighters, he was lucky enough to get bumped into business class twice in the same journey.

It was many years since Kovi had forgotten his briefcase at a public bus stop in Bulach. But that was a different time, and it did not generate a scare. Here, Kovi left the bag intentionally just outside the hotel in a secure compound. That day, Kovi learned a lesson the hard way: Never leave a bag unattended, anywhere, and if you see a suspicious-looking bag, call the authorities.

***

After his return home later that week, Kovi was sitting in a waiting area to see a dentist. He was reading his research paper, when a gentleman beside him started talking.

"So, what on Earth do you do?"

"I do research in particle physics."

"Oh! Are you one of these people?"

"Which people?"

"Well, these guys who claim to be looking for the God Particle."

"The God Particle?"

"Right! What does that mean, anyway? Do you mean when you find this particle you will find God?"

A nurse called for him. As he was going, he stepped on Kovi accidentally.

"Ouch!"

"Sorry, I guess I am just getting too excited."

"About the particle, God, or your dental work?"

"I need to ponder about that," he said as he disappeared in the corridor. He emerged many minutes later while Kovi was still waiting. As he was about to exit the dental office, he insisted.

"You still have not answered the question, my friend."

"Have a good day, sir," Kovi replied. "We already found the Higgs boson. Now we are searching for something new."

"Oh! So, you are looking for another God Particle?"

Kovi smiled, and he was thinking about the searches for new particles. The gentleman turned around, walked away while shaking his head, mumbling, "Unbelievable! These highbrow physicists! I am happy I am not looking for particles and I've already found God!"

Kovi was among the particle physicists that discovered the Higgs boson in 2012. But the discovery did not seem to make the donkey fat. It was an exciting time in fundamental physics research.

***

The day particle physicists announced the discovery of the Higgs boson, Kovi appeared on television to talk about it. They asked him many questions, one of which was what particle physicists meant when they claim that they observed a Higgs-like particle.

"Please explain to the audience what you people mean by 'observed a particle,'" the television anchor asked Kovi. So, there was Kovi on live television and he started to talk, "The analysis of the data showed a significant signal over the expected background. In the absence of a signal, the data would just be consistent with what we expect from the background in the detector. But when the data displays something significant on top the background, we refer to that as an observation of a signal, in this case the signal is from the Higgs boson-like particle."

The television anchor asked whether the "observation" might be a mistake? Kovi had to clarify that what they call "observation" results from a lengthy, reproducible, and thorough data analysis, with many tests and checks, supported by a tough and unforgiving peer review process. Also, scientists must make the discovery in different independent experiments.

Many friends and family saw Kovi on television that day. He did not prepare for the event. A few colleagues and Kovi had been discussing the recently announced discovery when they summoned them to the television station for a live interview. The call was unexpected, and after they applied some makeup to his face, they put Kovi in the spotlight, unshaved and in attire that he would not otherwise have considered for the occasion. He should have declined, for there were many more interviews after that day, for which he would have been more presentable. However, the excitement of appearing live on national television clouded his judgment. The result was a fiasco he regretted.

Later that day, Kovi sat with Aisha for a long while. It was a great evening. The sun set late. In the moonlight, her face was shiny. Aisha smiled at Kovi and spoke.

"You talked about the observation of a Higgs-like particle. We ordinary folks are observant. It is funny how a profound truth emerges from simple observations."

"What?"

"Nothing, I am just reflecting on what you said. Your observations seem to result from complicated, technical, and lengthy data analysis that only a few people claim to understand. For us laypeople, observations derive from common sense and alertness with profound and far-reaching consequences that many more people can understand. I mean there is no complicated mathematical formalism to justify an observation."

Kovi told her that was a deep, philosophical, and debatable statement; common sense, cleverness, and intuition are essential to all physics observations.

"Let's discuss this later, love. But you are right, it was my simple observation of your beauty and attractiveness that triggered and sustained my love for you. And I am sure that was an objective observation," said Kovi.

"Good try, love. Good try," she replied.

They sat in the breezy evening, and they were enjoying each other's company with wine and cheese, and they laughed at Kovi's earlier bad television appearance.

As it started to get chilly, they went inside the house. Their television was still on and drew their attention to a debate about inclusion and diversity, a debate in which someone defended intolerant views based on superficial racial differences not shown scientifically.

"Ignorance can be the root of many problems. Especially when people use hand-waving arguments to influence others," said Aisha.

"A place with racial and cultural diversity must be a blessed and rich one, for its people would learn a great deal from sharing with each other," she added.

"People should also travel around the rest of the world to develop tolerance and acceptance of others," Kovi responded.

Chapter Eighteen
A Safari

Kovi was grateful that his professional activities compelled him to travel many times. Occasionally, he was fortunate enough to journey to many places during one trip. He traveled to physics conferences with his djembes. In those days, Kovi thought he could make the world a better place by doing physics and drumming.

"Drumming! It is good for your health. You can punch the drum like a boxer, or tap it as a musician. Either way, you release frustration," Kovi used to say.

One of their periodic workshops happens at Les Houches in France. Kovi had attended this workshop a few times. Often, after full days of doing physics, Kovi and other physicists gathered at the bar after dinner for moments of fun and relaxation. Physics discussions continued in the night with coffee and drinks. A few played games while others improvised with a guitar and Kovi's djembes. The mountain slopes and the valleys shined under the clear night sky, creating a beautiful and mesmerizing contrast accentuated by the snow-covered mountaintops. The music echoed through the night until a neighbor came to complain. They invited him to join them, but he politely declined, citing the necessity of waking up early. They stopped playing music, but games, discussions and drinking continued late into the night.

***

They organized one of their conferences in Rome, Italy. Kovi had family there. Many colleagues and friends converged there for a one-week physics workshop. It was a gathering of the young and the old, all of them smart and gifted.

Each morning, they met in the hotel lobby, and they discussed and exchanged ideas on common research topics. After breakfast, they took a bus downtown, and then walked to the venue while the discussions continued. To laypeople, they must have looked like strange groups of individuals from different parts of the world, speaking English with various accents, and saying to each other incomprehensible mumbo jumbo that only the group members seemed to understand and follow. Observers must have wondered what brought these disparate groups together, and why in their beloved city? They must have gotten some relief—or not—when they noticed that the groups contained a few of their own who were also excited about whatever they were discussing. But then, perhaps the natives have seen it all in the big, international cities, where different people congregate for meetings, some of which they neither know nor care about.

At a street corner, they saw a gentleman walking back and forth and yelling different things. No one seemed to care. People were passing by unimpressed and ignored him. Most avoided eye contact with the man, who was disheveled and seemed like someone who was mentally ill. Kovi's attention drifted a moment from his group and its discussion toward this man, as Kovi was wondering what happened to him and how did he get there? "Imagine there were such people walking and telling each other a bunch of things no one around seemed to understand or care about—perhaps that's how we appeared to others," Kovi thought.

This man was unsuccessful at explaining to the passersby what was bugging him, and every morning he was trying again at the same place. Kovi and his colleagues too were passionate in discussing and explaining what they did, but they needed to reach out more to the public to galvanize and sustain support for the long-term viability and continuity of their research activities, i.e., make the elephant fat again!

One evening, Kovi skipped the conference dinner to visit with family. He ate food of Togo and he drank *Sodabi*. He heard hours of conversation in Mina, his native language. The last time when he felt so at home was during Kodjo's funeral many years ago. It was nice and grounding. During dinner, his cousin asked him what brought him to that city, and to explain to them the work he did. Kovi started lecturing passionately, waving his hands excited to tell them about his research and education activities, and all the while everyone around the table got quieter and quieter. When he noticed that he was not easily convincing anyone, he stopped with a fake smile and tossed down a shot of *Sodabi*. His cousin said, "Prince, you sounded like that mad fellow at the street corner."

They agreed to give Kovi another opportunity to explain himself, but for the time being, it was best to reminisce about their childhood years while they drank more *Sodabi*.

***

On a different trip, Kovi arrived in Tokyo Japan for a workshop on software for physics analysis. The workshop brought together many colleagues of Kovi's for one week of technical meetings and discussions. It was a long journey for Kovi. He wondered if there was any corner of the earth he had not yet visited. Maybe Antarctica and Siberia! He was tired of traveling and living out of suitcases. He missed Aisha and Hatshepsut. But frequently, there he went again, boarding a plane to somewhere. It was so boring to keep going to the same places and so narrow-minded to do little or no travel at all. Doing research in physics allowed him to visit many exotic locations, only a handful of which he could manage on his own vacation time and resources.

"Traveling broadens your horizons, not from the excitement to see the animals nor even to do the research work, instead from meeting and interacting with other people and cultures from around the world," he often said, and he felt grateful to learn more about other people!

One evening during the workshop in Tokyo, Kovi went out; he stayed off the tourist paths, and intermingled with the locals to see what it was like. He walked into a restaurant and sat comfortably at the counter. He could hardly understand the menu, but he knew the word biru. As he started to drink his beer, a well-dressed gentleman walked in, sat beside him, and mumbled something in Japanese. Kovi replied, "Sorry, I do not understand." Then the gentleman said sorry several times, bowing his head. After a while he stopped and added, "I must apologize a lot, the Japanese style."

Kovi could tell he was a regular as the bartender handed him a half-empty sake bottle without asking. He tossed down several glasses and asked Kovi to drink with him. Kovi agreed.

"You know, the Japanese invented two great revolutions," he said.

"What are they?" Kovi replied.

He tossed down one more glass of sake, and continued.

"The first one is the Toyota Revolution."

He smiled and added, "The second one is the lingerie pub."

"Lingerie pubs! I've got to check out one of those," Kovi exclaimed.

The man turned to other people around, talked to them for a while in Japanese and started on a second sake bottle. He asked Kovi for his name and how old he was. He wrote Kovi's name on the non-empty sake bottle, handed the bottle to the waiter, rubbed the top of Kovi's head twice, and said, "If you ever come this way again, you may drink from that bottle." Then, he walked out. As he reached the door, he turned around and said, "Lingerie pubs, for all kinds of special favors." And he disappeared around the corner without telling Kovi where to find a lingerie pub.

Meanwhile, two young ladies walked in and sat beside Kovi. After an unsuccessful attempt to communicate, they realized they had a common language, i.e., to laugh together, making fun of the inability of Kovi to speak Japanese and their struggles with English. Later, Kovi remembered being asked: how old he was, what was his blood type, if he had a partner, if his partner was Japanese... Kovi had to run to catch the last metro.

The next morning, before the session resumed, Kovi heard a colleague yelling.

"I have the solution. Can I have twenty minutes to present it?"

"How come? You must have been having sake until late last night."

"Yes, I just woke up this morning dreaming of the solution; it must have been the sake."

"Great! That is great, man! We have several problems to discuss and solve this week. I've got to keep you stocked with a constant supply of sake. Maybe then you can dream up all the solutions for us."

As Kovi walked away, he was thinking of lingerie pubs for special favors and then saw that with the right amount of sake, he could just dream up solutions to problems. Hum... Seemed like he'd come to the right place!

Kovi always meant to go back, drink from the bottle that perhaps still bears his name to this day, and do the lingerie pub thing, somewhere in Japan. He had not gone back yet; instead, he traveled to other places.

***

Kovi arrived in South Africa to explore joint research projects with colleagues he'd met during his postdoctoral studies there. At the invitation of local colleagues, Kovi traveled to South Africa where he gave speeches in different cities on his teaching and research interests. One afternoon, he approached a lady at the information desk in a store. She mumbled something to Kovi as he stepped closer.

"I am sorry. I do not understand," Kovi replied.

"You do not understand Xhosa?" said the lady.

"Koza, no."

She laughed and said, "Xhosa, with the click!"

In Mina, they have clicks, but not in words nor phrases—instead, to express anger, disappointment, or disgust.

"Xhosa is easy. You can learn fast with a Xhosa woman!" she stated.

"I have a friend fluent in Sotho, Zulu, Tsonga, Xhosa, English, and Afrikaans," Kovi replied with some pride.

"So, you are lazy then and you have no excuse."

"I speak Mina, Ewe, French, and English," Kovi attempted a comeback.

"Now you must add Xhosa," she insisted.

"So, you want to be my Xhosa woman?" Kovi could not resist the irony.

As she was laughing, Kovi smiled and thought that laughter is one universal language we can all relate to and understand. It must have been time for her to stop work. As she walked away, she said, "Ubenemini Emnandi." "Have a nice day," Kovi replied in Xhosa with the only Xhosa words he knew.

***

A week later, when Kovi finished with major business activities, Aisha joined him in South Africa, and with some local friends, they started a road trip they had organized months earlier. It was a seven-day journey to tour one of the Kruger Park. They stayed in a lodge just outside the park. On the first evening there, the staff at the lodge organized an entertainment for the guests. The performers were standing in the middle of the room. The lead artist had a hard voice, a bald head, and reddish eyes. He gave the impression of an accomplished musician. He played the djembe for a few seconds in a rhythm that took Kovi back to his ancestral village and ignited wonderful memories. Before he continued, the artist said, "I dedicate this piece to all those who are simply tired." Aisha turned toward Kovi, who was lost in his thoughts. "Are you good? You like it?" she asked him in a calm and soothing voice. His smile could not hide well his true feeling, "I wish to have an International Day, like Mother's Day or Father's Day, an International Day in honor of resourceful persons who have tried and are tired," said Kovi. She lay her head on his shoulder, with her fingers caressing his neck tenderly, "Yes, I understand," she said. "At the moment, let's enjoy this lovely music. It is for you, one of those tirelessly resourceful ones."

The music was vibrating in the entire room. The main artist was playing two djembes in some acrobatic fashion that defied description. The female supporting cast was dancing in movements that made their entire bodies shake, and their chests and behinds made lovely circular motions. The males were shirtless, showing their muscular physique. Sweat dripped along their bodies and accentuated the smoothness of their skins. The spectacle drove the crowd into screams and moans of pleasure and created a festive atmosphere that ultimately drove even the stiffest to dance. "What a pleasure to relax in dancing!" Kovi thought.

The next day, he was strolling on the property in the heat of midday. Kovi met the owner of the lodge near the reception area. He was interested in what they did. Kovi told him they had gone into the park at 6:00 a.m. for an early morning game drive and came out by 10:30 a.m. to avoid the heat of the day. He seemed surprised.

"You are the first persons I've met who came out of the park so early in the day. Did you see the carnivores?" he asked.

"Unfortunately, we did not," responded Kovi.

He seemed disappointed. Why go to the park and not see the carnivores?

"But among the big ones, we saw the buffalo, the elephant, the hippopotamus, and the crocodile," Kovi continued.

"So, you went by the river," the owner inferred, with a smile of relief.

"You must go back for an earlier evening game drive to see the carnivores," he instructed.

"Yes, then get into a private jet and fly straight to the Carnivores Restaurant for dinner!"

"Do you have a private jet?" the owner asked.

"No, I do not. Unfortunately!"

He laughed, "You are a dreamer, my friend. Even I would not have thought of that. Who knows, you might pull it off someday." The owner walked away saying, "That is a good idea. I might try it myself. Tjo! It is hot."

From that day, Kovi and Aisha followed the owner's recommendations. Each morning after breakfast or evening before supper, they went on game drives led by a ranger. In between, they hiked or drove in the park. For several hours, they enjoyed the diversity of the flora and fauna on a slow, leisurely drive. Each day, the scenario was different as they came face-to-face with dramatic struggles for survival between predators and preys.

They wanted to see the so-called Big Five—the lion, the elephant, the leopard, the rhinoceros, and the buffalo—before the end of their safari. So, they started a game of who could spot a new animal first, and the likelihood of the animal to be one of the Big Five.

One day, at a rest area, they engaged a family that was also on the quest for the Big Five. They told each other stories of which of the Big Five they'd seen, when and where. This family had seen one or two more of the Big Five than they did, in particular the elusive leopard. The family had a boy, about twelve years old. He was talkative and described to Kovi in great detail how he spotted the leopard. When he finished his narrative, Kovi asked him what he must do to spot more animals. The boy replied that he must look. The answer was not useful at first, but then on a second thought, the boy was right. One member of Kovi's group, Henry, a good friend of Kovi, had the talent of spotting animals and calling the attention of everyone when no one else noticed. Sometimes, Henry turned out to be wrong. But more often than not, he was right because he looked hard.

On one of their forays into the park, they saw nothing but impalas. They were unlucky and made wrong turns in the park, missing the actions, or arrived at the location after a spectacular event, such as the chase of an impala by a swift and graceful cheetah. They were returning to the lodge when they spotted a pride of lions. Many cars had gathered and people were watching.

At some point, the lions started to march along a paved road, with a procession of cars behind them. "Where are the lions going?" That must have been the question in everyone's mind. They were all determined to find out. The lion, the lionesses, and cubs all were taking lazy steps toward an unidentified destination, unmoved by these humans who were taking their pictures from the comfortable distance of their vehicles.

Suddenly, the aim of the lions became obvious, as they met up with a herd of buffalo. The lions knew the path the buffalo took on the way to quench their thirst late in the day, and the lions timed their journey to intercept and ambush them.

The game of cat and mouse they'd seen on television ensued live before their eyes. Sheer determination on both sides! The lions were trying to separate and isolate an elder, infant, or tired one, whereas the more vigorous and fierce buffalo repeatedly chased the lions away. The predators took a timeout and followed the prey at close range. Then, they regrouped and relaunched their attacks. The game went back and forth for hours until it was getting dark and the park was closing. Kovi and his friends needed to get out. One thing was clear: The lions had patience, they were unmoved by how long it would take. They would get their meal. A great example of perseverance and patience!

Early the next day morning, they hiked into the park with a ranger leading the pack. He was armed with a rifle and knives. He knew the bush well and commented on the plants they passed along the way, pointing out the poisonous and the medicinal ones. He also commented on the tracks left by animals when the tracks were visible.

They stopped and had breakfast in the bush while they stared at the expanse of green vegetation before them. In the undergrowth or on the leaves, they noticed movements of animals and birds. As they continued to walk, they started to guess at animals by examining their feces. Often, they guessed wrong, and the ranger explained to them which animal left that shit. They came upon some feces and the ranger asked them to guess the animal based on all things that he'd taught them. They all took wild guesses. Henry analyzed the feces as follows, "Noticing how the shit scattered when it hit the ground coming from the animal's ass, and given the radius of the scatter on the ground, I guess the animal must be tall with his butt high above the ground. One animal that fits the bill is the giraffe. It must be a giraffe."

The ranger was so impressed that he asked Henry, "What kind of work do you do?" To which Henry responded that he was a physicist. The ranger shook his head and turned around to lead the group further, saying, "Unbelievable. In all my years as a ranger, no one guessed that right until now. These highbrow physicists!"

In the early morning hours of the following day, Kovi and Henry stepped out of the lodge for a quick hike in the bush. The sun was rising. The cool air of the morning felt refreshing. They were walking at a comfortable pace and paid attention to singing birds. They stopped at every occasion to marvel at the diversity of the flora with many beautiful flowers. The dew on leaves attracted many creatures. Soon, they went far enough to no longer hear the noise of human activities from the lodge.

They could see the river ahead. Kovi was still taking pictures when Henry hurried to the riverbank. Suddenly, they were in a race for survival. An angry hippopotamus was chasing them. Instinctively, Kovi hid in the bush. The hippopotamus selected his target, and Henry made it easier for the hippopotamus by running on the unpaved road that went along the river. Kovi could see the scene unfolding and he kept thinking, "Dude, make a turn into the bush where it could be difficult for the hippopotamus to maintain speed." Kovi was feeling out of danger, but was worried for Henry.

Kovi took a snapshot of the encounter when the hippopotamus and Henry were about fifty-three meters apart, just as Kovi was running into the bush. The hippopotamus was about fifty times heavier and could reach thirty kilometers per hour at top speed, but might only sustain that for a few hundred meters or fewer. With the hippopotamus on his tail, Henry became the fastest human being alive. "Run, dude! Run like a bat out of hell!" But Henry could not sustain this speed over two hundred meters.

By Kovi's second snapshot, Henry increased the gap to about eighty meters. Both the hippopotamus and the prey were cruising at their top speeds. Safety was still about two hundred meters away, at a ranger station down the road.

The pair soon sped way past where Kovi was hiding and he could not see how it ended. He reached for his cell phone, but it was not there; he hadn't taken it with him. He kept wondering, "Did he make it to safety?" Against the odds, he hoped so.

A few hours later, the park rangers picked up Kovi. To his pleasant surprise, he saw Henry with them and he was unscathed. Henry was equally worried and feared that an angry hippopotamus had devoured Kovi. He complained that Kovi did not run with him on the road. He claimed that early in the morning the rangers were on patrol. Their chance for safety was to stay on the road to reach the ranger station.

It turned out that the rangers came to rescue Henry. They chased away the hippopotamus with rubber bullets and got Henry to safety. Kovi insisted that his friend took a riskier approach and like himself he should have disappeared into the bush to escape the hippopotamus. But anger did not linger for long and they were happy they got some excitement that morning.

To this day, they two men still argue about the event of that morning. What if the rangers did not notice Henry and come to his rescue? Henry and the hippopotamus were about eighty meters apart, both at their top speeds. But they could not sustain their speeds much longer before they became exhausted. Safety was still two hundred meters away at the ranger station. Henry insists that he would have made it, but Kovi is not so sure.

By their last morning at the lodge, they had seen four of the Big Five. The leopard was still eluding them. They checked out of the lodge and drove across the park on their way back to civilization. Perhaps, they might be lucky and see the leopard. They were. At one of the rest areas, they got word that people had spotted a leopard. They got into the car and drove there. Lo-and-behold, there was a leopard, and she was relaxing under the shade of a tree. She was the star, as many cars converged, and people made video recordings or took pictures of their celebrity.

That safari was one of Kovi's most memorable adventures in the wild.

Chapter Nineteen
Firm, Manly Handshake

After their safari in South Africa, Aisha returned to the USA and Kovi headed toward "Africa North" to visit André-Simon Le Beau, the Minister of Education of Zamumda. André-Simon was an old friend of Kovi's, the one who taught him to drive cars with manual transmission when they were in graduate school.

André-Simon Le Beau had returned to Zamumda at the end of his studies, and later he invited Kovi for visits. During his first visit, Kovi was in Zamumda City for a few days and traveling around in a rental car when a traffic policeman stopped him. The officer came over to his car.

"Driver's license? New York! Your passport?"

"I do not have it. It is back at the hotel."

"You must have your passport with you at all times."

"Sorry, sir. I normally do. I was hurrying and forgot."

"I want to write you a ticket."

"For what?"

"For not stopping at the stop sign."

"Oh! It is a four-way stop. I got there first, and I slowed down."

"But you did not stop."

"Sorry, sir."

"I want to write you a ticket."

"You can just give me a warning."

"What kind of warning?"

"I am not sure."

"You are the one who said I must give you a warning. You must tell me what kind of warning."

"You could tell me not to do it again."

"Oh! So, you want a verbal warning."

He left for a moment to check the car's registration. By the time he came back, Kovi had some money in his hand, and he noticed. Kovi said, "What about the warning of a firm, manly handshake?" The policeman laughed and said, "That is okay, you can go. Don't do it again." He did not take the money.

In the evening, André-Simon fetched Kovi from the hotel and took him to his house for dinner with his family. For a moment, they sat around the living room and watched the evening news on television. Excited, Kovi narrated his earlier interactions with the police to André-Simon, who became unhappy that Kovi had attempted to bribe a police officer. He contended that people like Kovi, with that kind of behavior, were inducing and sustaining corruption.

"You know well that where you come from, you cannot get away with such a despicable act. Yet, you come here and do that." He yelled as he walked back and forth in front of the television. André-Simon was a decent guy, always on the "right side" of every issue. Kovi thought he would laugh at the story, but he took it personally. He loved Zamumda deeply, with a determination to get rid of corruption at all levels of society. In his poor defense, Kovi said, "I agree that where I come from, I would not dare to do something like that. But here, that looks to be a standard practice."

André-Simon was even more enraged.

"Just because other people do it, doesn't mean you should do it, too. I expect you to know better."

"Well then, I will go back to where the police officer stopped me, search for the officer, and beg him to write me a ticket. Will that make you feel better?"

André-Simon lectured Kovi, saying he was mocking his comments, and did not understand the issue. Kovi listened to him carefully and when André-Simon finished talking, Kovi nodded in agreement, and changed the subject.

***

A few years later, Kovi watched, with pride and respect, the ascendance of André-Simon in the political realm. "That's the right individual we need in politics," Kovi thought.

André-Simon was energetic and passionate about helping the people. He did well for his community, and he held many positions up to the national level. One day, to the surprise of Kovi, they hit his friend with bribery allegations that smeared his image. They brought charges against him. He always maintained his innocence. André-Simon appeared in court, elegant, eloquent, dignified... and convicted. He went to do time.

***

One day when the research activities of Kovi brought him back to the country of André-Simon, Kovi paid him a visit in jail. André-Simon was happy to see Kovi, and they shook hands firmly. Many years behind bars had taken a toll on him. He appeared to have aged quickly, looked disheveled, and seemed to have lost his charm with people. Kovi listened to him for a while. He still insisted he was innocent and claimed they framed him. He explained that they had tried to bribe him many times, but he refused, and his downfall was because he was not doing like the others and, thus, they saw him as a threat. With some sadness in his face, he said he wished he had taken the bribes, and subsequently put them to some good use for the people. "Do you remember my firm, manly handshake?" Kovi asked him. He nodded and laughed to tears. But, he was still true to himself and insisted Kovi should not have attempted to bribe a police officer.

A few months later, there was a revolution and a change of government. They released André-Simon from prison and appointed him Minister of Education in the new government. He then embarked on the lengthy process of clearing his name. He insisted to form an independent committee to reexamine his case and all the evidence against him. Then, the committee would make a recommendation to the highest court in the land. The process took a while, but they cleared him of all charges.

Good man that he was, André-Simon pardoned all the people who had smeared his image with the allegations that caused his downfall and prison term. He was a true champion of reconciliation and tried to bring the people of Zamumda together to discuss and address issues of capacity and research development.

He set up an international committee of experts to come to Zamumda City to review the state of the education system and make recommendations for its improvement.

Kovi was one person invited, and he got involved in the task with enthusiasm. The review committee made a few trips to Zamumda, and each trip lasted two weeks. Also, the review committee had to analyze the scientific research priorities of Zamumda and their collaborations with the international community. At the end of the review, the committee released a roadmap document that became the reference for the Ministry of Education in setting the objectives, milestones, and progress evaluations in matters of education and research.

André-Simon Le Beau, the Minister of Education, also sought collaborations with other African countries to develop approaches to tackle common problems in education. Through the contacts made with the review committee members, André-Simon visited many major research laboratories around the world to develop partnerships with them and promote the improvement of fundamental research in Zamumda.

Serving on the committee gave Kovi the opportunity to meet his friend occasionally, and to discuss the African School of Physics—ASP. They founded the school while André-Simon was in prison and focused on tertiary education in physics and its applications. André-Simon argued that to improve the percentage of students who might later do scientific research, and to develop an effective education platform for the future, one must improve the scientific education in the secondary schools. At the bare minimum, secondary school pupils should be motivated toward an interest in the scientific disciplines, and also secondary school teachers should be trained for more effective scientific teaching strategies.

At the recommendation of André-Simon, they extended the ASP program to include an outreach activity for secondary education pupils and a workshop for high-school teachers.

The minister committed Zamumda to sponsor the school and encouraged his other African colleagues to do so. He often argued that if each African country contributed five thousand USA dollars every two years, African countries could entirely support the ASP. "And two thousand five hundred dollars every year is a negligible figure in the budget of even the least developed of the African countries," he reckoned.

The minister made efforts to bring ASP to the attention of other African heads of state, to review the ASP goals, and to develop mechanisms to make the school sustainable.

Kovi was pleased to be a part of the development and organization of the ASP, and to bring his contributions to the scientific development of Africa.

Chapter Twenty
Brain Drain

Two years after he completed the assignment in Zamumda, Kovi received an invitation to give a talk about ASP at a major conference in Russia. The organization of ASP was attracting international attention.

The conference started, and the room was full of people. Many presentations and discussions were being carried out. It got hot in the room and Kovi needed some air. He stepped outside and met a fellow lightly dressed and shivering in the cold, yet happy to be smoking a cigarette. Kovi looked at him, unable to comprehend the insatiable urge to step into the cold inappropriately dressed, to smoke. The man seemed to derive great satisfaction and pleasure from each inhalation. This was apparent from the elegant way in which he held the cigarette in between his index and major fingers, the contraction of his cheeks as he inhaled, and the somewhat pointed face and rounded lips as he released the smoke in a jet of particles that hung for a while in the cold air before it dissipated.

When the man noticed that Kovi was staring at him, he offered Kovi a cigarette. Kovi declined, but the offer made them feel comfortable and the two men engaged in a conversation after they introduced themselves by their first names. Edward was his name.

Edward was particularly interested to know about Kovi's country. Kovi said he was from an institute in the USA, but Edward responded that he already knew when he looked at his conference badge, and he was interested in his country of origin. He said he was from the USA, born and raised there, but his parents had migrated from eastern Europe. To this, Kovi responded that he was from the USA, too, but

Edward appeared annoyed. "But where are you from originally?" insisted Edward. Kovi said he was originally from Africa, West Africa, but he did not say the name of his country of origin. Edward knew of Ghana and Nigeria and, to Kovi's surprise, he correctly stated that these were countries in West Africa. When he learned that Kovi's country of origin was somewhere in between, Edward guessed it was perhaps the narrow and skinny country that protrudes inward from the coast.

"I do not know the name of that country," said Edward.

"Please guess."

"Did your country change its name recently?"

"No. The name has not changed since independence!"

"Interesting. Countries there have been changing names so often that one does not know their current names."

"Well, Edward, that does not apply for all the African countries, and I am sure you know that."

"You came from there and you do research in particle physics?"

"Yes, I do."

"Do they do particle physics research in your country?"

Edward never guessed the country name. To answer his question, Kovi said there was no such field developed into serious and concerted research efforts in Togo.

"You are the first person from Togo that I've met. And doing particle physics! How on Earth did you come from there, through the USA, to this conference in Russia?"

Kovi smiled, as it was not the first time he heard such questions. Edward appeared genuine and friendly, though naïve. Kovi asked him if he honestly had time to hear his story. Edward said with more cigarettes, which he had, he was eager to listen. "Tell me everything," he added. So, they sat comfortably in a smoking room around the corner.

Kovi started to tell his story with excitement tainted with disappointment and sadness in his face and voice. The mood in the room grew serious as Edward listened attentively.

"I had never failed in school, thus never repeated a class from the first grade all the way to the bachelor's degree. In the education system in Togo when a pupil failed the final exams, he had to repeat the class until he passed, to move up to the next grade. It was normal to see pupils who had failed many times and thus were too old for their grades." Kovi continued.

"At the beginning of the tenth grade, the pupils had to choose and declare their majors between mathematics and physics, natural sciences such as biology, or literature and philosophy. They required all the pupils to take all the subjects and exams, but to various degrees of depth and complexity, depending on the majors. The difficulty of the exam problems and weight of the marks also depended on the majors. If mathematics and physics were your majors, and you did poorly in them, because they weighted these subjects heavily for you, you were likely not going to pass even if you did well in all the other subjects. If you passed the written exams, they allowed you to go through the oral exams where you faced direct, live questioning from unknown professors and it was the combined weighted marks of the written and oral exams that determined the passing threshold. Some of the best pupils could not manage the stress and tension that built up during the days of the exams and failed."

"There were devils and traps in the written exams. For example, the physics problems could be a collection of short stories in which the answer to one problem fed directly as input to the next problem. A simple mistake at the beginning could then propagate throughout. The pupil was then at the mercy of the examiner—who had hundreds of papers to grade in a short amount of time—to notice that the pupil had the logical reasoning correct, but only made a minor numerical mistake early on, which led to the errors in the latter problems."

"In the hard sciences, the answers to the exam problems was undisputed and objectively unique—one could, therefore, attain a perfect grade. In other subjects such as philosophy or literature, where one might be asked to comment on or debate an excerpt from some famous writer, the answer was never clear. They believed one could never achieve the perfect mark; there might be somebody who could argue better and put it in a more eloquent and elegant written form. Therefore, the marks depended subjectively on the opinions of the examiners."

"With a single university in Togo which had a limited capacity, the university entrance exams at the end of high school seemed designed, somehow, to weed out a great number of pupils, who must travel from different regions to designated locations to take the exams."

"When I entered the university, my father wanted me to do medicine. It was a prestigious field that required several years of intense preparation, followed by more years of specialization. At the end of all these studies, the title of doctor conferred a lot of respect and was a sign of high intelligence, and the business of helping people to get well generated a lot of personal satisfaction and fulfillment. But, I decided to pursue a subject that might guarantee a job after fewer years at the university. So, I continued in physics. It was a decision I regretted later, since physics education, too, required many years to reach the PhD, then more years for postdoctoral studies, followed by constant and relentless requirements to prove oneself professionally in an ever-competitive environment."

"I was among a few students who majored in mathematics and physics at the university. In the first year, this group was about thirty students, but it shrank dramatically to about eight students by the third year. Progression to the next academic level was contingent upon successful completion of the end-of-year exams. In those years, the exams took place in June, and those who failed retook the exams in September. In case of failure at both the June and September exams, they allowed one to repeat the same level the following year only once. Two failures at the same level in two consecutive years resulted in automatic dismissal from the program. It was a harsh and unforgiving program that took three years to complete. Many who failed in the first year could not continue, and they also expelled those who reached the second or third year and failed there twice. One could spend up to five or six years in the program and not finish, but then had to face the tough decision to start a new program from scratch, or end their studies at the university."

"Much larger numbers of students went into other disciplines that were equally difficult to complete, and only a fraction of the students who entered the university ever finished their program successfully."

"French and local professors taught mathematics and physics. The exams contained theoretical problems and practical tests in which they required the students, in an amount of time, to carry out successfully physics or chemistry experiments and/or demonstrations. These were moments of highly intense pressure that could break even the best students."

"I was among the few who completed the program in the absolute minimum of three years. I passed each year at the university at the top of the class. When I graduated with the bachelor's degree, I faced a different problem: There was no possibility to continue higher education in physics at the only university in Togo. One must go abroad for the advanced degrees. To go abroad required a scholarship and getting a scholarship meant being well connected to the political establishment. Some people who could not find scholarships to go abroad became physics teachers in isolated villages and they did not pay them well."

"I was a good, young, and naïve student, with no connections. Many of my colleagues had scholarships waiting for them, and landed in France, Germany, Russia, and China within a few days after they announced the results."

"My father was supporting me and paying for the university fees and accessories, and he spent more than half of his monthly salary on me alone, and less than half on the rest of the family of seven siblings and two adults."

"Despite my achievements, I did not even get the national

scholarship that would have covered my local expenses. My father believed so much in me that he made the sacrifice. But after two years, the expenses became too much for him and he informed me that he could no longer carry the load of my studies. They announced on the national radio that I won the national scholarship in the final year. To this day, no one knows how that happened. The Lord works in mysterious ways!"

"When I graduated with the bachelor's degree, I did not have any scholarship to continue higher education abroad. I took a teaching position in a private high school where the principal was also the Minister of Education."

"The blessing of the Lord shined one more time on me. During my first year as a high-school physics teacher, the head of the physics department at the university advised the Minister of Education to find a scholarship for me. These men were good, may the Lord bless their souls! The scholarship the minister offered was an exchange student program. I had to sign an agreement that I was to return to Togo for a minimum of two years after receiving the master's degree in the USA, and my country would use me when I returned. So that was how I started my journey to the USA instead of France."

Edward, a serious chain smoker, stopped and said, "Wow! That's quite a story. That was a great program. It was obviously designed to reduce brain drain. But it looks like you did not go back after the master's degree. What happened? Tell me more," said Edward, and Kovi continued to tell his story.

"So, I arrived in New York City on a Saturday in August, and continued the journey to the Midwest, where I took an intensive English course for three months before I started the master's degree program. I did a master's thesis on photovoltaic solar cells as a cheap source of electricity for Africa."

"Two years later, at the end of the master's program, it was time to return and fulfill the two-year home country residency requirement according to the agreement I signed before I went to America. But I wanted to do the doctorate degree before I returned, so I petitioned the AAI for permission to continue with the PhD. The AAI informed me that the scholarship was for two years, that to continue further, I had to find my own sources of funding and show that I had the resources to cover my PhD education. I applied to many universities and got a teaching assistantship and fellowship, and thus could do the PhD. However, the two-year home country residency requirement still applied."

"It was during the PhD program that I tasted stiff competition from highly trained and skilled American, Chinese, and Indian students. It was then that I came to appreciate how my education in Togo, though it did not come with a sophisticated learning infrastructure, prepared me to perform well among my peers at the international levels."

"During my doctorate studies, I changed my major to nuclear and particle physics to earn a much-needed research assistantship, from my advisor's grant, toward completion of the degree. I went to Switzerland to collect and analyze data for the dissertation. After receiving the doctorate degree, I wanted to do postdoctoral studies. They granted permission for this, but the two-year home country residency requirement still applied. I had signed an agreement to go back for two years after my education in America, and I could not break that agreement even though my personal situation had changed. I had been away from Togo for a long time, and I argued that there was no support system for me to do nuclear and particle physics from Togo. So, I tried to get a waiver. I got a letter from the embassy of Togo in Washington, DC, stating that I was not needed in my country and I was free to go back or pursue my life elsewhere, as I wished. That letter did not waive the agreement."

"During my postdoctoral studies, I got engaged to an American citizen and began to get a comfortable living in America and Europe. I thought to play the 'I am engaged to a citizen, and we wish to make a family here, in America' card, and that still did not work. I learned that, even if I were married to an American citizen and my wife were to have a baby, that would not remove the requirement. They implemented the requirement so that a trained and qualified workforce would help their country. I had signed the agreement and enjoyed a scholarship under that agreement, therefore, I must fulfill my end of the bargain. My American wife-to-be enlisted the help of friends, family, Congress persons, senators, and highly skilled immigration lawyers, to no avail. As my postdoctoral studies were ending, my visa was expiring with no more possibility for any further extension. That was when I left America and spent time in South Africa on a long-term visa based on exceptional skills."

"Ultimately, I satisfied the home country requirement, returned to the USA with a Green Card, and later became a USA citizen. I got a USA passport and boarded a flight that same day to Switzerland for physics research. In time, I bought a house, lived close to the Old Lady of Oak Street, and became a Plant Whisperer."

Edward stopped smoking for a moment and said, "Wow! But you are a typical example of brain drain. Sent to a first-world country for education and never to return. Highly skilled and doing research not benefitting your country! Do you ever go back? Are you doing anything there?" To answer Edward's question, Kovi continued his story.

"Together with interested colleagues, I had created a school in Africa, a biennial school of physics and applications—ASP. That was my way to give back to Togo and Africa."

"ASP rotates every two years within different countries in Africa. The duration of ASP is three weeks. Biennially, we receive over four hundred applications from which we select sixty to eighty students from all over Africa. The selected students have a minimum of three years of university education in physics, mathematics, and computer science or engineering. We invite scientists from all over the world to lecture at the school. We later expanded the ASP program with the addition of a workshop for high-school teachers and an outreach to secondary schools in the host country. ASP has created a networking framework to help African students pursue higher education, and to keep a maximum fraction of the students within Africa, thus to lessen brain drain. The biggest problem has been to secure the funds for the school."

Edward was quiet and expected Kovi to talk further. Kovi smiled and said, "That's my story." Then, he asked Edward if he knew any funding sources that could help and invited Edward to teach at the school, provided he did not smoke anywhere in or outside the venue.

Edward became an active member of the ASP organization. During the school, Edward helps with fundraising, the design of the scientific program and the selection of the students. He is a regular lecturer at ASP and he continues to mentor many students. Edward always seeks a few good students that he diligently helps to pursue graduate studies at his university, provided the students agree to the two-year home country residency requirement.

Besides the organization and management of the ASP, Kovi continued to do research in particle physics.

Biography

Dr. Kétévi Adiklè Assamagan is a tenured research physicist in nuclear and particle physics at Brookhaven National Laboratory. He did his bachelor's degree in physics and chemistry at the University of Lomé Togo, and then he went to the USA to pursue his Masters of Science and doctorate degrees in physics at Ball State University and the University of Virginia, respectively.

Subsequently, Dr. Assamagan did postdoctoral studies at Hampton University. Since 1998, he has been working on the ATLAS Experiment. He is a member of the ATLAS Collaboration that discovered the particle known as the Higgs boson. Dr. Assamagan is one of the founding members of the African School of Fundamental Physics and Applications (www.africanshoolofphysics.org).

His current research interests focus on the search of dark matter and for physics beyond the Standard Model of particle physics. He is a member of the National Society of Black Physicists, the American Association for the Advancement of Science, and the American Physics Society. He can be reached by e-mail at keteviassamagan@gmail.com.